Praise for *Men in Prison*

"Novel or autobiography, the book is literature, for Serge was a wonderful writer."
—*New Yorker*

"If you know someone headed for prison, this is not the book to give him for a going-away present. It tells what prison is really like."
—*Book World*

"No purer book about the hell of prison has ever been written."
—Martin Seymour-Smith, *The Scotsman*

"There is nothing in any line or word of this fine novel which doesn't ring true."
—*Publishers Weekly*

"It is a stream of exquisite and refined consciousness undergoing man's most barbaric experience. Not even in *One Day in the Life of Ivan Denisovich* is there such a penetrating and disturbing account of what prison means to the body and soul."
—John Riley, *Los Angeles Times*

"Almost hallucinatory vividness of incident . . ."
—*New Society*

"This novel, properly so called by its author, being truth worked up as art, is strongly recommended both as a document and as a powerful work of literature."
—Robert Garioch, *Listener*

"He was one of those rare political activists who was also an artist, and his book is poetic and ironic, the account of a spiritual experience rather than a factual record. . . . Serge is almost unique (not quite—one remembers Dostoevsky and Koestler) in turning all this into art."
—Julian Symons, *Sunday Times* (London)

T0126110

"Here is Serge, the model upon whom George Orwell fashioned himself in his descriptive essays and in *Homage to Catalonia*. Here too, I think, must be the original spring of Jean Genet. Consider the homosexual Moure, alone in his cell, dreaming of boy friends called Georgette, Lucienne and Antionette. Moure links the most brutally obscene, obscene to the point of cruelty, with love words and coquettish diminutives. . . . Serge is not merely a political writer, he is also a novelist, a wonderfully lyrical writer. . . . He is a writer young rebels desperately need whether they know it or not. . . . He does not tell us what we should feel; instead, he makes us feel it."
—Stanley Reynolds, *New Statesman*

"This lucid and beautiful book. . . . The cool brevity of Serge's character sketches covers a deeply running sympathy for all human nature, however distorted and ignoble."
—Claire Tomalin, *Observer Review*

"This is a remarkable book. . . . Capable of Dostoyevskian intensity and power."
—Francis King, *Sunday Telegraph*

Men in Prison

Editor: Sasha Lilley

Spectre is a series of penetrating and indispensable works of, and about, radical political economy. Spectre lays bare the dark underbelly of politics and economics, publishing outstanding and contrarian perspectives on the maelstrom of capital—and emancipatory alternatives—in crisis. The companion Spectre Classics imprint unearths essential works of radical history, political economy, theory and practice, to illuminate the present with brilliant, yet unjustly neglected, ideas from the past.

Spectre

Greg Albo, Sam Gindin, and Leo Panitch, *In and Out of Crisis: The Global Financial Meltdown and Left Alternatives*

David McNally, *Global Slump: The Economics and Politics of Crisis and Resistance*

Sasha Lilley, *Capital and Its Discontents: Conversations with Radical Thinkers in a Time of Tumult*

Sasha Lilley, David McNally, Eddie Yuen, and James Davis, *Catastrophism: The Apocalyptic Politics of Collapse and Rebirth*

Peter Linebaugh, *Stop, Thief! The Commons, Enclosures, and Resistance*

Spectre Classics

E.P. Thompson, *William Morris: Romantic to Revolutionary*

Victor Serge, *Men in Prison*

Victor Serge, *Birth of Our Power*

Men in Prison

Victor Serge

Translated and introduced by Richard Greeman

SPECTRE
CLASSICS

Men in Prison
Victor Serge. Translated by Richard Greeman
Copyright © 2014 Victor Serge Foundation
Translation and Introduction © 2014 Richard Greeman
This edition © 2014 PM Press
First published as *Les hommes dans la prison*. Paris: Les Editions Rieder, 1931.
All rights reserved. No part of this book may be transmitted by any means
without permission in writing from the publisher.

ISBN: 978–1–60486–736–7
Library of Congress Control Number: 2013911528

Cover by John Yates/Stealworks
Interior design by briandesign

10 9 8 7 6 5 4 3 2 1

PM Press
PO Box 23912
Oakland, CA 94623
www.pmpress.org

Printed in the USA by the Employee Owners of Thomson-Shore in
Dexter, Michigan. www.thomsonshore.com

TO VLADY

Everything in this book is fictional and everything is true. I have attempted, through literary creation, to bring out the general meaning and human content of personal experience.

V.S.

Contents

Foreword

by David Gilbert

Men in Prison tells it like it was—and in too many ways still is—behind bars. Victor Serge is an inspiring example of revolutionary courage and principles. He gave his all and risked his life to defend the Soviet Republic as a proletarian revolution under ferocious attack by White Russians backed by troops from fourteen imperialist powers. He also gave his all and risked his life to defend dissidents and to oppose the rising repression and brutality of the Russian Communist Party.

Before being deported to Russia, Serge was an anarchist political prisoner in France from 1912 to 1917. This novel is based on those five years. His prose comes across seamlessly in Richard Greeman's fluid and lively translation. And Serge could write! No "socialist realism" here as we see the nuances, the quirks, and the resiliencies of a variety of individuals. The convicts we meet are neither demonized as depraved monsters nor romanticized as the noble oppressed. Some are sordid, many simply sad; almost all are poor; and a handful are conscious political prisoners.

"The Mill" where Serge did his time was an application of the "Auburn System," designed one hundred years earlier—the same two-hundred-year-old Auburn Correctional Facility in New York State where I'm being held today. Of course current conditions in the United States are not exactly the same as in France a century ago. The book's title would have to change *"Men"* to *"People,"* as the United States now has over two hundred thousand women behind bars, their numbers growing at a faster rate than men's. The rights of lesbian, gay, and transgender prisoners are a much more explicit struggle. Serge's brief mentions of gays are condescending if not negative. That's not surprising given the dearth of open struggle back then, but nonetheless totally inadequate and unacceptable today.

The rate of incarceration in the United States is totally unprecedented and astronomical at 1 percent of the adult population, with

2.3 million human beings in prisons and jails. Most telling, based on the history of genocide, slavery, and conquest, the U.S. criminal justice system is at the center of the surrounding stinking swamp of racism. The racism isn't just coincidental. The hyperexpansion of incarceration in the United States—with the number behind bars today eight times what it was in 1970—developed in response to the Black Liberation Movement, which was an inspiration and spearhead for a range of struggles and advances by the oppressed. The United States now jails Black males at four times the rate South Africa did under apartheid. The United States also locks up an unconscionable number of women. But the impact of the criminal justice system on women is far more pervasive as many more carry the burden of being single parents in impoverished communities decimated by incarceration, with one in nine Black males between the ages of twenty and thirty-four behind bars. The Latino/a community has also been hit disproportionately hard, and the U.S. mania for mass incarceration has swept up many poor whites as well.

While the numbers and the racial dynamics have changed, the continuities are amazing, and much of what Serge describes rings true today: the humiliations and degradations; the frisks where you have to bend over and spread; the obstacles to maintaining basic hygiene; the totally arbitrary authority the often contemptuous guards have. Serge writes of the terrible boredom; and to counter that, "it is a fundamental rule of mental hygiene to work at all costs, to occupy the mind" (p.36). *Men in Prison* also provides a couple of delightful vignettes of the creative little ways prisoners find to resist the restrictions and regimentation. Visits often provide warm rays of sunshine, and the vast majority of visitors are women. This holds true at today's women's facilities too, as men generally don't do nearly as well at standing by loved ones.

At the same time, there have been some notable changes due to the prisoners' rights struggle that flowed out of the Civil Rights and Black Power movements. We are now a little less isolated from the outside world because, even though there's still censorship, we have access to wider range of reading material, visits, and phone calls. We have more, albeit still minimal, educational programs. Those in general population are allowed to socialize, no longer facing enforced silence twenty-four hours a day. On the other hand, Serge's cell was 60 percent larger than mine, and back then there was a limit on how long someone could be sent to the total isolation of "the hole"—ninety days. It was recognized then that even that amount of time could do serious damage. As

Serge puts it, "Madness [is] the inevitable result of idle solitude" (p.60). In the United States today there are eighty thousand prisoners subjected to isolation, which many psychologists deem a form of torture, hundreds of whom have been held for years and even decades in segregation units at places such as Pelican Bay State Prison in California and the federal supermax in Florence, Colorado. In a 2008 report, the UN Special Rapporteur to the Human Rights Council expressed grave concerns about the widespread use of prolonged solitary confinement in U.S. prisons.

The guards we meet in *Men in Prison* range from friendly to sadistic. In 1913 France, as in the United States today, many of the guards are ex-soldiers just returned from brutal colonial wars. As we now know, cruelty and dehumanization have a synergy that flows in both directions, domestic and international. It's no accident that Charles Graner Jr., the ringleader of the soldiers who tortured prisoners in Abu Ghraib, Iraq, went into the army straight out of a job as a prison guard in Pennsylvania.

Serge's powerful meditation on capital punishment, which has since been abolished in France, serves as a ringing condemnation of the contemporary U.S. prison system, which has over three thousand human beings on death row. In the same paragraph that he condemns the state's use of the death penalty as a weapon against working people, he also squarely faces the duty of a true revolutionary to oppose any cruelty or misuse of power within our movements by stressing that even in the heat of intense class warfare, we must maintain "the greatest humanity" and fight "to build a new world, forever cleansed of killing machines" (p.83).

As gruesome as the guillotine is, Serge writes that many on the inside see life imprisonment as "worse, in reality, than death" (p.83). What would he think of the United States today, with over 159,000 individuals serving life, nearly 50,000 of whom are serving sentences of "life without parole" (LWOP), with no chance of ever being released? For older prisoners, any long sentence is in effect LWOP. The post-1970s penchant for draconian sentences has led to an explosion in the number of convicts fifty-five years old and above—roughly 125,000 today—despite the high costs of holding them and the miniscule re-offend rate of elders who do get paroled.

Men in Prison shows how "jail is a machine for grinding up lives slowly" (p.84), designed to stultify and efface people's humanity. Already perfect for that function, prisons aren't further perfectible; therefore, "there is nothing left but to destroy them" (p.43). Abolishing prisons is a monumental challenge for us today, but we can take big strides toward that ultimate goal with campaigns to decarcerate, to radically reduce the prison population, and most important of all to build the healthier, stronger communities needed to provide the only viable basis for safety, well-being, and justice.

Prisons are neither an insignificant nor an exotic sideshow but rather serve as a frontline of the rulers' offensive against the oppressed and their struggles. In this historical novel, a wonderfully principled revolutionary and vibrant writer takes us into the culture and realities behind bars in a different time and place but in ways that still resonate with relevance today.

Introduction

The author of *Men in Prison* was no stranger to his grim subject. Victor Serge spent more than ten of his fifty-seven years in various forms of captivity, generally harsh. He did five years' straight time (1912–17) in a French penitentiary ('anarchist bandit'); survived nearly two years (1917–18) in a World War I concentration camp ('Bolshevik suspect'); suffered three months' grueling interrogation in the Lubianka, Moscow's notorious GPU prison ('Trotskyite spy'); and endured three years' deportation to Central Asia for refusing to recant his oppositional views or confess to trumped-up charges (1933–36).

The present novel, completed in 1930, is based on Serge's experience of 1,825 days in a French penitentiary (solitary confinement, rule of absolute silence, chronic undernourishment) to which he was sentenced essentially as punishment for his refusal to testify against his comrades at the infamous 1913 trial of the 'Tragic Bandits' of French Anarchism. Like Alexander Berkman's better-known *Prison Memoirs of an Anarchist*, Serge's book is a cry for justice fueled by bitter experience and personal sacrifice. Yet at the same time, Serge's novel is also literature, a fiction created by a serious novelist. "Everything in this book is fictional and everything is true," wrote Serge in the epigraph to *Men in Prison*. "I have attempted, through literary creation, to bring out the general meaning and human content of a personal experience."

As Serge recalled in his *Memoirs*, "While I was still in prison, fighting off tuberculosis, insanity, depression, the spiritual poverty of the men, the brutality of the regulations, I already saw I kind of justification of that infernal voyage in the possibility of describing it. Among the thousands who suffer and are crushed in prison—and how few men really know that prison!—I was perhaps the only one who could try one day to tell all . . . For me, that is the *raison d'être* of this novel. I emphasize that it is a novel, for the convenient use of the first person singular may lead to misunderstanding. I don't want to write memoirs. This book is not about me, but about men . . . There is no novelist's hero in this novel, unless that terrible machine, *prison*, is its real hero. It is not about 'me,' about a few men, but about men, all men crushed in that dark corner of society."

Ironically, Serge returned to writing (after a long career as a revolutionary activist) upon his release from another spell in prison—this time in the same Communist Russia for which he had fought in the Civil War (1919–21) and whose revolutionary promise glimmers in *Men in Prison* like a candle at the end of the long, dark tunnel of incarceration. In 1928 Serge was arrested and interrogated by the GPU secret police for his declared opposition to the bureaucratic tyranny of Stalin's monolithic Communist Party. Writing under the shadow of another arrest, Serge sent his chapters abroad one by one as soon as he finished them. Serge managed to complete *Men in Prison* and two other novels in what he called 'semicaptivity' before being re-arrested and deported to Central Asia in 1933.

Reviewers have compared Serge's classic prison novel to Dostoyevsky's *House of the Dead*, Koestler's *Spanish Testament*, Genet's *Miracle of the Rose*, and Solzhenitsyn's *One Day in the Life of Ivan Denisovich*. Nonetheless, his notoriety as a revolutionary has always overshadowed his achievements as a writer. We will return to the literary qualities of *Men in Prison*, but first let us look at the remarkable life of the man behind the novel.

The Life of a Revolutionary Maverick
The briefest chronological summary of Serge's career as a rebel reads like a roll call of the radical movements and revolutionary uprisings of the first half of the twentieth century.[1] Born Victor Lvovitch Kibalchich in 1890 in Brussels to an unmarried couple of penniless Russian revolutionary refugee students, Serge was by birth a stateless exile and remained a lifelong internationalist. From his parents he inherited the critical spirit of the radical Russian *intelligentsia* and the heroic ideals of the *Narodniki*—the Party of the People's Will who executed Czar Alexander II in 1881. By his mid-teens, Victor was already an activist, signing his radical articles *Le Rétif* (Maverick). Alone in the world after

---

1   See Serge's *Memoirs of a Revolutionary: 1905–1941*, the first complete English translation of which was published in 2012 by NYRB Classics, with a translator's introduction by Peter Sedgwick, a foreword by Adam Hochschild, and a glossary by Richard Greeman.

his parents' breakup, he bonded with his crew of teenage comrades. They were "closer than brothers," idealistic, overworked apprentices, who devoted their rare free time to reading dangerous books and hardening their bodies through all-night hikes. They all met tragic ends.

Raymond Callemin, a.k.a. 'Science,' with his baby-face, myopic squint, and sarcastic tongue, was Victor's oldest friend—and rival. [See jacket cover, photo B4 (bottom row, fourth from left)]. On the steps of the guillotine, Callemin taunted reporters with a sarcastic: "A beautiful sight, eh, to watch a man die!" Tough Edouard Carouy (M1, middle row #1, with beard and moustache), built like a circus strongman, newly awakened to reading and 'ideas.' Sentenced to Devil's Island for life, Carouy took poison in prison. Serious Jean de Boë, a.k.a. 'Printer' (photo B5), was the organizer of their Brussels Revolutionary Group. Sent to Devil's Island for life, he managed to escape, after several attempts.[2]

Together, these serious young rebels evolved from the Brussels Socialist Young Guard, through anarchist 'communes' (where they learned printing and put on their own four-page *Rebel!*), to anarchism, which, unlike reformist socialism, demanded deeds not just words. By 1909, their strident militancy had provoked repression in Brussels, and one by one they drifted to Paris, to anarcho-individualist circles where 'illegalism' (individual expropriation) was *à la mode*. There the group was swelled by new comrades: handsome, violent Octave Garnier (photo M2); pale, tubercular André Soudy (B2), a.k.a. 'Out-of-Luck,' who on the morning he was guillotined didn't even get his 'last request,' coffee and a croissant (the cafés were still closed); Victor's red-headed Left Bank soul-brother René Valet, a.k.a. 'Carrot-Top' (M3) a square-jawed 'young Siegfried' who loved poetry and shot himself with his last bullet after a twelve-hour gun battle with the police; and sentimental Eugène Dieudonné (T1), condemned to death although known to be innocent.

In Paris, in the Summer of 1911, Victor and his lover Rirette Maitrejean had been uneasily sharing the suburban print shop–commune of the anarcho-individualist weekly *anarchie* with Victor's Brussels homeboys, who had been more-or-less living off small 'expropriations' (thefts) and needed to disappear. The boys soon teamed up with an

_____

2 De Boë and Serge were reunited in Brussels in 1936, when Serge was freed by the Russians. De Boë was by then a respected leader in the printers' union.

Victor and Rirette c. 1911. This photo appears on the cover of *Confessions* magazine with Rirette's account of the 'Tragic Bandits' affair.

anarchist chauffeur—an older desperado from Lyon named Jules Bonnot (T2)—and embarked on a series of bloody holdups that literally paralyzed Paris for half a year. They have gone down in French judicial history as the 'Tragic Bandits of Anarchy'—the subject of dozens of books, radio and TV dramas, graphic novels, and a popular film with Jacques Brel.[3]

The 'Bonnot Gang' have also gone down in history as the first bank-robbers to use a stolen getaway car (the cops only had bicycles), but their robberies, although bloody, were not very successful. On the run for months, they were joined—out of solidarity—by other comrades who offered them asylum according to the unwritten laws of anarchism and who ended up sharing their tragic fates. When finally cornered, they defiantly held off regiments of police and military units in gun-battles so spectacular they pushed the sinking of the *Titanic* off the front page. Victor, who in his writings had defended the expedient of 'illegalism' *in theory*, had nothing to do with the robberies, whose bloodiness rather

---

3   Curiously, the only serious, reliable, and politically astute book on the gang was written by an Englishman, Richard Parry. Malcolm Menzies has written an excellent novel about the tragedy, *En Exil chez les hommes*, which sticks close to the facts and brings to life the characters and atmosphere.

horrified him. However, writing in the pages of *anarchie* as Le Rétif, Victor was bound by solidarity and loudly proclaimed, "I am with the wolves" in their war against society.[4] He had just turned twenty-one.

Arrested, Victor refused to 'talk' and was kept in solitary at the *Santé* prison for thirteen months. At the sensational 1913 mass trial, he and his lover Rirette (the business manager of *anarchie*) were cast in the role of the ideological 'brains' behind the gang. Against them, the evidence of two stolen pistols found during the police search at the office of *anarchie*, where Victor, Rirette and her children also lived. Neither had had anything to do with the robberies, indeed by then were out of sympathy with illegalism, but their 'not guilty' defense was compromised because their comrades, the surviving members of the Bonnot Gang also pleaded 'innocent.' This transparent masquerade lead to the conviction of Eugène Dieudonné, who really *was* innocent.[5]

This non-political 'not guilty' defense was in any case pointless since the Prosecution's evidence was as overwhelming as was the judges' thirst for vengeance. Only Dieudonné's repeated cries of innocence rang true, yet he too was sentenced to the guillotine (later 'pardoned' to Devil's Island for life, whence he managed to escape).[6] Raymond ('Science'), Victor's oldest friend from Brussels, was sent to the guillotine, along with luckless Soudy, another close comrade. Rirette got off with time served. Victor, for refusing to cooperate with the law or renounce his anarchist ideas, was given the unusually harsh sentence of five years for possession of the pair of stolen pistols apparently bought by Rirette. The night of the verdict, Victor heard prolonged moans from the next cell: Carouy, the strongman from Brussels, managed to

---

4   For Serge's articles as Le Rétif, see *Anarchists Never Surrender: Essays, Polemics, and Correspondence on Anarchism, 1908–1938* (Oakland: PM Press, 2015).

5   Bonnot and Garnier, the two most hardened killers in the gang, each sent an open letter to the press and police proclaiming Dieudonné's innocence, then fought it out to the death, surrounded by police and army units. At the trial, Raymond pretended to have nothing to do with the robbers and so waited until after the verdict—when it was too late—to shout out Dieudonné's innocence. The bandit's 'innocence' pleas contrasted with the 1905 trial of the anarchist burglar Marius Jacob, who proudly admitted: "I have burned down several townhouses, defended my freedom against the aggression of the agents of power. I am a rebel, living off the product of his thefts . . . I beg no indulgence from those I hate and scorn," and reportedly "took over the trial," expounding his anarchist principles.

6   Dieudonné and Serge were reunited in the 1930s in Paris, where both worked in print shops as proofreaders.

poison himself rather than accept a life of sentence. As for Victor, he resolved to drink the bitter cup of prison to the lees and survive to tell the tale you are about to read.

Men in Prison, Serge's first novel, is thus based on the author's experience of five years' incarceration: thirteen pre-trial months in solitary at *La Santé* followed by forty-seven months in the Penitentiary at Melun. From January 31, 1912, until the end of the 1913 trial, Victor was kept in solitary under Maximum Surveillance among the Death Row prisoners, 14th div. cell 32, then 10th div. cell 20 of Paris's *Santé* prison.[7]

Although the name *Santé* (Health) derives from a former hospital that stood at the site in central Paris, the appellation is appropriate. The *Santé* was designed during the heyday nineteenth-century scientific progressivism for reasons of 'philanthropic hygiene' to replace traditional dungeons which were dark, filthy, malodorous and the source of epidemics like cholera.[8] Billed as a 'model prison,' the *Santé* was designed to offer its inmates 'light and air' as well as central heating, gaslights, washstands, toilets, and sewer evacuations—luxuries only dreamed of by its honest neighbors in 1867 when *La Santé* opened (or rather closed) its heavily reinforced door—and it is still in operation, albeit much overcrowded and degraded, today. Its towering stone walls loom over the 14th *arrondissement* on the Left Bank, lending a somber tinge to the whole quarter. Up through the 1940s on days of public (executions) the guillotine was erected in the street under its shadow.

As Serge notes in his chapter of meditation on carceral architecture, prison is "impossible to mistake it for any other kind of edifice. It is proudly, insularly, *itself.*" According to Serge, except for the American skyscraper, the modern city's "architects have added practically nothing to the legacy of the past except, for its victims, this scientifically imperfectible hive of crimes, vices, and iniquities." Inspired by

7   Which I was permitted to inspect on August 6, 1993, accompanied by M. Didier Voituron, a young *directeur adjoint* who was interested in Serge. Grim. The architecture of the *Santé* and its bare cells had not changed, but the 1974 prison riots all over France had led to some visible humanization of the regime as M. Voituron explained to me as he greeted unescorted prisoners in the halls. Apparently these reforms did not last. A sensational 2012 exposé, *Chief Doctor at the Santé Prison* by Véronique Vasseur, describes a "pathogenic universe" of overcrowding, "which secretes its own arbitrary rules of despair, boredom, violence, forced cohabitation, promiscuity, domination by the strong, and corruption with no prospect but passing time badly."

8   Michel Fize, *Une Prison dans la ville. Histoire de la "prison modèle" de la Santé, 1ère époque, 1867–1914.* Ministère de la Justice, Coll. Archives pénitentiaire. June 1983.

the *Panopticon* of eighteenth-century philanthropic reformer Jeremy Bentham, modern prison is "a model of functionalist architecture . . . From the center of the hub a single man can keep his eye on the whole prison without difficulty, and his glance can ferret into the most remote corners. Maximum ease of surveillance is ensured with a minimum of personnel. The lines are simple, the plan faultless."

Prison is "imperfectible," writes Serge in ironic praise, anticipating Foucault's *Discipline and Punish* by a half century. However, Serge is writing from a very different viewpoint than the late postmodern philosopher. In the words of Marshall Berman, "Foucault is obsessed with prisons, hospitals, asylums, with what Erving Goffman has called 'total institutions.' Unlike Goffman, however, Foucault denies the possibility of any sort of freedom, either outside these institutions or within their interstices."[9]

For Foucault, criticisms of the system (including his own) only add to the triumphant of the all-pervasive 'discourse of power.' "Any criticism rings hollow," he writes, because the critic himself or herself is "in the panoptic machine, invested by its effects of power, which we bring to ourselves, since we are part of its mechanism."[10] Perhaps. But much depends on *where* one is situated within that inhuman 'mechanism.' Foucault the university professor writes from the point of view of the guard in the power center of the hub, spying on the prisoners (and on society in general). Serge writes from the prisoners' viewpoint, testifying to and affirming the triumph of that freedom and that subjectivity whose existence Foucault's postmodern philosophy denies.

After sentencing, Victor was transferred to the Penitentiary at Melun on the Marne, where he was held until his release on January 31, 1917. Serge's summary: "solitary cell at night, ten hours of forced labor by day (printer, later corrector). Permitted studies: living languages, religion. Arbitrary punishments. Rule of absolute silence. Chronic undernourishment. Stays in the infirmary every eight or ten months thanks to the sympathy of a doctor allowed me to survive." These harsh rules were modeled after the Quaker-inspired U.S. Auburn System. Isolation and solitary confinement, today recognized by the UN as torture, were

---

9   Marshall Berman, *All That Is Solid Melts into Air: The Experience of Modernism* (New York: Simon and Schuster, 1982), 34.
10 Michel Foucault, *Discipline and Punish: The Birth of the Prison*, quoted by Berman.

supposed to provoke meditation and penitence while preventing the spread of bad influence among inmates.[11]

Soon after the 1913 verdict, Victor and Rirette applied for permission to marry in order to have the right to correspond. Approved by the warden, their request was twice vindictively overruled at the highest level of the Ministry of Justice. Finally, in May 1915, the prison authorities granted permission to Victor and Rirette to marry with the proviso that "following the marriage he must immediately be reintegrated into the Penitentiary."[12] Similarly, two separate appeals for clemency were overruled, and Serge was made to serve the full sentence of 1,825 days (the original title of *Men in Prison*), but at least granted twelve days in Paris before being expelled from French territory as an undesirable 'Russian subject.'[13]

Released in 1917 at the age of twenty-six, Victor was deported to Barcelona, where he slowly came back to life, racked with survivor guilt. Rirette followed him to Barcelona, but with a living to earn and two little girls to support, she could not stay. Victor worked in a print shop, joined the anarcho-syndicalist CNT, participated in the preparation of an anarcho-syndicalist uprising and began signing his articles *Victor-Serge*, marking a kind of rebirth. This was his first experience of mass revolutionary activity and coincided with the outbreak of revolution in his ancestral Russia.

When the Barcelona revolt faltered, Serge heeded the call of the 1917 Russian Revolution and set off across war-torn Europe to join the longed-for revolution of his exiled anti-Czarist parents' dreams. Arrested

---

11 Ironically, David Gilbert, author of the foreword to this volume, is interned at Auburn in upstate New York. Another irony, it was Alexis de Tocqueville, revered by U.S. liberals, who as Justice Minister imposed this harsh, dehumanizing system in France. As a result, the French penitentiary system remained more repressive than the Spanish, even under Franco, as testified to by Serge's comrades from the Spanish POUM who were incarcerated in both. The late Wilebaldo Solano laughingly told me the story of receiving in his French prison a postcard from a comrade in one of Franco's jails that read: "It's Paradise here! The guards even play soccer with us." And of course Spain permitted conjugal visits.

12 Préfecture du Marne, May 19, 1915. In fact, the couple were left alone in an office for an hour or so.

13 It was unusual for a non-violent inmate to serve out the full sentence, and Serge's clemency appeals, organized by Rirette, had influential sponsors. However, a high ministry official considered him an anarchist firebrand 'dangerous to good order' and kept him in the pen. Nonetheless, enemies in anarcho-individualist circles spread the rumor that Victor had been let off early.

in Paris, he spent nearly two years in a wartime French concentration camp for subversives before arriving in frozen, besieged Red Petrograd in January 1919. In his 1931 novel, *Birth of Our Power*,[14] Serge brought to life this odyssey across war-torn Europe 'burning at both ends' with the flame of revolution.

Once in Russia, Serge threw himself into the Revolution and fought with the Reds in the Civil War—along with other 'Soviet' anarchists like the Americans Bill Chatov and Bill Haywood.[15] Along with another 'Soviet Anarchist' and ex-prisoner, Vladimir Mazin, Serge was drafted by Zinoviev to improvise the press services of the new Communist International—finding paper, setting up print shops, working as a translator, editor, journalist, and propagandist. When his soul-brother Mazin was killed during the White siege of Petrograd,[16] Serge joined the Communist Party—all the while retaining his anarchist scruples about Bolshevik authoritarianism and hoping that, once the Civil War was ended, he would be able to fight for his libertarian ideals from *within* the Revolution.[17]

Meanwhile, Serge used his daily contact with the top Bolsheviks to help save anarchists and other dissidents from the clutches of the Cheka secret police, and privately revealed his fears to a few trusted European anarchist comrades visiting Russia. Ten years later, he would express the tragedy of the revolution savagely turned in on itself in his 1931 novel *Conquered City*.[18] Meanwhile, he addressed letters to his comrades back in France 'for insertion' in the anarchist press in the hope of winning French anarchists over to the cause of the embattled, starving Soviets, beleaguered by Allied-financed White armies supported by Czech, French, British, Japanese, and even a few U.S. troops. Serge's pro-Soviet arguments were taken up in France by revolutionary syndicalists

---

14   Translated by Richard Greeman (Oakland: PM Press, 2015).

15   Dave Renton cites among the Russian 'Soviet anarchists' the names of Benjamin Aleynnikov, Herman Sandorminsky, Alexander Shapiro, Nikolai Rogdayev, Novomirsky, Grossman-Roschin, and Appolon Karelin, http://www.dkrenton.co.uk/research/serge.html.

16   Serge's son Vladimir, my late and dear friend, was named after Vladimir Mazin, not after Vladimir Lenin as has been surmised.

17   See Serge's 1921 "The Anarchists and the Russian Revolution," translated by Ian Birchall, in Serge, *The Revolution in Danger: Writings from Russia 1919–1921* (Chicago: Haymarket Books, 2011).

18   Translated with an introduction by Richard Greeman (New York: NYRB Classics, 2010).

and anti-war internationalists like Pierre Monatte, Alfred Rosmer, and Marcelle Martinet, but rejected by mainstream anarchists like Jean Grave, who had patriotically supported France in World War I.

Not surprisingly, Serge has been attacked over the years both by anarchists (for collaborating with the Bolsheviks) and by Trotskyists (for his criticism of the Cheka secret police under Lenin) as well as for his political 'inconsistency' and even 'schizophrenia.' These critics fail to see that he was guided by an underlying revolutionary principle of 'double duty': to defend the revolution from its external enemies (the Whites, the imperialists) and its internal enemies (intolerance, bureaucracy, corruption).

In 1921 as the Civil War was winding down, the Bolshevik leadership harshly repressed of the revolt of the Kronstadt sailors' Soviet. Serge was shaken to the core by this tragic conflict among revolutionaries, and he attempted to help the mediation efforts organized by U.S. anarchists Emma Goldman and Alexander Berkman. Serge was particularly revolted by the lies in the Communist press as well as the continuing massacres of defeated Soviet sailors by the Cheka. Dispirited, he retreated to a French anarchist agricultural commune north of Petersburg. When it collapsed, he then accepted a job as a Comintern editor, journalist, and revolutionary agent in Berlin, where he hoped the German revolution would triumph and by so doing liberate the USSR from isolation and increasing bureaucratic tyranny.[19]

After the fiasco of the 1923 Communist *putsch* in Hamburg, Serge fled to Vienna. It was there, working along side Gramsci, Lukács, and Lucien Laurat, that he finally found time to seriously study Marx—and discover Freud. In 1925, with his hopes for a European revolution dashed and in conflict with the bureaucratic leadership of the Comintern, Serge returned to Russia to participate in the Left Opposition's fore-doomed struggle against Stalin. As the Opposition's *rapporteur* on China, Serge was the first writer published in the West to analyze Mao Zedong's Hunan Report, with its perspective for a peasant-based revolution.[20] In early 1928 Serge was expelled from the Party after blaming the massacre of workers at Canton on Stalin's policy.[21] Arrested, interrogated

---

19 See Serge's *Witness to the German Revolution*, translated by Ian Birchall and published by Haymarket Books.

20 "The Class Struggle in the Chinese Revolution," 1927–28, http://www.marxists.org/archive/serge/1927/china/index.html.

21 Serge (writing as 'Paul Sizoff') "Canton, December 1927," http://www.marxists.org/archive/serge/1927/china/canton.html.

for weeks, released after protests in France, Serge was politically dead. A few days later, Serge came face to face with physical death, struck down by an intestinal occlusion. On his hospital bed, he resolved that if he survived, he would devote whatever time he had left to writing, and that is how he was reborn as a novelist.

Serge turned to literature as the best way to serve the revolution—by preserving its truth for future generations. He was living with his family in 'semicaptivity' in Leningrad, harassed by GPU spies—even within their collective apartment. However thanks to his self-discipline and long apprenticeship as a writer, editor, translator, and literary critic, Serge managed to finish three novels as well as a history of the *Year One of the Russian Revolution* and to publish them in Paris before being arrested again in 1933. Interrogated for months in the GPU's notorious *Lubyanka*, accused of espionage, Serge stubbornly refused to confess to any 'crimes' other than his public opposition to the Party line and was deported, without trial, to Orenburg on the Ural in Central Asia.

Out on the Ural, the tragic experiences of Serge's anarchist youth continued to haunt him. Around 1935 he completed another novel, *The Lost Men*—the 'prequel' to *Men in Prison*—based on Tragic Bandits and the collapse of French anarchism in the face of World War I patriotism. Ironically, the forty-five-year-old author of *Men in Prison* and *The Lost Men* was once again in detention, now as a Communist Left Oppositionist deportee in GPU custody. Alas, the typescript of *The Lost Men* may never be found. Serge painstakingly retyped multiple copies of his novel and sent them abroad, but they were 'lost' (confiscated by the GPU) and despite years of effort have not been recovered.[22] As the twenty-year-old anarchist Victor the Maverick had famously predicted: "The present order crushes us, tracks us down, kills us. The revolutionary order will crush us, will track us down, will kill us."[23]

In 1935, protests in France by well-known writers and teacher unionists demanding that Serge be either tried or released eventually persuaded Stalin to permit Serge to emigrate with his wife (driven mad

---

22   A copy found its way inside the Kremlin, where the French writer Romain Rolland, a guest of Stalin, read it and returned the manuscript (which he had agreed to take to Serge's Paris publisher) to GPU chief Yagoda. See my "The Victor Serge Affair and the French Literary Left" in *Revolutionary History* 5, no. 3, http://www.marxists.org/history/etol/revhist/backiss/vol5/no3/greeman.html.

23   "The Revolutionary Illusion" (1910) translated by Mitch Abidor, http://theanarchistlibrary.org/library/le-retif-the-revolutionary-illusion.

by persecution) and children.[24] However, for a year no 'free' country would grant a visa to this notorious revolutionary. He was finally granted asylum in Belgium in April 1936, just before Stalin unleashed the Great Terror that would certainly have spelled his doom. However, the GPU arrested his relatives in Russia as hostages and confiscated his manuscripts. These included two novels: *The Lost Men*, about the Tragic Bandits; and *Men in the Storm*, about the Russian Civil War (the sequel to *Conquered City*).[25]

From the moment Serge returned to Europe, he was subjected to a Communist-inspired campaign of slander ('anarchist bandit') and effectively marginalized. Unable to get published in the French press under the CP-dominated 'Popular Front against Fascism,' Serge was reduced to working as corrector in the print shops of the very Socialist papers that refused to print his first-hand, well-documented exposés of the Moscow Trials—the frame-ups and false confessions of Old Bolsheviks that fooled the world.[26] In 1939 he published a new novel, *Midnight in the Century*, about the imprisoned Oppositionists in Russia.[27] He also found time to publish two substantial essays on anarchism, *Meditation on Anarchism* (about his early experiences in Belgium and France) and *Anarchist Thought*, which looked forward to fruitful synthesis of the purity of the anarchist ethic with the efficacy of Marxism.

When Paris fell to the Nazis in 1940, Serge, his son Vlady and his lover Laurette Séjourné made their way on foot to Marseille, where they shared a villa with Varian Fry of the American anti-fascist Rescue Committee and the surrealist André Breton while waiting for visas and a ship to escape from Vichy France. Serge and his artist son Vlady eventually found their way, after various arrests *en route*, to exile in Mexico where Serge continued to agitate for 'Socialism and Freedom' (the name

---

24 See Greeman, "The Victor Serge Affair and the French Literary Left."

25 So far our efforts to recover them in the Russian archives, partly open since *glasnost*, have come to naught. On the other hand, Serge was able to reconstruct from memory his book of poems, *Resistance,* translated into English by James Brook with an introduction by Richard Greeman (San Francisco: City Lights, 1972)

26 Serge's brilliant and prescient articles appeared in the small-circulation syndicalist magazine *La Révolution prolétarienne* and in one union-owned large-circulation local paper in Liège, Belgium, *La Wallonie*. They have recently been collected and published in France (Agone, 2010) under the title *Retour à l'Ouest: Chroniques, juin 1936–mai 1940* (preface by Richard Greeman), which we hope to see translated in the near future.

27 Translated with an introduction by Richard Greeman (London: Writers and Readers Publishing Co-op, 1982; New York: NYRB Classics, 2014).

of the group he formed with exiled comrades from Spain, France, and Germany). Isolated, calumnied, and physically attacked by the Mexican Stalinists on orders from Moscow, he soon found the pages of Mexican publications closed to him.

In 1947, Serge died in poverty and obscurity at the untimely age of fifty-seven. His rugged constitution had been undermined by ten years of harsh imprisonment and the altitude in Mexico City was terrible for his heart. Among the last things he wrote were a letter to the far-left French journal, protesting the publication of an anti-Communist article by an American,[28] and an essay called "30 Years after the Russian Revolution" (generally considered his 'Political Testament') once again vindicating the historical rightness of the 1917 Russian Revolution, however much it may have degenerated later. Despite this 'deathbed evidence' to the contrary, critics keep speculating that *if Serge had lived*, the lifelong revolutionary would have become a (posthumous!) pro-Western Cold Warrior.[29]

Be that as it may, Serge will be best remembered as the novelist who best incarnated the tragedy of the twentieth-century revolution movements that were his life. He died leaving three masterpieces in his desk drawer—considered unpublishable at the time—*Memoirs of a Revolutionary* and two novels, *The Case of Comrade Tulayev* and *Unforgiving Years* (the latter remaining unpublished until 1972). Serge's comrades chipped in for a cheap funeral, only to find that his lack of nationality made it illegal to bury him in a Mexican cemetery! Eventually, they put him down as a citizen of the 'Spanish Republic'—a nationality that, after Franco's victory, no longer existed. Serge would have been pleased.

French novelist and leftist publisher François Maspero, who revived Serge's books (all but forgotten in post-war France) during the rebellious '60s, remarks: "There exists a sort of secret international, perpetuating

---

28 "If the Soviet regime is to be criticized, let it be from a socialist and working-class point of view." Quoted from Ian Birchall, "Letters from Victor Serge to René Lefeuvre," *Revolutionary History* 8, no. 3 (2002).

29 Serge's posthumous 'rightward evolution' is posited (most recently in the *New Left Review* 82 (July–August 2013) on the basis of guilt by association: since the editors of *Partisan Review* (where Serge published two articles) later moved right as did some of his comrades in exile in Mexico, Serge too is guilty of joining the Cold War consensus. Please see my "Victor Serge's Political Testament," Postface to the 2012 NYRB edition of Serge's *Memoirs*, online at http://assets.nybooks.com/media/doc/2012/07/02/Greeman-Serge.pdf.

itself from one generation to the next, of admirers who read, reread [Serge's] books and know a lot about him." As Adam Hochschild notes in his foreword to Serge's *Memoirs*, "It is rare when a writer inspires instant brotherhood among strangers." As one of Serge's translators, it has long been my pleasure (and revolutionary duty!) to welcome new readers into the 'English-language section' of this Invisible International.

Men in Prison as Literature

After such a spectacular career as an activist and historical witness, it is not altogether surprising that Serge-the-revolutionary has overshadowed Serge-the-novelist. Ever a maverick, Serge remains totally ignored in French academia, and his name does not even appear in voluminous dictionaries of French Literature. In any case, as a Belgian-born, Francophone Soviet-Russian writer, he falls through the cracks between academic literature departments. Moreover, along with the hostility of fellow-traveling critics, Serge's standing as a novelist has suffered from the bourgeois prejudice ('art for art's sake') against politics in literature, indeed against the very notion that a committed Marxist militant could also be a serious literary artist.[30]

On the other hand, back in 1968, when this translation of *Men in Prison* was first published, British and American book reviewers immediately recognized its value as literature:

> It is a stream of exquisite and refined consciousness undergoing man's most barbaric experience. Not even in "One Day in the Life of Ivan Denisovich" is there such a penetrating and disturbing account of what prison means to the body and soul. (John Riley, *Los Angeles Times*, December 14, 1968)

---

30   Paradoxically, we find similar Philistine attitudes—reducing Serge's novels to useful sociological documents—on the Left as well. For example, Trotskyist Susan Weissman, in her *Victor Serge: A Political Biography* (formerly *The Course Is Set on Hope*, 2001 and 2013) concludes: "Writing, for Serge, was something to do only when one was unable to fight. . . . Serge wrote with a mission: to expose and analyse the significance of the rise of Stalinism" (the subject of Weissman's PhD dissertation). Meanwhile Weissman's colleague, the celebrated Trotskyist literary critic Alan Wald, ignores Serge's novels entirely, viewing Serge through the lens of *his* particular academic specialty, the 'New York Intellectuals,' forgetting that 99 percent of Serge's writings were published in Paris in French (a language which Wald, like Weissman, doesn't know).

This novel, properly so called by its author, being truth worked up as art, is strongly recommended both as a document and as a powerful work of literature. (Robert Garioch, *Listener*, August 24, 1970)

[Serge] was one of those rare political activists who was also an artist, and his book is poetic and ironic, the account of a spiritual experience rather than a factual record. . . . Serge is almost unique (not quite—one remembers Dostoevsky and Koestler) in turning all this into art. (Julian Symons, *London Sunday Times*, July 19, 1970)

Novel or autobiography, the book is literature, for Serge was a wonderful writer. (*New Yorker*, March 1, 1970)

Serge [is] the model upon whom George Orwell fashioned himself in his descriptive essays and in *Homage to Catalonia*. . . . Serge is not merely a political writer; he is also a novelist, a wonderfully lyrical writer. . . . He is a writer young rebels desperately need whether they know it or not. . . . He does not tell us what we should feel; instead, he makes us feel it. (Stanley Reynolds, *New Statesman*, July 17, 1970)

Few other professional writers have ever endured the experience if prison's living hell, among them Dostoyevsky, sentenced to four years at hard labor in 1849 for his participation in a liberal discussion circle, Oscar Wilde, persecuted for his sexual preference, and of course Russian dissident Aleksandr Solzhenitsyn. There is no doubt about the authenticity of Serge's witness. But how, as a novelist working in the 1920s, did he raise it to literature in *Men in Prison*? His techniques are curiously modern.

To begin with, *Men in Prison* has is no 'plot,' no 'hero' in the conventional sense. Although the novel begins with 'Arrest' and ends with the narrator's release, its internal structure deliberately undercuts this outer appearance of a kind of fictional 'memoir' through a process of abstraction, irony, and distanciation.

Despite the author's "convenient use of the first person singular," Serge's 'I' is a slippery subject, which the postmodern reader will have no problem identifying as an 'unreliable narrator.' For example, the first chapter, "Arrest," begins with a blanket affirmation: "All men who have truly know prison know . . ." followed by a series of generalizations in which the narrator's 'I' alternates with the more general

pronoun 'one' or the passive voice—interrupting the facile identification between the reader and the 'narrator-hero' to the point where
we don't really know who the latter is and why he is in jail. Indeed,
under the heading 'Arrest,' Serge gives us not one, but three accounts
of that 'icy moment.'

Similarly, the second chapter, "The Lockup," although *logically* and
chronologically the next stage in the processing of all prisoners, opens
with the same device of distancing by generalization: "A man imprisoned differs from man in general even in his outward appearance,"
and continues: "He feels as if he has been stripped of part of himself,
reduced to an impotence inconceivable an hour before." The name-
less prisoner's effects are confiscated by anonymous "jailer's hands—
fat, hairy, soiled, accustomed to handling these cast-off objects. From
now on, they are only Number 30's 'bundle.'" But who is 'Number 30'?
The gritty details ("fat, hairy, soiled,") embed the reader in the physi-
cality of the situation and satisfy her legitimate expectations for novelistic atmosphere, without inviting identification with the elusive narrator. These modernist stylistic devices, no doubt deliberate, reflect
Serge's literary project:

> Individual existences—beginning with my own—are only of inter-
> est to me in relation to the vast collective life of which we are only
> parcels, more or less endowed with consciousness. Thus the form
> of the classic novel seemed impoverished and dated. The banal
> French novel in particular, with its dramas of love and ambition,
> centered at most around a family, seemed to me a model not to
> follow in any case. My first novel had no central character. It is
> not about me or about a few, but about men and about prison.[31]

Serge handles the problem of presenting general truths while sat-
isfying our novelistic expectations by alternating ironic first-person
meditations on topics like "Capital Punishment," "The Guards," and
"Architecture," with author omniscient chapters filled with character,
dramatic and stream of consciousness. For example, in one such scene,
Serge enters the mind of a prisoner named Moure, interiorizing his
crude and strangely poetic homoerotic obsessions, rather daring for
1929. As *New Statesman* book critic Stanley Reynolds remarked, "Here,
too, I think, must be the original spring of Jean Genet. Consider the

31   Serge, *Memoirs*, 305.

homosexual Moure, alone in his cell, dreaming of boy friends called Georgette, Lucienne and Antionette. Moure links the most brutally obscene, obscene to the point of cruelty, with love words and coquettish diminutives."[32]

In 2013, political prisoner David Gilbert had another response to this passage: "I don't think I can see the passage on Moure (who is also a sex offender and had sex with 'corrupted adolescent[s]') as affirming gay desire. The 'unctuous' Moure is introduced as the one who snitched on Duclos, a man of 'integrity,' who loved reading and did favors in violation of the rules, and got him sent to the hole. Then Moor got his job. Maybe I'm too much of a hardened con, but I can't see a snitch as a positive figure." Gilbert concludes that Serge, although a man of universal sympathies, was to an extent a captive of the homophobic prejudices of his times.

Serge's strategy of alternating such narrative scenes with extended generalizing meditations, also serves to slow down the pacing of his novel. This alternation gives the reader the impression of the slow passage of time—time being of the essence in a story about 'doing time' in a place where essentially nothing is allowed to happen to mark time's progress. After each intellectual flight, we land right back in the daily brutalizing regime of prison, where time has stood still—perhaps for a day, perhaps for a year.

When embedded more directly in the narrative, Serge's ironic and generalizing 'digressions' provoke a proto-Brechtian 'distancing' or alienation effect. For example as the narrator is being led up a stone spiral staircase to be fingerprinted, he suddenly realizes that he is inside the tower of Paris's medieval Conciergerie and ironically remarks, "They used to question suspects on the rack in the cellars of this very tower. Today they apply Bertillon's scientific fingerprinting upstairs. This is the stairway of progress." Much of Foucault could be deduced from a thorough unpacking of this ironic definition of progress.

Although Serge's narrator tells us nothing about his history, personal life and relations outside the prison, he does allow us into his spiritual world. He recounts the struggle to maintain his spirit, symbolized by the "crystal sphere" (*sphère de cristal*) of the philosopher Taine and the "Azure!" of the poet Mallarmé. It is a constant struggle against the encroachment of madness and obsession, symbolized by "*le cafard*" (the

---

32 Stanley Reynolds, "Courage & Blood," *New Statesman*, July 17, 1970, 63.

cockroach, French slang for depression). "The image fits. The ugly black bug zigzags around under the vault of your skull" (p.48).

Serge's narrator also evokes the religious retreats of earlier times. There are meditations on the joys provoked by the sight of a patch of color, by the passage of a thin ray of sunlight across the ceiling of a cell. There is the fierce ironic joy of the narrator, who as a prisoner is *forbidden to know* any news of the Great War taking place on the Marne, when he hears the German bombardments approach his prison and reads the panic in the face of the guards as the old world crumbles about their ears.

Yet for Serge's narrator, (as for Stendhal's heroes Fabrice and Julien) imprisonment is also a privileged situation. The world may be crumbling, but the insane prison-machine grinds implacably on as if nothing had changed. The guards themselves are trembling, for the German advance on the Marne has come almost within artillery range of the prison. But the deadly routine must continue. Serge's narrator derives a fierce satisfaction from the idea that his prison—that microcosm of a brutal society—may soon be destroyed by the cannon, the ultimate symbol of that society in its most inhuman, and therefore most natural, incarnation. Far from sharing his captors' terror, he experiences an apocalyptic sense of release, a savage joy:

> Our church steeple seemed to us a perfect landmark for artillery. Poule, [an inmate] asked me, terrified: "Do you really think they'll shell us?" "Naturally," I replied. I lived *alone*, feeling the fear spread from one man to the next. I felt a sort of exaltation which gave birth to a great serenity. The old world was being smashed by the cannon. The Mill would be crushed by the cannon. The law of kill-and-be-killed- was reaffirmed for my generation . . . There was profound joy in thinking about this resurrection of the world through the cannon, which had at last interrupted our round . . .
>
> We were the only men on earth forbidden to know about the war; but, though we read nothing and could only glimpse, through the double smokescreen of war and administrative stupidity, the general outline of events, some few of us were blessed with exceptional clear-sightedness. I knew enough about the inner decay of the Russian Empire to foresee, at a time when the Cossacks still incarnated the hope of several old Western countries, its inevitable fall. Long before Europe ever dreamt it, we were discussing, in whispers, the coming Russian Revolution. We knew in what part

of the globe the long-awaited flame would be born. And in it we
found a new reason for living . . .

The bell gave the signal for lights out. Squadrons of airplanes
flew over the prison on the way to Paris. The sky was golden.

The tone is at once ironical, lyrical, apocalyptic. The bitter irony of
being "privileged" through loss of liberty, of being forbidden to know
war; the paradox of feeling joy and serenity in the face of catastrophe,
the lyricism of the final image of bombers against a golden sky. And
yet politics informs and organizes this vision of the totality of a world
organized for repression and finding its ultimate expression (and its own
negation) in the brutalities of prison and war. Without this savage irony
there would be no exaltation, no apocalyptic vision. And the image of
the Russian Revolution, that dim candle flickering at the end of a long,
dark corridor, evokes the ironic theme of the whole passage, indeed of
the whole novel: victory-in-defeat.[33] As literature, it is a powerful and
compelling vision; as politics, a kind of poetic equivalent of Lenin's
1917 "revolutionary defeatism."

Men in Prison Today

As David Gilbert's foreword indicates, inmates in times and places far
from Serge's own context continue to appreciate Men in Prison. As an
inmate in a Minnesota prison wrote in 1970: "My prison is separated
from Victor Serge's by half a century, half a continent and an ocean and
yet we have shared the same experience . . . Nothing changes. Absolutely
nothing changes."[34] Indeed, if anything, things have gotten worse as the
number of human beings in captivity has increased incrementally, resulting in overcrowding, increased brutality, and deteriorating conditions.

The construction and populating of prisons is apparently dying capitalism's answer to massive youth unemployment, and Serge would
certainly have seen today's so-called war on drugs as a war against the
poor. Nearly half of America's two million prisoners are 'guilty' of
non-violent crimes, mostly low-level marijuana and coke dealing—the
principal occupations open to Black and immigrant youth, nearly half
of whom have 'done time' by age thirty-five. The United States, once

---

33 Coincidentally, Alexander Berkman, in The Bolshevik Myth, called the day he first
    heard of the revolution in Russia the "happiest day" of his life.
34 Harley Sorensen, an inmate at Stillwater Prison and former editor of the Prison
    Mirror, writing in Book News (Minneapolis), Sunday, January 18, 1970.

a model of liberal democracy, has now surpassed Russia and China in percentage of its population behind bars, with about two million men and women trapped in the criminal justice system. Mandatory long-term sentences, which Serge correctly termed 'slow death sentences,' have created a whole population of wheelchair-ridden inmates, while undocumented immigrants and small children are increasingly being confined under unnecessarily brutal prison-like conditions.

Indeed, privatized prisons have become vastly profitable, and the building of new high-tech maximum-security and 'supermax' prisons where inmates are kept in solitary twenty-three hours a day and allowed zero contact with other prisoners, is one of the few remaining growth industries. If history is likely to remember the twentieth century for Hitler's Auschwitz and Stalin's Gulag, the young twenty-first is already marked by Guantánamo, Abu Ghraib, and the U.S. 'supermax' penitentiaries on which they were modeled.[35]

As Serge wrote in his *Memoirs:* "The fact that nobody in more than a century has considered the problem of criminality and prisons; the fact that since Victor Hugo, nobody has really raised the issue reveals the power of inertia in our society. This machine whose function is to turn out felons and human refuse is expensive without fulfilling any useful purpose." Serge said it all eighty years ago: "Modern prisons are imperfectible. Being perfect, there is nothing left to do but destroy them."

I ended my original 1968 introduction to this translation of *Men in Prison* with the sentence: "If this book doesn't make you angry, nothing will." I was twenty-eight and fresh from the barricades of the Columbia University student strike. A *New York Times* critic archly described my introduction as "somewhat overwrought." Meanwhile, prisons have grown exponentially, conditions worsened drastically, and I have waxed ever more overwrought. The recent prolonged hunger strikes at Guantánamo and across California attest to the courage and indignation of its victims, just as the official response of cruel and humiliating force-feedings attest to the inhumanity of U.S. capitalism's deciders, from the White House on down. Indeed, since 2003, effective public protest 'on the outside' has been increasingly restricted and criminalized as 'terrorism,' with whistle-blowers and non-violent ecological, anti-war, and human rights activists now facing long prison terms.

---

35 Many of the U.S. soldiers accused of tormenting Iraqi prisoners were prison guards in civilian life.

What with intrusive government surveillance and use of vague 'conspiracy' charges, one doesn't know who will be next. Veteran inmates inform me that, among other things, *Men in Prison* is a reliable guide to what one may expect there.

Meanwhile, as the saying goes, "If you're not overwrought, you're not paying attention."

Richard Greeman
November 2013

ONE

Arrest

ALL MEN WHO HAVE EXPERIENCED PRISON KNOW THAT ITS TERRIBLE GRASP reaches out far beyond its physical walls. There is a moment when those whose lives it will crush suddenly grasp, with awful clarity, that all reality, all present time, all activity—everything real in their lives—is fading away, while before them opens a new road onto which they tread with the trembling step of fear. That icy moment is the moment of arrest.

The revolutionary living under the shadow of the prison wall or the gallows, who, suddenly, in a busy street, feels he is being watched; the underground agitator coming home at night, having finished his work as organizer or journalist, who is suddenly aware of a shadow clinging to his shadow, of firm footsteps dogging his own; the murderer, the thief, the deserter, the hunted man, whoever he may be—they all know that moment of panic. It is a moment as painful to anticipate as to live through, courage and will power notwithstanding. The only difference between cowards and other men is that the others, after living through this moment without revealing their emotion by the slightest gesture, recover full possession of themselves. The cowards remain broken.

I have experienced this moment several times. Once it came after I had actually been under arrest for five or six hours. A plainclothesman had picked me up at the office of the anarchist paper I was editing. He had said it was merely a question of signing receipts for the documents that had been seized during a search that morning at my home. I caught on, but was not really alarmed. For prison is also something we carry within us. I had allowed for this as an occupational hazard, not to be taken too seriously. At police headquarters a fat sergeant of the Sûreté, gross in gesture and speech, told me calmly:

"I've got you. You'll do at least six months awaiting trial. Talk, or I'll arrest you."

Through the window over his shoulder, I could see some bricklayers working on a scaffold. I thought to myself, "Maybe this is one of your last views of life," but without believing it, without any fear. The moment had not yet come. I answered with a shrug:

"Go ahead. Arrest me."

And I was left in that large room, which was furnished with desks and filing cabinets and decorated with anthropometric diagrams ("Nose shapes, Ear shapes, How to read and draw up a description"), for several hours, calmly reading newspapers from one end to the other, ads included. That evening they took me into the comfortable office of the Assistant Chief of the Sûreté. Two leather armchairs before a broad desk, the soft light of a table lamp. Across from me in the shadows, the refined, slightly elongated, regular features of the urbane, well-mannered policeman whom I had guided that morning from our editorial office to the print shop. His behavior on that occasion had been courteous: the intelligent affability of a clever sleuth who knows the value of taking in his opponent, of seducing him a bit. He had told me:

"I sympathize with you. I am quite familiar with your ideas. In the old days I even used to go to meetings where F*** spoke; a marvelous speaker, a marvelous speaker . . . But you people are too advanced; you're bound to be a minority . . ."

Then, with cold, almost negligent, but predatory, glance, he had scrutinized faces, papers, objects—and had arrested just about everybody.

Now he was again extremely polite, rather sad, and seemingly distressed at having to carry out his duty. And once more, ingratiating and persuasive, he invited me to talk. "We know everything; all you can tell us are a few corroborative details; none of your comrades will ever find out; you'll spare yourself months, if not years, of prison; you have no moral obligation toward these miserable wretches; you have nothing in common with them . . . Come now!"

While he was talking to me, the moment came. All I could see in the shadowy room was the dull, wan oval of his face across from me. I felt a choking sensation in my throat. Like a drowning man, I saw a series of incoherent images pass, with extraordinary rapidity, before my eyes: a street corner, a subway car, the scaffolding I had glimpsed earlier. Things were fading away. I took a deep breath and forced myself to speak in a normal tone of voice:

"Lock me up. But I'm terribly hungry. I'd be much obliged if someone could bring me some supper."

It was late; it would be a problem. But as soon as we started talking about it, I felt different, calm again, strangely *free*, and in control of myself. The moment had passed. I had crossed the invisible boundary. I was no longer a man, but a man in prison. An inmate.

I was to live one thousand eight hundred and twenty-five days in prison. Five years.

A few months later, while searching the empty apartment of an anarchist storekeeper, that same policeman came to a dark, tightly shuttered back room. Bravely, and at any rate unaware of any immediate danger, he entered; an instant later, he was locked in a violent hand-to-hand struggle with the man he had been tracking—a desperate anarchist bandit. In the wild embrace of the two bodies thrashing about on the floor, three bullets—fired point-blank—put an end to his career.

Another time, the moment came in a golden Mediterranean city on a brilliantly sunlit day, heavy with heat, a day of rebellion. We had lived for weeks waiting for the battle. That evening, feverish crowds seethed in dark, quiet waves against the foot of the rock where the citadel stood. In the streets, patrols of comrades filed silently past the patrols of gendarmes. Four o'clock in the afternoon: the hot, orange-tinted hour. The stucco façades of the squat, workers' homes, usually ocher, glowed red; the trampled earth underfoot, orange or pomegranate red. A muffled din could be heard coming from a nearby boulevard, blocked off by troops, where the police were charging into running crowds. Walking rapidly, I left a house, surrounded by police, from which one of the leaders of the growing insurrection had just slipped away. My heart was still pounding with the joy of his escape. What light! As I emerged abruptly into the street, two plainclothesmen looked me up and down, hesitated . . . Then their steps fell in with mine—rapid, more rapidly; close, closer . . . Better not turn around. If only I could get to the street corner just ahead! My mind was absurdly fixed on that corner, as if it offered me some unhoped-for chance of safety. A voice hailed me:

"Señor! Hey, Señor!"

The man was already beside me; his dark eyes looked me over coolly. He pronounced the formula:

"In the name of His Honor the Civil Governor . . ."

Another ran up. The street suddenly seemed to darken. It closed in on me. The moment! In my mind, I started immediately to prepare a vigorous protest.

That time it was nothing serious. The police of that city knew they were living on the edge of a storm of revolt. And they were afraid. The workers' power could be felt hanging in the air. An old police sergeant who was very correct, very polite, talked to me about Esperanto—one of his hobbies—and set me free after an hour.

Paris, the war, waiting to be mobilized. Camp Mailly? The front in Champagne? Stages to be passed through, luck providing: It would really be a shame to fall along the way. In the distance, the goal: the revolution unfolding its red flags in the streets of Petrograd. A day of high tension, anxious apprehension. Kornilov goes down in defeat. The Revolution lives! Over here, old Clemenceau carries out his slogan: "Make war!" Almereyda is dead, strangled in Fresnes prison. People are spied upon, arrested. Suspects and informers everywhere. The end of a workday, working clothes, the contented weariness of evening. Coming out of a friend's house—chancy—I run into a slovenly, badly dressed, pallid little man with shifty eyes. I've noticed those shifty eyes several times during the past few days. Just to clear the suspicion from my mind, I turn around and walk right toward him. He slips away. This place is one of the most attractive spots in Old Paris: a modest little street between tall buildings, a little-known byway they say Balzac used to haunt. The street is not deserted this time. A gentleman waits at the end, idle. Another walks slowly away. Behind me, in a hallway, a third.

I have a record: anarchist "bandit." There is an expulsion order out against me. I am "Russian." Under suspicion. The day before yesterday—after meeting those shifty eyes—I put my papers in order and left detailed instructions with a comrade "in case of arrest." Now this placid old street in the heart of Paris, whose silence I love so much, has become a vise tightening around me. I stop. I raise my head toward familiar windows. One of them is edged with flowers.

Le ciel est par-dessus le toit
Si bleu, si calme![1]

---

[1] The sky above the roof
So blue, so calm!
—Verlaine (Tr.)

The shifty-eyed man sidles shiftily up to me. I can feel his fear. My God! It's all so stupid and tiresome! Let's get it over with quickly. The moment has passed. I start walking again, I can hear the other man's footsteps; I know he is afraid and that there is nothing to be afraid of.

"Your name?"

He expects a false one. His face is pale. The others are still far off—ten paces away. But they are walking faster. I give my name.

"That's a lie! Your papers!"

He expected a false name so much that he automatically contradicts my answer, barely moving his bloodless lips! I put my hand into my pocket to take out my letter of transit, but my movement is checked. Violent hands grab both my wrists from behind. Hot breath blows into my ear: "Don't try anything!" Three men, three bodies, brutal and heavy, bear down and crush me. Our faces almost touch. At last they realize that I am not struggling—I have no weapon, I am weak. They take a deep breath. So do I. We walk through the pale-blue street like any other passers-by . . . Those three men around me already constitute a prison, unseen by everyone but me.

When I finally recovered my freedom—after nearly dying in the meantime—I was fifteen months and twelve hundred and fifty miles from there, during a night barren of stars but velvet with snow, on the Finnish border.

There, keeping the watch, stood an emaciated soldier. The red star on his cap seemed almost black in the darkness. The trenches of the Revolution were behind him.

TWO

The Lockup

MAN IMPRISONED DIFFERS FROM MAN IN GENERAL EVEN IN HIS OUTWARD appearance. Prison marks him from the very first hour. Incarceration begins with the search. Necktie, collar, belt; suspenders, shoelaces, pocketknife, anything that might be used in secret to free a desperate man from the power of the law by stabbing or strangulation; papers, notebook, letters, snapshots, everything that characterizes a man, the little objects that accumulate around his private life—all this is taken from him. He feels as if he has been stripped of part of himself, reduced to an impotence inconceivable an hour before. His clothes hang loose, with nothing to fasten them, constantly in the way. His shoes yawn open. He is disheveled from head to foot. Personal effects and toilet accessories are gathered up in my handkerchief by a jailer's hands—fat, hairy, soiled, accustomed to handling these cast-off objects. From now on, they are only Number 30's "bundle."

This first night's cell is apparently nothing more than a lockup set aside for prisoners in transit. A windowless hole, ten feet deep and eight feet wide, somewhere down a corridor. During the day a pale light filters in through the dirty panes of the wire-mesh door. At night an electric bulb screwed into the ceiling gives off a dirty yellow light just strong enough to weary the eyes and aggravate insomnia. Along the wall, an old wooden bench, worn smooth by countless sleeping bodies. In the corner, a fairly clean toilet. Every quarter hour, the toilet flushes automatically, making a great racket. Every time I manage, despite the wearisome glow of the electric light which seeps through my closed eyelids, to doze off stretched out on the bench, my neck flat on the wood, my head thrown back—like a dead man, the racket of the toilet flushing drags me out of my torpor.

On the bench, etched in with pinpricks, I find inscriptions. There are more on the walls; they are everywhere, barely visible. You have to examine the walls very closely to make out these graffiti; but they are always the same, in every prison cell: only four or five themes, sex predominating. It is as if the throngs of men thrown together by prison needed only thirty words and a phallic symbol to express the essence of their suffering and their lives. At first glance, the cell is empty, silent, sepulchral. But after the first five minutes, every square inch of wall or floor has its tale of woe to tell. A thousand hushed voices fill it with their changeless, unremitting murmurs. You soon grow tired of listening, tired of the constant repetition of the same miseries.

Night. Even the city's rumble seems to have stopped. Nothing. Nothing. Sleep is impossible. Yet this wakeful state has something in common with sleep and dreams, perhaps with hallucination as well. I am already in a sort of tomb. I can do nothing. I am nothing. I see, hear, and feel nothing. I only know that the next hour will be exactly like this one. The contrast between this vacant, empty prison time and the intense rhythm of normal life is so violent that it will take a long and painful period of adaptation to slow down the pulse of life, to deaden the will, to stifle, blot out, obliterate every unsettling image from my mind. The first days' total disorientation. My inner life pursues its feverish course in a silence void of time.

Nerves strain with curiosity about tomorrow, with the feeling of being at the mercy of an anonymous, fearsome, many-faced enemy who must be resisted, deceived, defied, shown no weakness.

We climb a long spiral staircase. We are in one of the medieval towers of the *Conciergerie*, I discover. We: a bizarre company that has just been formed in the gray murk of a corridor. I catch a glimpse of a dozen terrified faces. Their clothes, unfastened and disheveled, hang loose. Wrists handcuffed. We climb ponderously, with guards preceding us, separating us, following us. The stairs are narrow. Clumsy feet stumble over the steps. A muffled "Goddamn." I am led by a single plainclothesman, a nondescript blond fellow who doesn't even seem to notice me. In earlier times they used to put their victims "to the question" on the rack in the cellars of this very tower. Today they apply Bertillon's scientific system upstairs. This is the stairway of progress.

A kind of waiting room, fairly well lighted, furnished with benches divided into square compartments. A man is seated in each square. Immobility, silence, stares of various kinds: stupefied, curious, anxious, angry. Mostly stupefied. Every five minutes the squares empty and fill again. After hours in a cell, the narrow staircase, the grayness of the corridors and faces, these large, well-lighted rooms of the anthropometric service, with their wooden apparatus, are somewhat disconcerting. The clerk, attentive but with perfect professional indifference, measure the prisoner's skull, foot, hand, forearm; note the scars and the tiniest marks on his body; examine and record the exact color of his eyes, the folds of his ear, the cut of his lips, the shape of his nose; gently take his fingerprints. I observe these automatons, noting that they are free men occupied in compiling an exact scientific description of the prisoner: me. They don't notice me at all. They ignore me. For this man who, with three rapid, deft movements, stretches my forearm out on a kind of short measuring rod, I don't exist. There is nothing in front of him but a forearm, so many inches long, bearing this or that peculiarity. Two numbers, ciphers to be entered, always in the same place, on a file card. Each day, the man enters these numbers several hundred times. He has neither the time nor the inclination to look at faces. But in the evening he probably enjoys looking at the picture of the Ménilmontant murderer in the *Petit Parisien*.

After these silent manipulations, the measured subject lands in front of the photographer's lens. The same indifferent hands raise the subject's chin, place the back of his skull against a metal stanchion, hang a plate bearing a number on his chest. A violent flash of light startles him as the camera operator releases the shutter. A gallery of lost souls. There are only two or three varieties of expression: animal passivity, confusion, humiliation—each modified by anger, despair, defiance, or taciturn sullenness, depending on the case. Experienced prisoners have explained to me the way, to fight the camera, to fool it. Some men stubbornly close their eyes, make faces, screw up their features. These are soon made to submit; and not by friendly persuasion . . . The clever ones know how to distort their features in advance, how to put on an abnormal expression, make it seem calm and natural, hold it as long as necessary. The stiffness of the pose, the fixed stare of the eyes, the dishevelment of the clothes, all add to the effect: the image they leave on the photographer's plate differs enough from their normal appearance to deceive an unpracticed eye.

An enormous hall, lofty, gray, cold, with a vaulted ceiling reminiscent of a monastery except for the tiled corridors, the heavy padlocked doors, the bars, the grilled windows, the mournful comings and goings in silence— a silence broken by calls, sharp orders, and the murmured confidences

of frightened voices. There are a handful of us here, walking clumsily
in shoes without laces. We come to rest on a broad oak bench polished
by countless daily contacts, as everything here is polished, nearly black
from the touch of flesh, clothes, and grime. A pale, gray light falls from
the window above us; we sit in the dimness like wood lice under a rock.
Each man thinks of his own troubles. Each observes the dismal movement of this room with weary curiosity. Each whispers a confidence, a
question, a word of advice, or a complaint to his neighbor. There are
four of us: an older man of about fifty with the poise and bearing of an
officer or casino gambler—Rumanian or Greek—a handsome black mustache, and pomaded hair. He wears a fashionable overcoat of the very
best cut. Lack of sleep has puffed up his big, dark, expressionless eyes.
Now that he no longer has a collar or tie under his blue-black chin, he
reminds me of one of those flashy, big-time adventurers whose police
photographs are always published in the papers when there is a big financial scandal. He holds his derby politely on his knee. I notice his gnarled,
hairy hands; their well-manicured nails are grimy after a single night in
the lockup . . . There is also a poor, bedraggled wretch slouching in the
corner, feeble and pasty-faced, so crushed he seems ill. His mustache,
stiff and sporty only yesterday, droops, half-eaten and frayed by nervous
fingers. The last traces of a vulgar elegance are fading from his sorry
figure . . . And a twenty-year-old guttersnipe with a cap and the prog-
nathic jowls of a Spanish Bourbon . . . The fourth: myself.

The guttersnipe tells us:

"Me, I'm done for! Goddamn, goddamn, goddamn . . ."

Under his breath he reels off his monotonous litany of swear words.
I already know all I need to know about him: He is twenty-one years
old and has had seven convictions ("all small-time stuff! but goddamn,
goddamn . . . I'll get life . . ."). This time, even though he was picked up
for a minor offense only, he'll get at least a year and a day, plus recommitment for being a repeater: in other words, hard labor for life. He
picks over the linings of his pockets attentively, looking for flakes of
tobacco to suck on.

"You know, that makes two days without one . . . Ah, shit!"

There are four of us. Others like us, forty or four hundred of them,
are filing right now through the corridors, rooms, and offices of this
building. The prison machine sweeps these bits of human flotsam along
from one compartment to another. We watch the parade of prostitutes
arrested last night by the vice squad. Inmates for only a day, we are

not yet aware of how miraculous the most ordinary female shape can seem. The men usually laugh when this grotesque, ill-assorted company goes by. Every woman you have ever passed in the street seems to be there, every type, every age. A stout, fussy lady becomes indignant: It's really not her turn, they pick her up too often, they have it in for her. Hardened hustlers go by, indifferent, their hands in their apron pockets. Some of them giggle. Young, modest women also file by, crestfallen, bedraggled, choking back the tears. A nice working girl, a secretary in a raincoat, a streetwalker from Les Halles, seething with rage, her wrists held by a city cop. It's a deluge—the same deluge every night, every morning at the same time—hundreds of them. A smell of cheap perfume and dirty underwear thickens the air. I notice a well-dressed woman carefully holding a pretty feathered hat in both hands, wrapped up in a blouse. Her bust is ample; she fills out the necessary papers decisively. That's life, eh! Once every two weeks or every month you have to go through this: It's just part of the business.

Actually, the police are only "doing their job," that is, hauling in a specified number of girls each night; and since they are human, they tend to take those with unfamiliar faces or the ones who refuse to do them favors. They also hunt out the nonprofessionals; for every new registration places another creature under the power of men whose law is absolute on the sidewalks of doubtful streets.

The formalities go on and on. How many printed forms are inscribed with our surnames, Christian names, descriptions! From window to window, the same surly prison-rat faces question us without seeing us. Our height is measured; huge green books, so big that two hands are needed to manage them, are opened to register each wretch. Sign here! The indifferent wretch signs.

The hybrid of bureaucratic scribbler and turnkey, who works at desk jobs here, is a singularly monotonous breed; they are all thick-set, their bodies grown fat from sitting and lack of exercise. Two types of faces: one ruddy, wine-soaked; the other livid and bloated, stamped by the murky grayness of the prison bureau. Their eyes have grown dim with the horrid dullness that emanates from the forms, receipts, registers and filing cabinets, where the same inanely bureaucratic descriptions of hopeless victims and miserable wretches pile up *ad infinitum*. Vegetative brutes, old police-station scribblers, registrars from provincial prisons transferred to Paris through favoritism. Their faded uniforms, greasy at the collar, shiny at the elbow, have lost all definite color and shape. A musty odor of wine-soaked breath, cold tobacco smoke, old clothes, ink, dust, and yellowed paper clings to these men; they emerge from their total indifference—and then just barely—only to insult or to make a clumsy, stupid joke at the expense of a man whose misery they have just recorded. Some poor old devil murmurs his ridiculous name to them in a whisper:

"Lecornu, Alcide-Marie!"

Three low guffaws follow, three piglike grunts. A winy voice drawls:

"Well! I hope you earned your horns, Mr. Cuckold!" But most often the registrars' silence falls on the prisoner like a first layer of dust.

From window to window, from measurement to search, from search to shower, from shower to compartment, we move on. I think of grains of sand sifting through a complicated, extremely dirty sieve, and falling deeper with every instant into sordid obscurity. They already searched us when we were first arrested; there is nothing more they can take, it seems, except perhaps that pin, that cigarette butt, that tiny pencil stub, even that gold piece which experienced prisoners know how to carry past any obstacle.

The ceremony is repeated, nonetheless, and in a slightly more odious form. Two or three hulking guards strut out in front of a line of naked men. "Open your mouth! Bend over! . . . More . . . Lower, dammit, you jerk, lower! . . . Legs apart . . . Come on . . . Next man forward!" A fat thumb prods the inside of a suspicious jaw. A guard with a crumpled *képi* inspects the rear end of a tough-looking mug who has been put over the bar; the bar is designed to make you bend over in such a manner that any object hidden in the anus is supposed to be revealed . . .

The grimy gang of new arrivals rushes toward the showers—a gallop of bare feet smacking on the tiles of the wide corridor. The first ones in run into the last of the group coming out, cleansed and ridiculous. Their physiques are grotesque: Men dredged up and thrown together by the accident of their misfortune are usually misshapen and ugly in the nude, deformed by their misery. They gesticulate, shiver, struggle with heaps of clothes. While they were in the shower, the clothes they had been wearing were sent through the steam press: an instantaneous disinfecting from which—pulverized under the enormous pressure—they emerge like rags, honeycombed with wrinkles that can almost never be removed. I catch only a quick glimpse of them getting dressed: a grotesque scene. We are herded forward, hustled, bullied by shouts of "Come on, faster, get a move on! Hurry, goddamn it! Hurry!" The machine works so fast that now we are already lined up in the hot, sticky wooden tubs. A shower of nearly boiling water; the slimy black soap sticks to the skin. "Out! Get a move on! Hurry up!" Another gallop of bare feet smacks down the corridor.

Roll call again. Each one of these ritual operations begins with a roll call. Nonetheless, I find myself interested each time by the different tone of the voices answering, "Here": stifled by physical fear; hurried with that special haste of the bashful, who are somehow always a little late; low, lingering, coming out almost reluctantly; nonchalant, among the old-timers. After roll call we file, two at a time, into rather well-lit compartments along a wide corridor. A little light is good for the eyes. We have at least an hour to wait: rest (which turns to boredom in a quarter of an hour; our inner agitation will only calm itself after a long time) and vacant time. My companion in this cage is my neighbor from the lineup: the poor wretch with drooping mustaches who now looks like a casta-way. He cheered up momentarily when he saw our Rumanian-officer-financier-adventurer coupled with a fidgety little fag. Alone together, we can talk in whispers. After all, it makes a comfortable noise.

"Things going badly?" I ask.

He answers with a meaningful glance and a nod.

"What a lousy break. I got nabbed in the Galeries Lafayette. I was warned: It shouldn't have happened to me. You see there's a store dick there, a real bastard . . . He had me spotted right away . . . Oh, boy, now I'm in for it . . ."

He is still wearing the cause of his good or bad fortune—the tool of his trade—an ordinary beige overcoat. But this overcoat is full of false pockets and false linings. Hands in pockets, he looks like a gentleman walking through the crowd, brushing against the counter of the store; in reality, his hands, free within the folds of the open garment, are operating with great dexterity. Booty drops into the lining. If this professional overcoat passes unnoticed, my companion of the moment will get off with a few months in prison. If not:

"I'm in for it. Up for recommitment."

You are up for recommitment after three convictions for theft; the amount of the theft itself doesn't matter in the least. Three times a hundred *sous*—these things happen—can mean an "additional" life sentence for a twenty-year-old, three-time loser . . .

The cell door has finally closed on me. The bolts have been drawn, the Judas shut. I'm on the ground floor. My cell has two large, semicircular barred windows with panes of frosted glass. It is large and dirty. A low column divides it into two unequal parts. Three gray straw mattresses on crude cots—gray with filth, spattered with all sorts of stains, stinking of dust, old straw, sleeping animality—make up the furniture. Bolted to the wall, there is a little oak table; the wood is an oily brown and covered with inscriptions. On the table, an earthenware jug and a "quarter"—a tin drinking cup—that holds a quarter of a liter. The mattresses and the drinking cup are apparently never cleaned. After the first hour, I wanted a drink. I was clumsy enough to shake the jug, and a greenish slime rose to the surface where wisps of straw, odd leaves, hair, bits of thread, and a broken match were floating. Before quenching your thirst, simple prudence advises allowing this "brew"—which is changed every day—to settle to the bottom. I am already used to the graffiti. They will interest me only later on, during the months of isolation, when every sign in the cell will become a life-giving word for my brain in its struggle against stupor and madness. The only thing I find here, at first glance, is the name of a wayward comrade, a murderer and thief—a man overboard. When mountain climbers scale the highest peaks, they tie themselves together with a stout rope; thus, if one should happen to fall, he may drag his companions down with him into the abyss. Among us—rebels and revolutionaries, so different from one another, ill-assorted idealists, bohemians, adventurers, cranks, proletarians, bandits—blind solidarity, knowing only comrades, plays the role of that life-saving or ill-fated rope. We too, are conscious of striving obstinately to climb upward. But for us the peak, more dreamed of than glimpsed, is inaccessible, and a fall is always fatal.

> *Par les airs sidéraux*
> *Monte en plein ciel, droite comme un héros,*
> *La claire tour qui sur les flots domine . . .*[2]

Ballade Solness, "Anarchy! Oh torchbearer!" Here I am, suddenly transfixed with awful clarity, before a name and a date on the sordid

---

2   Through the starry air
      Climbs into the very sty, erect like a hero,
      The bright tower which rules over the waves.

wall of a detention cell. The name of a wayward comrade, a murderer and thief, a man overboard—my poor friend!

I am not alone. My chance companion is a tall devil of a workman with a tanned, forty-five-year-old face and a long, drooping mustache. Black—a dull black, eyes black, hair black (graying nonetheless), features black, it would seem, because of their blank fixity and the rough, lusterless skin, cracked like old leather. Squatting on the foul mattress, we talked as the hopeless night drew slowly over us. My cellmate told me his story in a gloomy voice, in short, rudimentary, incomplete sentences. Workman, widowed, a fifteen-year-old daughter. The whole paycheck drunk up. (Why? There is no "why." Or rather, why live? If life is always hard work which hardly keeps you from starving, with nothing afterwards.) Staggering home to a filthy hovel, falling heavily onto the mattress where his little girl is sleeping. After that, he can't remember very well how it happened in the double darkness of night and alcohol: He had never even thought of it before—no, never!—rape. Man is not too far removed from the brute: A beast of burden, even after forty-five years of misery and work, has these bestial revolts of the flesh. The usual punishment in such cases is at least ten years at hard labor.

Six years later, I was to enter one of these detention cells again, perhaps the same one. Nothing had changed: not even the greenish slime at the bottom of the earthenware jug. This time I was alone. On the second day, having procured pen and paper from the prison store— prizes of inestimable value for which you have to wait at least twenty-four hours in total idleness—I began to write a story. In prison it is a fundamental rule of mental hygiene to work at all costs, to occupy the mind. So I was writing; the Judas of the barred door was half-open; there was that peculiar silence of jails, peopled by a hundred lifeless sounds: bolts being drawn somewhere among the galleries, a patrol of guards making the rounds, mess tins being washed, a chow wagon rolling down the corridor . . . Suddenly the silence was broken by a soggy thud like the sound of a bundle of wash falling onto the tiles—and a strange cry, not very loud, but sharp:

"Ou-i-iiiiii . . ."

Like a bird whose neck is being wrung.

The sound of hasty steps resounded, not too loudly—the sound of guards wearing boots and the muffled, padding tread of trustees on the cleanup squad. The half-open Judas closed with a bang. I listened for a long time with that premonition of evil which comes so accurately to old prisoners that they no longer question it. I heard the footsteps multiply; whisperings; an unprecedented number of footsteps, now moving away; water splashing on the tile floor; rag mops swishing; an unusually lengthy washing-down. Soup was brought in. The silence continued. The Judas opened again; I glimpsed two civilians discussing something in low voices in the gallery: they were sizing up the height of the stories with movements of their hands . . .

The next day a trustee from the cleanup squad told me: "You know, one of 'em took a dive from the third gallery almost in front of your door. Hardly made a sound."

"Who was it?"

"I don't know; an Italian, they say. A deportee. Maybe that ain't so. But there sure in hell was a lot of blood, believe me: a whole bucketful, he made!"

The old trustees on the cleanup squad had done a good job sopping up the blood with their dirty rag mops: the tiles were as shiny as usual.

Once inside prison walls, the use of the familiar *tu* is practically a rule among inmates. At the house of detention, where crowds of transients are always coming and going—in that sudden physical indignity of arrest which is so much harder on new prisoners than on underworld "regulars"—the guards call almost everyone *tu*. Elsewhere, after a rapid process of classification by social categories, they reserve this vulgarly familiar address for inmates who command no respect or consideration. One of my first observations—the accuracy of which was confirmed many times later on—was that this use of the familiar form by guards to inmates, or by policemen to criminals, is an instinctive recognition of a common existence and a common mentality. Guards and inmates live the same life on both sides of the same bolted door. Policemen and crooks keep the same company, sit on the same barstools, sleep with the same whores in the same furnished rooms. They mold each other like two armies fighting with complementary methods of attack and defense on a common terrain. I have learned from long experience that, if there are any differences of mentality and morality between criminals and guards or policemen, they are generally, and for profound reasons, all to the advantage of the criminals. Even when it comes to everyday honesty, the comparison leads to that conclusion. Most of the guards and policemen I have run into were themselves thieves or crooks, sometimes pimps. An hour after my arrest, while I was reading the newspapers in the office of a sergeant of the Sûreté, I saw one of those professional finks, known as "plainclothesmen," come in. (They are called *plain*clothesmen precisely because their civilian disguise—derby hats, canes as thick as billy clubs, heavy shoes—makes it impossible for anyone to mistake them for ordinary plain people in the street.) This one reported a difficult "tailing" job to his superior; then, embarrassed, lowering his voice, he explained his misadventure of the day. His wife had just been arrested, red-handed, for shoplifting in a department store. The sergeant reassured him without appearing at all surprised. It would be taken care of.

The next day, while being taken to the anthropometric service by a man from the Sûreté or from headquarters—I wasn't sure which, because we never opened our mouths—I heard my guard become vehemently indignant to an acquaintance:

"Really, what a lousy joint! What bastards! You know what? I leave my overcoat on the coathanger, see? Well, somebody came along and stole my handcuffs! I had to borrow a pair to bring over this customer."

I wasn't in a happy mood, but I had to stifle a wild desire to break up laughing. Steal a pair of handcuffs! This low point in thievery could only have been reached by a cop. A genuine thief would have seen it as a low point in perversion.

THREE

Transitions

THE TRANSITION—THE TRANSFER—FROM THE HOUSE OF DETENTION TO THE Santé Prison takes an hour in the darkness of a Black Maria, or police van. Thirty men as unlike each other as thirty kinds of misfortunes, are dragged one by one out of the gray void of their cells, bustled for the twentieth time down corridors lined with Judases, dazzled for an instant by the bright daylight of the courtyard, and swallowed up by the blackness of the waiting vans. A city trooper hustles them up the step. The van is divided down the middle by an iron-plate corridor half a yard wide. Inside, another trooper armed with a key opens one of the narrow lateral doors. The man drops in there like a billiard ball into a pocket. The inside is so narrow you can't turn around, so low you can't stand up: hunched up, automatically seated. The darkness seems to melt little by little. Your dilated pupils capture the faint light that sifts in through a dusty ventilator. On the wall I read:

> *Mon coeur à ma mere,*
> *Ma tête à Deibler,*
> *Mon corps à la terre.*
> *H. bon pour la tronche.*[3]

An "I love Louey-the- . . ." in small block letters partly covers over this allusion to the guillotine. The wall is covered with inscriptions. Another one reads: "Petty theft, May 2. Shit on the Republic and long live Rochette!" The van is now rolling along through the soft smile of the Paris lights. The Seine has been crossed; here we are on the Boulevard Saint-Michel. I can hear the sounds of the living Boulevard: even the

---

3   My heart to my mother,
     My head to Deibler,
     My body into clay.
     H. ready for the blade.

sudden bursts of conversation from strolling passers-by. Pulling myself up to the grill of the air filter, I attempt to look out; I see the corner of a building: *Pâtisserie* in big gold letters, a horse's head, two students hurrying along . . . Nothing about this astonishes me yet; I sit down again. What is astonishing is to be going up Boulevard Saint-Michel like this, exactly like a dead man in his coffin.

My coffin is perpendicular.

From one coffin to another, a conversation begins:

"Hey, Martingale! You there?"

Martingale gives vigorous evidence of his presence:

"Ay!"

In covert language, half-slang, half-Javanese—Javanese being a language, unknown to philologists, formed by interposing made-up syllables between the syllables of each word—Martingale and his buddy tell each other a strange story—punctuated by scatological exclamations (in French) and laughter.

Glimpsed in transit:

The outer wall, towering, gray; the paved inner court; the gate, yawning open like a grave.

On the inside, cleanliness, light filtering down from an open transom twelve yards above, wide hallways forming little streets. The impression of entering a subterranean vault—impossible that this pale light should come from the free sky over the city! A buried city, peopled with shades. *The House of the Dead*, someone called it.

The same seedy sempiternal scribblers are working in a sort of glassed-in cage at the crossroads where all these inner avenues come together. Vague silhouettes in front of a grilled window. To the right, splashing sounds from the showers, naked forms, clouds of steam, the tired voice of a turnkey:

"Will you get the fuck under there . . . Get the fuck out in the hall."

A guy emerges, still dripping, wearing his shirt, arms full of clothes: gray tweed suit, soft felt hat, detachable collar, duds of comic elegance.

"Are you deaf? Move on there!"

In front of me the blue-black nape of a neck bobs up over rounded shoulders, and I hear:

"Carder, Pierre-Paul-Marie . . . What's the matter, one name isn't good enough for you? . . . thirty . . . Under a warrant from Examining Magistrate Billot . . . Charged with intentional homicide . . ."

The clerk recording these details looks like a Gavarni caricature of an old Foreign Legionnaire. Beard specked with tobacco flakes, *képi* over one ear.

"Intentional Homicide." The administrative term makes the murderer standing there smile. The clerk-registrar writes a beautiful round hand: the "H" is surrounded by a winged flourish. I wonder: Is it stone or sponge under that greasy *képi*?

"Cartier, Pierre, Twelfth Gallery, Division Twenty, Cell Number One."

A broad winding staircase, on which barred windows cast a strange green glow, for the leaves of old linden trees rustle against this corner of the prison.

FOUR

Architecture

I KNOW OF ONLY ONE PERFECT AND IRREPROACHABLE WORK OF ARCHITEC-
ture in the modern city: prison.

Its perfection lies in the total subordination of its design to its function. A modern prison is as different from an old crenelated castle—
whose every loophole and battlement betrayed the need for defense
against the surrounding countryside or town—as today's all-power-
ful capitalist society is unlike the absolute monarchies of olden times,
so limited in their real power. Set up in the center of town, or in the
suburbs, a modern prison feels totally secure. Behind its thin walls, its
frail buildings spread out in a star-shaped pattern. Only the barest minimum of thick walls, barred windows, metal doors and purely deco-
rative battlements has been retained from the convent or fortress of
yesteryear. Its perfection is revealed at first glance: It is impossible to
mistake it for any other kind of edifice. It is proudly, insularly, *itself.*
The design is almost invariable. There is only one opening in the outer
wall, around which the guardroom, the registry, and the administrative offices are gathered. Inside the wall, the cell blocks, arranged in a
star, converge on a central hub. Within each cell block, the narrow galleries running along in front of the cells rise tier upon tier over a wide
corridor. Each stretch of wall is like a beehive honeycombed with rectangular cells. From any point along any gallery, as from the corridor,
nearly the whole beehive enclosed in one of the branches of the star
is visible. From the center of the hub, a single man can keep his eye
on the whole prison without difficulty, and his glance can ferret into
the most remote corners. Maximum ease of surveillance is ensured
with a minimum of personnel. The lines are simple, the plan faultless. Uniform daylight comes down through the glassed roof, getting
grayer and grayer as you get closer to the ground floor: This solves
the problem of daily lighting with a maximum of thrift. The empty

spaces between the branches of the star are used as exercise yards for the inmates.

A modern city has no forum. It contains no circuses for the diversion and amusement of its throngs of people. It provides no day nurseries. Nor does it nurture, with all its lodgings and gathering places, the labor, the meditation or the relaxation of *all* men. In America, its skyscrapers, those mechanical creations of the business mentality, bring together apartments, banks, movie theaters, hospitals, schools, and churches in carefully ordered confusion, all behind the same totally anonymous and undistinguishable façade. Its architects have added practically nothing to the legacy of the past except, for its victims, this scientifically imperfectible hive of crimes, vices, and iniquities.

A modern prison—the Spanish more openly call it *Carcel Model*, or *model prison*—successfully resolves the problem of economy in space, labor, and surveillance. Housing a crowd, it effects the total isolation of each individual in that crowd. Busier than a beehive, it is able to accomplish, silently and systematically, as many different tasks as there are lives tossed into its grinding cogs. The chance of escape is reduced to infinitesimal proportions. They used to escape from the Bastille. They used to escape from Noumea, in spite of the ocean fraught with squalls. They still escape from Guiana, across the virgin forest. No one escapes from the model jail.

Modern prisons are imperfectible, since they are perfect. There is nothing left but to destroy them.

FIVE

In a Cell

HERE I AM BACK IN A CELL. ALONE. MINUTES, HOURS, DAYS SLIP AWAY WITH terrifying insubstantiality. Months will pass away like this, and years. Life! The problem of time is everything. Nothing distinguishes one hour from the next: The minutes and hours fall slowly, torturously. Once past, they vanish into near nothingness. The present minute is infinite. But time does not exist. A madman's logic? Perhaps. I know how much profound truth there is in it. I also know that a captive is, from the very first hour, a mentally unbalanced person.

My cell is one of those whose perfect order and irreproachable maintenance are probably noted in official reports. On the second story of galleries a shiny door, bolted, exactly like the others: Fourteenth Division, Number thirty-nine. I am Number "14–39." Three or four yards in length, the same in width. A little oak table, bolted to the wall; a heavy chair, attached to the wall by a chain to prevent it becoming a weapon in the hands of the unknown man whose despair and fury have been anticipated. A camp bed of satisfactory cleanliness folds up against the wall during the day and hardly takes up any room. The inmate makes his bed in the evening at a signal given by a bell, after which it is forbidden to be seen standing up. It is folded in the morning at a signal. Even in case of illness, it is absolutely forbidden to lie down during the day without the doctor's permission. There is also, in a corner, a board which is used as a shelf: For the moment, only the tin "quarter" and the wooden porringer which serves as a spoon can be seen on it. Two windows at the top of the back wall, long and low, with bars and frosted glass. In one corner, a porcelain toilet and a water faucet. In the door, the Judas, a shelf for the food that is pushed through. Inside the Judas, the spyhole, an eye whose metallic blinking is heard every hour when the guards make their rounds. The walls are painted a dark brown up to the level of one yard; above that a yellowish, light ocher. The light which falls on you is always dirty.

It is not like a room; it is more like an oversized bathroom or a monk's cell. It's habitable, nonetheless. I came to understand this with time. For man needs but few things to live! Hardly more than the six feet of earth necessary for his rest when he has finished living. As in the monk's cell, the proximity of death can be felt here. It is also a tomb. Prison is the *House of the Dead*. Within these walls we are a few thousand living dead . . .

I have nonetheless done a great deal of living there, and very intensely. I have changed cells several times. It has never been without feeling a certain sadness at having to leave walls which could speak, whose every secret I knew, between which I had spent such hours of plenitude. My memory of an iron-gray death cell—despite an infinite fifteen-day nightmare—contains an element of authentic clarity.

The first days are the worst. And in the first days, the first hours.

Here is man, between these four walls. Alone: nothing around him. No event. No possibility of an event. Total inactivity. His hands are idle. His eyes soon tire of that uniform yellowish light. His feverish brain spins in a void.

There is a furious agitation in the city's life and in the lives of those who live there. Yesterday you had a thousand worries, a bustling schedule of activity; the hours rushed by, you were barreling along in the subway, pushing your way through the living sea of the avenue; you were surrounded during the day by thousands of faces; you had newspapers, the motley lure of the billboards, the persuasive voice of books. Yesterday, in the very center of life, there were your woman, your child, your friends, your comrades. People and objects surging forth in ceaseless motion, like you, with you. And all at once: nothing. Silence. Isolation. Inactivity. The dullness of empty time.

A runner, suddenly immobilized, experiences shock. So does a captive. In the total disorientation of his inner life, everything is thrown out of proportion; things in the foreground become exaggerated. The slightest worry aggravates itself, becomes an obsession. The imagination immediately fleshes out thousands of hypotheses that the normal mind disdainfully discards. From a large number of observations I have drawn the conclusion that the immense majority of captives, during the first hours of isolation, live a shortened version of their whole future life in jail with a peculiar intensity. They immediately run off the rails, the rapid transition from active life to dead claustration being an entirely sufficient cause for mental disorder. Two or three obsessions dominate them from the very first, which are usually: preoccupation with their "case," family worries, sexual obsession.

Every man who is thrown into a cell has an *idée fixe* as a companion. Every man who is thrown into a cell immediately begins to live in the shadow of madness.

. . . You bring nothing with you into a cell. Sometimes you find a book there. Never a sheet of paper. Nothing to work on. Prisoners awaiting trial have the right to ask for work, but several days go by before they get it, and it is invariably ridiculously underpaid work of stultifying monotony: sorting coffee beans, making paper bags, making paper fans, folding school notebooks. The same dull gesture to be repeated several thousand times a day. I admit that, however stupid it may be, this work is still a physical distraction, a diversion from obsessive thoughts. But this diversion is too weak; it merely serves to inspire the individual with a horror of work, pure and simple. Prisoners awaiting trial can also get permission from the examining magistrate to receive books for study from the outside; that is salvation. Unfortunately, this procedure takes several days. I got the permission without any trouble, but I recall they refused to give me two novels by Anatole France and Pierre Loti, these books doubtless having seemed unsuitable for study to the functionary in charge of censorship; and since prison, even preventive prison, still persists in the medieval notion of *penitence*, an inmate is not supposed to spend time reading things whose value is purely distractive. Fortunately, this rigor was tempered by bureaucratic imbecility: Having offered the argument of "literary research," I was allowed to receive anthologies. The penitentiary administration, by the way, is very proud of having libraries in every prison. At the Santé Prison, they lend a book of one to three hundred pages a week to every inmate, but without any choice. The Judas opens, a voice calls "Books." You hand over the book you have had for a week; the prisoner in charge of this distribution throws you another, taken at random from the little pile he has with him. The book I found in my first cell was an adventure novel by Mayne Reid: scalp hunters, trappers, virgin forest—all that is necessary, after all, to keep at half-cock the instincts of neighborhood "toughs." About one fifth of the pages were missing; on the other hand, the margins were ornamented with various inscriptions and even with erotic drawings in a marvelous primitive style. The covers and the corners of the pages were so shiny with grease that I struggled for several hours against the emptiness of the hours before making up my mind to touch that book.

The bulk of the Santé Prison library seems to consist of bad adventure novels, old graduation-prize books, Mayne Reid, Jules Verne, unknown and mediocre amateur novelists, probably bought by the obliging administration precisely because they are unsalable to the public, and a heaven-sent collection of Balzac. Later on, I had the privilege of choosing my book from a list which included about twenty titles of this sort. I almost forgot to mention those ancient little treatises of somniferous morality. To judge from the relative cleanliness (of the pages), they are the ones least read; but the ferocity of certain commentaries written into the margins reveals that they are the best understood. Here at least bourgeois morality dupes no one . . .

I learned, alone with these books, that the most mediocre printed page can have its value. Everything is in knowing how to read and how to make the book a pretext for meditations. Even if only on human stupidity . . .

Have you ever seen caged wolves at the zoo? There are lean ones, with grizzled pelts, who circle, circle tirelessly in a rapid trot around their prison. A man in jail, before the end of the first hours, discovers that expedient: walking. He begins to walk. He paces around his cell, his steps mechanical or self-conscious, depending upon his feeling at the moment. He counts his steps. Eleven!, Bad! He gets his pace into rhythm and smiles at having eluded the trap set by an ill-omened number: He gets around the cell in twelve steps. There are many other things to do: you can figure out the necessary time in seconds, note the number of times around, then undertake a complicated calculation of miles traveled. You can make bets with yourself, improvising fascinating games of chance. How many steps, how many times around before the next check by the man on duty, revealed by the faint click of the spyhole? Thirty-eight trips . . . Lost, lost! No, won! Right, thirty-eight. The captive comes to a halt with a great silent laugh, one of those laughs of solitary men that the psychiatrist recognizes so well. Or, like a whirling dervish, you can walk until you're dizzy, until your breath gives out, until you collapse in the heavy wooden chair, your ears buzzing, your pupils dilated, while the four walls of your cell seem to stretch out obliquely, twisting themselves into diamond shapes and spinning around a fantastic axis. More often you walk with a meditative step and your brain grows weak winding its skein of offensive-defensive tactics. When this has gone on for a certain number of months or years, the expression of your eyes and the lines of your face begin to change. A certain inmate will look at you in a distracted way, listen to you with detached politeness, and, by means of ingenious shifts and changes, constantly bring the conversation back to his system of defense. I met some who had been ruminating over theirs for eight to ten years.

A man marching in circles around his cell—twelve steps, never eleven!—has an invisible companion who is sometimes cruel, but who more often calms him, stultifies him, or releases him from the weight of his idle hours: insanity.

I immediately developed my own way of walking and of resisting the influence of my cell. Certainly not original. In his *Memoirs*, Peter Kropotkin tells the story of the years he spent in the Peter-and-Paul fortress at St. Petersburg. For a long time they gave him neither books nor paper. To prevent himself from going mad from idleness, he invented the idea of editing a newspaper every day, methodically, with the greatest seriousness; lead article, bulletins, features, scientific and artistic columns, society items . . . In this manner he mentally wrote thousands of articles. I did the same thing. For me it was an opportunity of undertaking a methodical classification and reexamination of my meager stock of knowledge, my memories, and my ideas . . . A huge internal labor which one never undertakes in the heat of action, but which makes you understand the value of "retreats" as they were practiced in past centuries in the Catholic world, and are sometimes still practiced today. Contemplation brings about a reexamination of all your values, an auditing of all your accounts with yourself, and with the universe. Introspection opens up the endless vistas of the inner life, shines a penetrating light into the most secret recesses of our being.

. . . But the invisible companion remains. Observing yourself, you become familiar with her. She is always there, watching and waiting for the moment when the will grows weak, when some spring in that complex cerebral mechanism which the metaphysicians call the soul begins to slip: Then an obsession invades your meditation and begins to bore its way slowly into your weary brain.

The French call this state of depression *"le cafard"*: the cockroach.

The image fits. The ugly black bug zigzags around under the vault of your skull.

The walls speak. To the careful eye, every surface reveals signs, most often scratched in with a pin or, in dark corners, in thin pencil lines. Four unchanging themes basically sum up the essence of the lives of the successive inhabitants of this cell. Man and woman. A heart pierced by an arrow. *"Fred-of-the-Catalan-Bar to Tina-of-the-Alley—for life."* Or, abbreviated: *"Big-John of the Bastille to Lena-the-Mouse f.l."* To give or take for life: This is the ritual dream inscribed on these walls by the hands of pimps. Does the idea of true self-abandonment really take hold of them? I think, rather, that they suffer, with a certain amount of self-complacency, from the feline violence of love: Violence is in the domain of the absolute. Other love motifs, brutal commentaries on the previous ones: The phallic symbol, the crude urchin's sketch of pointed or fleshy breasts, the slit of the secret lips, and, less frequently, the ass or the whole outline of a woman. Of the face, only the characteristic hair-do remains. Primitive drawings which evoke the sex act, with the unimaginative lewdness of dirty postcards . . . How can we avoid the obvious conclusion, looking at these haunting symbols, that a kind of phallic cult persists in the slums of our big cities? The eternity of love is expressed in writing; the permanence of animal lust and all the suffering it brings in these circumstances cries out in these drawings . . . M.A.V., or M.V., means *mort aux vaches:* death to the cops! This phrase or its abbreviation follows most of the signatures. For there are two fundamental duties: love woman, hate the enemy . . . Another duty: solidarity. The betrayed man, like the captain of a sinking ship who tosses a bottle into the sea, throws out his warning to any and all:

"Dédé of Montparnasse is a queer." This is signed by B.H. followed by five periods and a date. Or again: *"Riri, squealed on by the Alsatian, two years, burglary,"* a concise history! Many names are followed by similarly terse statements of fact.

I found the following words carved deep into the floor in a corner of my first cell:

"Only seven months more and I'll kill her."

Below, a sort of little calendar. The inmate had drawn a line for each day, a cross at the end of the month. He had spent five months and two days in this cell . . .

The walls also speak with voices of the present. The guard has scarcely made his round when a faint noise, a mouselike scratching, makes your ears perk up. Three discrete little taps, a pause, three more taps. A man is calling me from the other side of the stone wall.

I answer: three, pause, three. Then, coming regularly now, the taps are spaced out evenly in long series. As many taps as are needed for each letter of the alphabet: 16, p; 9, i; 5, e; 18, r; again 18, r; 5, e. The tapper's name is Pierre. It takes a great deal of concentration to avoid making a mistake counting up these hasty little taps to which you must listen with one ear tuned to the noises from the corridor so as to avoid getting caught. After long minutes, "Pierre of the Gang of the Four" managed to tell me: "Hello. Sent down for murder. And you?" Personally, I have nothing to say to Pierre of the Gang of the Four. This conversation made up of mouse noises and alphabetical additions wearies me. I tap:

"Goodby!"

And I fall back into my silence . . . To work.

You soon learn to tell time by the sounds of the prison. A long clattering of mess tins announces the next doling out of food. Soon it is four o'clock, end of the day. Doors are hastily opened and shut: the prison mailman making his rounds.

All at once the man pacing in his cell stops short, dumbstruck. From the guard's desk at the bottom of the gallery a voice has just announced:

Number 13–21, released!

Upstairs, in their cement cubicles, both number 13–20 and number 13–22 are shaken by an icy shudder. They listen, anxious, their chests tight, cowering against the door. In the distance, heavy footsteps mount the stairs, move closer down the gallery. Here it comes. Here it comes. The door of cell 13–21 opens with loud clang. The following dialogue is heard:

An indifferent bass voice:

"Number 13–21, Michaud, Oscar-Leon, that's you, right?" A palpitating, eager, choked voice:

"Yes, officer, yes, that's me."

The poor wretch has heard. He knows. But he doesn't believe it yet. He is afraid. He would like to grovel before this mustachioed, ruddy-complexioned guard who holds his destiny written on a scrap of paper. And at the same time he would like to unchain his heart, which is ready to burst from his chest, to cry out:

"That's me! *Me! Me!*"

The bass voice continues calmly:

"Get your things together. Provisional release."

The other voice, muddled, effusive, like a thankful schoolboy's:
"Thank you, sir."

They leave. The poor wretch can be heard telling his story loquaciously. Numbers 13–20 and 13–22 straighten up, taciturn, their stern brows doubtless wrinkled by the same frown. Number 13–20 has at least two more years to go. Number 13–22 has ten more years . . .

Another shout, at the end of the corridor:
"Number 13–23, released!"

Number 13–20 bites his lips, wrings his hands. Number 13–22 glances in bewilderment around his cell, which has grown darker from one moment to the next; his mounting rage vents itself in vague imprecations:
"Oh! the bastards! Of all the dirty, stinking . . ."

In one of his novels, Alexander Dumas describes a horrible execution in Venice. Three miserable wretches were to undergo an excruciatingly refined torture. They marched calmly to the scaffold, ready to die, already dead in the depth of their souls. Suddenly a messenger appeared, bringing a pardon for one of them. And the other two went into a frenzy of indignation. To see someone survive was worse than death for them. This fictional passage contains a terrible psychological truth. In here, every announcement of a release brings an uncontrollable nervous shock to those who hear it. The average prisoner, in spite of habit, feels it like a sudden blow. Those who feel that freedom has brushed by them, since they were the neighbors of the man released, feel the outrage of an injustice.

Calls to the visitors' room cause the same reaction. A fearsome jealousy gnaws at the hearts of those who have been abandoned or betrayed when their brothers in misfortune are visited by their dear ones. I met two cellmates, one of whom hated the other with mortal passion. The one had been betrayed to the police by his mistress. The other received passionate letters every day from his . . .

When evening falls, other cries rip through the silence . . . The gloomy time of day passes slowly. Suddenly, from outside, a resonant voice calls out:
"Good evening, mates, good evening!"

A moment's pause. The whole prison is listening. The impassioned voice soars and wheels with fury:
"Didi of La Chapelle wished you a good evening! Courage and blood!"

Sometimes it's the farewell cry of a man about to leave; sometimes the revolt of an impatient man who must remain—and who will be punished that very night in the "hole." An appeal, an exhortation, a promise.

The fierce exhortation strikes deep. This cry, reaching up from the lowest depths of Paris, bears true witness to a tradition of courage and blood.

Sometimes, especially in the evening, a noise from the street may reach the prisoner in his cell. An automobile sounds its horn. The bell of a trolley car rings out in the distance. Instantaneously, the image of the illuminated streets and of that trolley car appears in your mind's eye. You see the conductor taking the steering bar into his wool-gloved hands. You see everything. You breathe in the smell of asphalt and gasoline. And then everything vanishes.

Two eyes under the visor of a *képi* appear and disappear in the rapidly opened spyhole of the door. You feel buried alive. Depending on whether you are an old inmate or a newcomer, the calm grayness of time sooner or later resumes its usual hue.

The city and life are nothing but unreality.

These walls: That is reality. And those one hundred and sixty little lines on the dark corner of the floor under a sentence etched in by an unknown hand:

"Only seven months more and I'll kill her."

SIX

The System

AT SEVEN IN THE MORNING A BELL RINGS, GIVING THE SIGNAL FOR RISING. A quarter of an hour later, the cell door is opened by the guard on duty for a quick inspection. The cot is folded up into the wall, the bedclothes folded according to regulations. An inmate in overalls, accompanied by a guard who opens the Judas for him, throws in a *boule de son*, 700 grams of black bread, which hunger alone enables you to eat. An hour later, morning soup. The mess tin, passed through the Judas by a grimy hand, generally contains nothing but a rather abundant portion of luke-warm yellowish water on which—sometimes, but not always—some odd scraps of cabbage are floating. It is lightly salted. When you are very hungry and, in winter, if the "soup" is hot enough to warm up the stomach, you dip your black bread in it. Most often, even those who are starving throw this insipid water—which is neither food nor drink, but more like dishwater—down the toilet. The administration, nonethe-less, delivers fixed quantities of dried vegetables, fats, even fresh vege-tables to the cooks. But, aside from the fact that the only check on the way the regulations are carried out is left to personnel with interests at variance from those prescribed by the rules, a large number of succes-sive plunderings, coming one on top of the other, ends up by reducing the inmates' usual fare to a bare minimum. The ill-paid guard on duty in the kitchen is not above a little pilfering. Before him, the quarter-master-sergeant took his share before delivering the quantities of pro-visions—weighed, for form's sake, quickly and under the benevolent eye of his cohort or the accessory eye of the prisoner-chief-cook. Then the prisoner-cooks take care of their own interests. They naturally eat as well as they can, and put together special dishes or packets of provi-sions for some of their pals. They need money. By carrying on a sharp trade in fats and onions with inmates who have positions of trust and even with certain not-too-scrupulous guards, they are able to obtain the desired funds: Then whatever nourishment is left in such a well-skimmed soup goes first to feed the boys on the maintenance squad and then to their "buddies." If you give a modest reward to your regular soup server, you can get a fair amount of cabbage in your mess tin. The feckless and the penniless get nothing but yellowish water.

Around four o'clock, a second meal. The same soup, plus a dish of vegetables, alternately beans, mashed green peas, mashed potatoes, rice. These vegetables are boiled, salted, apparently without any fat added; this is a bare subsistence, a tasteless nutriment which you absorb out of necessity. The mashed purées are gelatinous, shiny like glue. Sometimes they serve you kidney beans which break your teeth and make a lovely metallic clank when you drop them into your mess tin from a height of a few inches. On Thursdays and Sundays the little bit of meat juice which they add to this administrative pittance is enough to make it delectable. On the latter day, "eighty grams of cooked beef" are added to the evening vegetables: a few thin scraps of cold meat strung out on a wooden stick or threaded onto a tough piece of tendon.

The diet of prisoners awaiting trial at the Santé Prison is considerably worse than that of convicts in the penitentiaries. The administration obviously takes the following reasons into account. Prisoners awaiting trial are divided, from a dietary point of view, into three categories: rich or middle class, aided, abandoned. To tell the truth, they are only interested in the first category, who are frequently visited by well-known lawyers, protected by deputies, capable of bringing the attention of the press to bear on the House; but these people throw away or disdainfully refuse the administrative pittance. They are allowed to have their meals brought in from restaurants; they receive bottles of wine and ample baskets of provisions. The less fortunate ones, who are nonetheless aided by their relatives, live on food sent in from the outside or bought from the canteen; the subsistence allotment is of secondary importance to them. Those who are abandoned, without money, without relatives, drink down the lukewarm, yellowish morning water in fury, have devoured their loaf of black bread by noon, and apply for an extra quarter loaf from the doctor. These common-law prisoners, whose sham defense is hurried inattentively along by a court-appointed lawyer, have no complaints to make: This is made quite clear to them. The slightest comment is enough to send them off to the hole for several days. Shrugging his shoulders, the guard in charge of punishments tells them:

"Go ahead and croak, if that's what you want. I don't give a shit!"

They're stuck. They croak all right, but slowly, without saying a word, sometimes dreaming of the hard-labor colonies from which you can escape, where you can take revenge.

("Ah, I swear to God, if the screw messes with me, I'll shove my shiv into his gut . . .")

The evening cries—courage and blood!—send long, invigorating shivers through the marrow of their spines.

There is always the expedient of signing up to visit the doctor. You get extra bread, a ration of cod-liver oil, and pills—God knows what kind of pills!

Moralists sometimes compare the practice of medicine to a priestly calling. The mission of the doctor, the priest, the lawyer; aid to the sick, the disabled, the innocent victim and the guilty. How little of these old hypocrisies remain once the walls of prison have been entered! Victim or guilty man—a subtle distinction!—the prisoner awaiting trial who cannot pay, has no lawyer in reality. When, in the fourth or fifth month of pretuberculosis, the starving man's tonsils swell up painfully, when chronic ear infection sends neuralgic pains through his head, he signs up for a "visit with the doctor."

Around eleven o'clock, a guard rounds up the sick. Ten or so prisoners come together with joyful surprise in their sullen eyes and line up in the ground-floor corridor. While they're waiting for the last of those who have signed up, a man with a swollen cheek discreetly makes the acquaintance of a man with varicose veins who complains of not being able to walk anymore; a consumptive gives a slight cough as he contemplates the blood-specked sputum in his handkerchief, on whose display he is counting to get some medicine. A fishy-looking financier— delighted to escape for a few minutes from solitude so cruel for an ex-playboy—engages in a hasty conversation with tall, cunning-eyed Jadin ("You know Jadin, from the Bagnolet holdup . . ."), who has only signed up for the visit himself to pursue some subtle scheme . . .

"Forward march!"—in Indian file under the direction of a guard. In front of the ground-floor cell which is used as the doctor's office, more meetings, exchanges of furtive signs, top-secret missives passing from hand to hand concealing more than one criminal secret—and also more than one message of friendship. The whole value, even purely medical, of the visit to the sawbones consists in these meetings and correspondences. Psychosomatic afflictions subside in these moments of contact with *other men.*

A white table. On it, a large register. Seated behind it, a gentleman in a white coat flanked by two inmate-orderlies. A kind of administrative tribunal. A guard calls the patients.

"Pirard, Marcel . . ."

Pirard, Marcel, emerges out of the gray corridor wall and appears before the table of the sawbones, who is still busy with the previous patient (Crispin, Gustave-Leon, twenty-two years old; bronchitis), for whom he is writing, under the *prescriptions* column in the big register: "tinct. iod." Eight *tinct. iod.* for today: November! Without lifting his eyes from his register, where he reads the records devoted to Pirard, Marcel, the sawbones questions:

"What's your trouble?"

Pirard, Marcel, a teamster by trade (in the register: "assault and battery"; he broke his whip handle over the back of a dishonest subcontractor), has been preparing his lesson for two days. Being in a cell is driving him mad. He can't sleep anymore; he has cold sweat, nightmares, buzzings in his ears: He can't go on! He would like them to "pair" him off—that is to say, give him a companion, a living man, to talk to, since these walls, these naked empty, silent, cold walls are driving him out of his mind! . . . But how to say everything in this fleeting minute!

"Doctor, I don't know what's the matter; I'm going crazy . . ."

The two orderlies—two augurs—standing behind the doctor smile indignantly. Another faker! ("He's going crazy! What's that to us, buddy?") The doctor at first raises his head, but immediately remembers that he has forty-seven men signed up for consultation this morning, and that this is only the twenty-third. Without even having seen Pirard, Marcel, the doctor himself clarifies:

"Headaches?"

"Yes, that's it, Doctor!" murmurs Pirard, Marcel, in ecstasy.

He is already being gently pushed outside. The doctor writes "Bromide" in the *prescriptions* column. Maekers, Henri, is called in. Each visit lasts from forty to sixty seconds, the time necessary to fill out the *prescriptions* column with a rapid scrawl. Pirard, Marcel, returns to his cell weak and dejected. He continues "going crazy" noiselessly until the day—if his pretrial examination drags out—when we hear him dashing himself furiously against the door, beating his head against the wall, howling like a wild beast. Then they knock him senseless for a while, give him a shower, throw him into the hole; afterwards they "pair" him without medical assistance.

I have never seen the sawbones touch a patient with his stethoscope.

But it sometimes happens that an inmate is found dead in his cell—of natural causes.

The regulations prescribe a twenty-minute exercise walk each day; you have the right to refuse. I have refused it times out of dread of the wads of phlegm in the exercise yard.

The yards are twelve to fifteen feet wide by twenty-five to thirty feet long. The buildings of the Santé Prison, taken as a whole, form a vast quadrangle whose middle is occupied by the exercise yards. A vast courtyard is divided into more or less equal compartments, all of them closed. Some are enclosed by walls on three sides only; on the fourth, a grillwork looks, from a height of seven feet, onto the windows of the inside ground-floor cells. A covered catwalk forms a circle over these courtyards, which are very like middle-sized bear cages. Above, the guard. Twenty men can take the air under his eyes without ever emerging from their total isolation. Some parts of the courtyard are covered.

You go through the corridors in a racket of slamming doors; you see your cell-block neighbor passing out ahead of you; suddenly you find yourself in the bear cage. A landscape of mud-colored walls; above, the rectangular buildings, also mud-colored, with their infinity of little barred windows. You notice those that are open or closed.

Between seven and ten o'clock, nine men have passed through this hole; the tenth finds the cement literally covered with cigarette butts and greenish mucus. I have often resisted the temptation of those twenty minutes of fresh air, so great was the nervous repulsion I felt for that slimy mucus. For twenty minutes you walk in circles in the cages among the spittle. Sometimes a note rolled into a ball jumps over the wall or a voice calls from the grill side. Returning, you are nauseated by the stale odor of your cell.

Twice a week the inmates' relatives gather, a little early, in front of the prison gates, forming one of those odd groups that can also be seen, on visiting days, in front of hospitals. Women, especially older women, are the majority in these groups where people whisper, commune with each other's sorrows, or remain apart in oppressed silence. All of them look like widows. The old men, who have come from poor neighborhoods with their baskets of provisions, have mourning faces.

Their gestures are constrained by embarrassment, their glances veiled with shame. Some of them draw together in sympathy. The mother of a thief glances, with a look full of inexpressible commiseration, at the murderer's mother. No one dares speak aloud; idle hands fuss over packets of foodstuffs and linen. Respectable people are afraid of being recognized there by a passing neighbor.

The visitors' room is made up of two opposing rows of wire-meshed compartments separated by a space about a yard wide . . . The mother sits down in a compartment on the administration side. The son sits down in a compartment on the prison side. They are unable to touch each other. They can hardly see each other, barely communicate. Each has his face glued to the dusty grillwork. On both sides their eyes become inflamed trying to make out the familiar features in the semi-darkness. *The other person is there:* corporeal, yet ghostly; present, yet inaccessible. These partitioned compartments stretch out in long parallel rows. They are filled with a confused tumult of voices, sobs, sighs, cries, exclamations, admonitions, and advice which must be overcome in order to project a word from one cage to another. You leave this howling hall with your ears buzzing, full of clamors. But how many pardons, how many promises, how many sorrows, how many dashed hopes soar by each other there in painful flight—and fall there, heavily, with broken wings, in the mud . . .

A man, a woman. He: magnificent athletic shoulders, short neck, forehead low with compressed power, a kind of black fire in the deep sockets under the ridge of the brow. He: terror . . . a murderer. She: supple and feline from buttocks to breasts to golden hair. She: love, sold by night, given by day, a bogus "sister" come today to look at her man and to cry out to him:

"I'm yours, you see! Down to the depths of me! You're my man!"

She is glued right against the wire mesh, straining toward him. Because it was for her that he bloodied his knife! Teeth clenched, he stares with dull eyes at that mouth which is proffered, given, but unreal; murmurs with the affectation of disdain for love proper to a male:

"Send me some tobacco."

On the right, a mother and her son.

Twenty minutes. The mother, somewhat paler, leaves her cage with a hesitant step. She looks drunk. Her hat has slipped down over one ear. Her damp eyes are burning, her lower lip trembles . . . She is probably ashamed of crying "in front of people." She is in a hurry to leave:

"The street will do me good," she thinks—and the walls of the jail turn about her, angular, shattered, crooked, falling in. "So it's true, it's all true, everything the papers said. My God! My poor little Marcel! My poor little Marcel! . . ."

. . . On his side, he moves off, staggering a bit himself, his eyes still clinging to the image of an old mama's pained, ruined face. His shouted confession keeps vibrating in his throat. But it's over, over. What a relief! She knows everything now, everything: that he did it in order to become a pilot . . .

In his cell he finds the gift of maternal hands: a jar of jam, some white bread, a can of sardines which has just been opened. A clean shirt. The shirt is spotted with grease.

In the neighboring cells, the jealousy of abandoned prisoners stirs with the clanging of the bolted door.

From time to time, inspectors come through. A gentleman in a silver-braided *képi* stands haughty in the doorway. Behind him, the guard on duty, chief guard—bedecked with braid from cuff to shoulder—or some fat sergeant.

"Do you have any complaints to make?"

I have none. No one has any. Nobody wants to get on the wrong side of the omnipotent authorities. The pale, skinny kid whose guard calls him a "stinking little bastard" from dawn to dusk (lucky when his guard's heavy key doesn't whack him between the shoulder blades "on the sly"), gazes, full of deference, at the three rows of silver braid on the *képi,* squints at his torturer's lantern jaw, stares out with the hate-filled eyes of a beast at bay—and keeps quiet.

Whistling, humming, talking to yourself out loud, making any noise, is forbidden. It might seem easy to maintain discipline in a cell. But punishments of dry bread, loss of canteen privileges, even of being sent to the hole, are dealt out each day to a steady number of celled prisoners, Most of whom are guilty of attempting to communicate with each other, either by tapping, by writing, or by other means. The use of the "telephone," for example, is severely punished. The toilet bowls are connected to wastepipes which pass perpendicularly from story to story, so that when you speak into the opening you can be heard on the floors above and below you. By means of this bizarre "telephone," it is possible to have actual conversations, albeit conversations interrupted by untimely waterfalls and requiring a great deal of skill: The whole thing is to talk loud enough to be heard on the next floor without being heard from the guards' catwalk.

The regulations could be summed up in three peremptory words: *Living is forbidden!*

But is it possible to forbid living men to live? With all the weight of its mighty edifices of stone, cement, and iron, the hulking prison affirms that it is possible.

The large number of inmates makes it impossible for the prison authorities to respect the principle of isolation. Thanks to an insufficient number of cells, a handful of culprits escape this special torture. Three men are put together. There is only one bed: Two spread their mattresses on the floor. I spent only two days under that system. Certainly, whatever its disadvantages may be, it usually presents one great advantage: Madness, the inevitable result of idle solitude, is somewhat delayed. But for the man who is able to master himself and discipline his mind, solitude is better. Being put in with two others can become intolerable to him.

Three men are brought together in a cell by chance. Whatever their differences, they must tolerate each other; relentless intimacy twenty-four hours a day . . . Rare is the day when at least one of them is not depressed. Irritable or gloomy, at odds with himself, he exudes a sort of invisible poison. You pity him. You suffer with him. You hate him. You catch his disease . . . If, among the three, one has the advantage of being well cared for by his relatives, then a jealous hatred hovers over all of his movements as he drinks the wine of inequity or reads the letter which the others didn't get . . . If there is one abandoned starveling, then hunger and hatred may move in with him alongside the two other inmates. The presence of a slob fills the cell with snoring, spitting, belching—nauseating smells and filthy gestures.

The cube of air, hardly sufficient for one, is so insufficient for three that the air never really changes. You wake to a rank stench—a compound of putrid exhalations. The bitter smell, at first pleasant, then asphyxiating, of tobacco smoke, is mixed in with it. A bluish fog fills these four yards of space where three men wander around, gesticulating, like phantoms. Human beings give off an animal odor, and it takes a great deal of hygiene to keep it from getting rancid. The cell fills with a warm stench.

Each does his business in front of the other two. But perhaps the worst intimacy is not that of bodies. It is not being able to be alone with yourself. Not being able to remove your face from the prying glance of others. Betraying, with every tic, at every moment, the secret of an obtusely disturbed inner life. Not being able to work.

SEVEN

Burial and Victory

HOW IS THE PULSE OF LIFE EXTINGUISHED? IT IS IMPOSSIBLE TO SAY: WITH TIME. The same feelings, repeated indefinitely, grow dull. You lose count of the hours and the days. What moved or terrified you during the first days no longer moves you. Suffocation? Drowning? A torpor sneaks into your veins, between your temples: All of life takes on the faded-ocher hue of the cell. You can no more escape this torpor than you can escape from these four walls. The rhythm of your inner life slows down. I will speak of the exaltations later on. Their rhythm is slow too; they come and go against this unchanging background without shattering the deeper torpor.

Men become childish again. The joys of the seventh year of child-hood return. Gregory Gerchuny, an intrepid revolutionary of the time of the first Russian Revolution (1905), has described what a joy it was for him to receive a bar of soap in his death cell. Even less will do! I have witnessed—and other men have told me of the same experience—the profound drama of the appearance and disappearance of a ray of sun-light . . . On the ceiling, in a corner, around ten in the morning, a rec-tangle of sunlight appears: a few square inches. The cell and its inmate are instantly transformed. The rectangle draws itself out, becomes a ray. The presence of this warm light, which neither lights nor warms, cre-ates an inexpressible emotion. Your step quickens, your back straightens, the day takes on a brighter aspect. But the ray of sunlight draws itself out, becomes narrower. This tiny bit of life-bringing gold becomes a thin thread ready to snap. Dull anxiety. The thread has snapped. The man-child grows cold.

Dreaming is another thing you soon learn about. Opium. This path, too, leads to insanity. Like all the cell's paths.

The unreality of time is palpable. Each second falls slowly. What a measureless gap from one hour to the next. When you tell yourself in advance that six months—or six years—are to pass like this, you feel the terror of facing an abyss. At the bottom, mists in the darkness.

So as not to lose track of the date, you have to count the days attentively, mark each one with a cross. One morning you discover that there are forty-seven days—or one hundred and twenty, or three hundred and forty-seven!—and that it is a straight path leading backwards without the slightest break: colorless, insipid, senseless. Not a single landmark is visible. Months have passed like so many days; entire days pass by like minutes. Future time is terrifying. The present is heavy with torpor. Each minute may be marvelously—or horribly—profound. That depends to a certain extent on yourself. There are swift hours and very long seconds. Past time is void. There is no chronology of events to mark it; external duration no longer exists.

You know that the days are piling up. You can feel the creeping numbness, the memory of life growing weak. Burial. Each hour is like a shovelful of earth falling noiselessly, softly, on this grave.

The first day in a cell contains, in miniature, the months, years, decades which will follow till death, which may wait for you at the end, and whose terrors you live through more than once. The effects of living in a cell develop according to a constant curve: I tend to think that only their rhythm may vary among individuals.

In the main, they are characterized by three phenomena. First, *exaltation,* whose causes may be frivolous to the point of total insignificance. I have known inmates to live twenty-four hours or several days of radiant inner joy in expectation of an exchange of glances, during fatigue duty. A fifteen-minute visit is enough to fill long days with expectation and long days with memory afterwards. A word, a gesture, a detail can feed the inner flame indefinitely. What extraordinary events letters are! War veterans probably remember what these little paper rectangles covered with familiar writing coming from *the other world*—from the strange, storybook world of the living—meant to them in the trenches, which are in many respects like prisons . . . They know how some brows used to darken after mail call and how other radiant or tragic faces pored over their letters. The exaltations of a man confined in prison take on the most varied forms. An exacerbation of emotional attachments, sex drives, the instinct for survival, religious faith, or political convictions is its most frequent manifestation. The periods of exaltation are followed, as a reaction, by periods of apathy. Dejection: dull torpor, indifference.

I believe that this exaltation belongs to the *period of struggle*—which varies in length, and ends, once a man is freed from a decisive mental aberration and no longer puts up much resistance, in a state of vegetative, slow-motion existence in which sharp sufferings and sharp joys no longer play a part. I have met convicts like that who were astonishingly placid in their sixth, seventh, or tenth year of confinement.

This exaltation gives birth to obsession. The brain, at once anemic and feverish, is overcome by an idea, an image. In the absence of contact with outside reality, in the unreality of this deathlike existence, in the ruins of one's former mental equilibrium, an *idée fixe* can move in and take over. There are those, usually males, who are haunted by a hallucinating carnal memory. Some are led to morbid lewdness by persistent sexual obsessions. Some are tormented by jealousy day and night, night and day. When you speak to them, they don't understand at first, "return from somewhere" blushing all at once, and are delighted by the unexpected diversion. There are also those, hardly less numerous, who are obsessed by their "case," who never stop weighing, trying, analyzing, and examining the details of their imaginary briefs. These are the ones who are really "guilty," drowning men clutching at straws. Tireless, they write out long memoranda, underlining their "essential" arguments two or three times, arguing over the legal Code, which they have learned by heart, piling defense upon defense to the point of absurdity, sometimes to the point of an indirect but unmistakable admission of what they are denying . . . Some are devoured by the obsession of death, and these will die in prison. For the fear of death is already death's lure, the weakening of the organism, death itself . . . Some, desperate with anxiety, yearn for someone who is absent, beyond these walls. Obsessed by the thought of an accident, by the absolute, unreasoning certainty that the other person will die . . . Some, obsessed by hate, bear a grudge against a judge, a cop on the vice squad, a "fag," a "female." These are the ones who kill when they get out of prison. *They* never die in prison. It is possible to live on hate and murder.

The *manias* and *superstitions,* common in varying degrees among all prisoners, are phenomena related to obsession. The connections between these various aspects of mental imbalance, unreason, and failure of the will are sometimes quite apparent. Many prisoners awaiting trial, obsessed by anxiety over their defense, become afflicted (quite rapidly, within a few months) by a kind of procedure mania. They know the Code thoroughly. They quote paragraphs, articles, interpretations, and jurisprudence. They find new defenses in it. They are incapable of carrying on a few moments' conversation without dragging in their case and quoting such and such a paragraph of the law. The authors of memoranda have the writing mania. Long after they are convicted, sometimes in the sixth or tenth year of a sentence, they are writing, still writing—petitioning for a new trial—and this gives their lives a meaning. They can always recite their irresistible arguments by heart, and they do so with voluble passion. Failure doesn't discourage them. But if their application for permission to write is refused, this plunges them into fury or despair . . . In the long run, an inmate's life is regulated by a quantity of less important little manias produced by the lack of any normal object over which he can exercise his will power. The few personal objects he owns are arranged and put away in an invariable order: Any disturbance of this housekeeping arrangement will throw him into a frenzy. (The guards, fully aware of this, weakness, deliberately exasperate it through unnecessary searches in the cells and workshops.) He puts on his clothes in a certain manner, he has his own special way of doing up his buttons. In his cell, he has his own way of walking: so many steps in such and such a direction. Never in another . . .

Personal superstitions are harder to get to know, for they are only revealed through confidences. My impression is that they are very common, especially among men with a certain intellectual development . . . It would seem that the more complete, refined, and perfect the cerebral mechanism, the greater the chances of its going off the track . . . Dumb brutes get off the lightest. Rare is the man who is not superstitious about lucky and unlucky dates, meetings, dreams, numbers, mental incantations. "If I count up to eleven three times before the next time a door slams, that will be a good omen."

Mysticism often develops, but it is clearly an abnormal phenomenon. The return to religious practices in convicts or prisoners awaiting trial can usually be explained merely by the need for distraction and the hope of protection or minor privileges. True believers are quite rare today. In prison, a certain rather impoverished mysticism is common to practically everyone who begins to wonder about life's great problems. The system tends, in a continuous manner, to weaken the mind, destroy the will, obliterate the personality, to depress, oppress, wear down, torture. If you don't want to relapse into something close to a primitive form of religious mentality, you need regular intellectual labor, which is just about impossible to find—or else well-thought-out convictions of exceptional firmness.

The only healthy reaction of the organism against the incessant, multiple, insidious, and harassing pressure of madness is joy.

We all have great powers of vitality. We are filled with such a deep love of life that sometimes it takes only the slightest outside impulse to make the flame of joy suddenly rise up in us. And we are elevated above ourselves, the present, despair, prison. I once asked a comrade—whose life, I knew well, had been hopeless, full of suffering, a savage struggle in city slums and in jail—what had been the happiest hour of his past existence. He answered me:

"It was in V*** Prison, one Christmas night. I was alone. It was warm. I had a good book and some wine . . . All at once I felt so well, so calm, so glad to be able to think, so glad to be alive . . ."

Among those who succeed in resisting madness, their intense inner life brings them to a higher conception of life, to a deeper consciousness of the *self,* its value, its strength. A victory over jail is a great victory. At certain moments you feel astonishingly *free.* You sense that if this torture has not broken you, nothing will ever be able to break you. In silence you struggle against the huge prison machine with the firmness and stoic intelligence of a man who is stronger than the suffering of his flesh and stronger than madness . . . And, when a broad ray of sunlight inundates the barred window, when good news comes in from the outside, when you have succeeded in filling the dismal day with useful work, an inexpressible joy may ascend within you like a hymn.

The guards, peering through the peephole, are astonished to discover a radiant brow and oddly silent lips: for all the joy of living is poised on them in one unuttered cry.

EIGHT

Yet Life Goes On . . .

THE CELL IN WHICH I SPENT THE LONGEST TIME—A YEAR—DAZZLED ME WHEN I first entered it. The light, it seemed to me, poured in abundantly between the black stripes of a large, high, barred window. A stay of two months in a dingier cell had already atrophied my vision. The corrugated panes only permitted a hazy view of the gray wall on the other side of the court. With the transom open and standing on tiptoes, I could, in the right position, glimpse a triangle of sky: less than one square inch. Especially in summer, I often gazed, as if from the bottom of a pit, at that touching bit of sky whether it was that light blue, tinged with ashy gray, of Paris skies after a rain; or white and heavy when the mists hang low; or luminously, implacably blue, that hard blue which made a poet cry out:

> Où fuir dans la révolte inutile et perverse?
> *Je suis hanté*. L'Azur! L'Azur! L'Azur! L'Azur![4]

and which brutally overwhelmed me, beyond all thought of "literature." It was an inexpressible feeling. What was its deepest source: Joy? Suffering at once denied and embraced? Serenity at once profound and active? It matters little.

In winter the skeleton of a leafless tree raised its scraggy branches over the top of the wall. I used to think: "That's the street out there." I didn't know which one. The central heating hardly worked at all. You were numb with cold several hours a day. The electricity went on early; but the bulb, which was weak and placed too high, never cast enough

---

4   Whither can I flee in this futile and perverse revolt?
     I am haunted. Azure! Azure! Azure! Azure!
     —Mallarmé (Tr.)

light on your book. Your eyes burned. Nonetheless, this was better than grimy daylight.

My turn in the exercise yard often came early in the morning, around eight o'clock. Pacing briskly up and down—caged, but under an open sky in the cold air, in the half-light of dawn. A closed horizon: the quadrangle of square, massive, black buildings; the rows of oblong barred windows glowed against this background of dark masonry. It made you think of some bizarre furnace seen from the outside. Once in a while a gasping cry might be heard somewhere, clinging to those bars. A man, having hoisted himself up to his window—a genuine feat of acrobatics—was howling at the light, at the open air, from within his brick and concrete cage. The howlings would die down, rise up again, fade away like a flame flickering in the wind. You could imagine the struggle between the "screws" and the desperate man, first beaten senseless, then dragged off toward the hole.

Another event: the cat passing by. This prison cat was a horrible beast, horribly intelligent. He used to slither around the exercise yards with expert insolence. He never paid attention to a man; he ate the scraps of foodstuffs that were brought to him without hurrying. And then went away, undemonstrative, indifferent, without a friendly purr for the man bending over him in the unfathomable surprise of fondling a little life which was warm, primitive, free, and vaguely feminine. When you had nothing to give him, the cat would pass you by without a look. His dirty white fur seemed to have taken on the color of the prison stones.

Sometimes, at the very beginning of spring, we were lucky enough to enjoy the marvelous warmth of the first vernal sun. If you shine a ray of light on a drop of water under a microscope, you can see the tiny organisms that live inside gathering together in the light. A prison yard spotted here and there with sunlight has often reminded me of that experiment; and the men shivering in their ray of sunlight, pale and joyful, reminded me of microbes . . .

The silhouette of the walls almost never let the sunlight bathe the whole of the exercise yard; but one corner of the cement cage was gilded. The men stood there: an old man with turned-up collar smiling through dull-green eyes at the renewed warmth; a young convict happily stretching his limbs with a few gymnastic exercises; a chilly, sick man, holding in his shivers, breathing in the beneficent light through all his pores. I felt a sudden "whiplash" through my whole organism.

My imagination gallivanted about, whims, desires, memories, dreams, projects abounding, inner rhythms awakening . . .

What microbes we are!

Then, above the outside wall, at the point where branches made crazy hatchmarks against the whiteness of the sky, green patches of leaves would appear.

One day, one of my extremely rare visitors looked at those faraway leaves and exclaimed:

"Why, the chestnuts are in flower!"

Together we stared at those bright-green patches through the milky glass; we were finally able to make out white borders on them like motionless snowflakes. There were flowers there. As long as they remained, albeit half-invisible, I greeted them several times a day. Later on, I realized, from the deep, darker green of the leaves, that they had gone away; but of all the flowers I have seen in my life, these—which I never really saw—have left me the most charming memory.

Our eyes need colors. Because for whole seasons I had seen no colors other than that green patch of inaccessible foliage, I developed an obsessive *desire for colors*. The letters I received sometimes came in envelopes lined with red, violet, blue, or green silk paper. I used these shreds of paper as bookmarks. It was a joy for any eyes to come upon a red square between two pages. Like a child, I would sometimes spread out these colors on my table. Or close my eyes to remember some dazzling material.

NINE

Encounters

ALTHOUGH THE GOAL IN PRISON IS TOTAL ISOLATION, COMMUNICATIONS ARE eventually established among the inmates. There are accidental meetings, glances exchanged on the way to the exercise yards. Somebody throws a "telegram," a wad of paper weighted with breadcrumbs, into your exercise yard. Friendships are born, correspondences start up . . .

For many long months my neighbor was a pale convict, broad and heavy-set, with an oversized head like a sad clown's. I had no wish to make friends. He overcame my indifference by hailing me during an exercise period.

"Listen! This is good!"

We were in two different exercise yards on either side of a dividing wall. Whenever the guard, making his rounds on the circular gallery above our heads, was down at the other end of the vast courtyard, we had a good thirty seconds to talk. "This is good!"

I could hear my neighbor laughing quietly on the other side of the wall.

"You're listening? Yes? Well, your buddy B*** just killed the Chief of the Sûreté . . . *Oremus!*"[5]

I had heard nothing of "my buddy B***" for several months. All I knew was that they were hunting him down from hide-out to hide-out and that he would sell his skin dearly. The joyful voice put off my questions:

"That's all I know, pal. One of the boys on the clean-up squad told me. They're all laughing. They're as happy as little women since they heard about it. Do you hear them every night, the girls?"

I heard them . . . The nights were beautiful, heavy, starry—those summer nights when you feel surrounded by all the warmth and primitive fervor of life. Only ten yards from our windows, under the heavy

---

5   See translator's introduction.

70

branches of the chestnut trees, couples used to lurk in the darkness of the deserted street. And we often heard the piercing laughter of young women—that prolonged laughter which is a nervous reaction to the struggles, caresses, and uneasy games of desire.

"You hear them, right? . . . They sure in hell treat themselves to a good time, the bitches! . . ."

Then, as if to seal a mutual understanding based on a common joy linked to a common suffering, my neighbor concluded without any transition:

". . . Anyway, it sure feels good to hear he got what was coming to him, the bastard."

The ice had been broken. Our relations became friendly. A true *Apache,* our sad-faced clown was serving out his fourth sentence for theft: eighteen months, I think. The prosecution was preparing various other accusations against him. One two-year sentence was hanging over him, on appeal. At the end of all of this, nothing—except death, or a miracle. He believed—quietly, without fervor—in a miracle: escape. And he was prolonging "the pleasure" of being here, in the Santé Prison, dressed in threadbare denim, spending his days making paper fans, smoking on the sly now and then, getting letters from his "wife."

"When they add all that up, you understand, I'll get at least five years in Guiana. Once I get there, I'll see if I can't escape . . ."

"How much have you done already?"

"Eight months, pal, with nothing to eat . . ."

He earned a few centimes a day, which he spent on illegal tobacco. But three times a week I heard the mailman noisily unlocking his door and then I understood his silent joy, dissolving into a long, stifled laugh; his sad clown's joy; the joy kindled by a little square of pink paper . . .

This joy brightened his dead-end existence so much that he finally confided in me. But not without first making sure he wouldn't be open- ing any old wounds, causing any hurts ("you've got a wife too, right? . . . I hear the mailman every day when he comes to you . . . I says to myself: Only his woman would write him so often . . ."). He threw me a few of his precious letters over the wall in the exercise yard. They were writ- ten in a big, childish hand, and full of "my dear little man" and "your woman for life."

The woman who wrote them wandered up and down Boulevard Sebastopol every day from five o'clock on, provocative and on the look- out. She knew her lover was a lost man. And she knew the score.

I made the acquaintance of two other neighbors, more conveniently, and less intimately. The guards sometimes give in to the pleadings of a man in isolation who is too weary of solitude, and allow him a yard companion during exercise period. It happened to me two or three times a year. In this way I met a neighbor from across the hall who intrigued me, a little old man, all white, spic and span, a little shabby, who looked a lot like the portraits of President Combes . . . When he learned I was an anarchist, he shook my hand effusively. In the "bear cage" he minutely observed the rules of a childlike and untainted courtesy. His tiny eyes, blue as motionless pools, fixed me with a watery stare while he rubbed his hands together and repeated, as if he were in a *salon:*

"Delighted, Monsieur, truly delighted . . ."

This man, a dead ringer for "little papa Combes," had been a lawyer and had known Prince Kropotkin and Pierre Martin at the time of the Lyons trial; their memory filled him with a respect which was, perhaps, under the circumstances, only politeness. Then, having gone into business, and after long years of financial speculations, he had brought down on himself a large number of suits for fraud, violations of corporation law, etc. The pretrial examination of his numerous cases had been going on for two years. He explained to me that, since he knew more about the legal Code, procedure, jurisprudence, the brief, petitions of appeal, and delaying tactics than anyone, he would be able to prolong it for at least a year longer.

"You understand, Monsieur, at my age you don't like change. Here, at least, I'm left alone, I am respected. The Chief Warden is very nice. I get my food from a restaurant . . ."

He expected to be sentenced to five years—he only spoke of this guardedly—and he hoped to do at least half of his time in the preventive-prison system and then to be let out on parole.

Years later, in another prison, I heard him mentioned as one of the cleverest men in France. I asked what had happened to him. They told me that he had died in prison before the end of his trial, but after having crowned his career with a last dazzling exploit. It seems this swindler was able to inspire such confidence in the Chief Warden that the latter, led on by the prospect of a "nice little investment," entrusted him with his savings . . . The Chief Warden's savings had naturally gone into buying white wine for the old charmer.

The other neighbor, whom I met the same way, was a rather tall gentleman with the bearing of an ex-officer. His chest was embellished by a broad, fan-shaped beard. But his face, pockmarked to the forehead, was dark, with sharp little black eyes. He was an ex-colonial official— he said—charged with embezzling and wearing unauthorized decorations, and he bore a historical name—a name admirably suited, in this century, to seduce the plebeian wealth of Yankee lard-and-leather heiresses. The occupant of Cell Number 24 (I believe), Tenth Division, was the last direct descendant of a crusader who had been King of Jerusalem and then Emperor of Constantinople; and of a Cardinal who had been Finance Minister under Louis XVI.

People generally don't realize the place held by the old nobility in this world. On various lists of old offenders I have seen the name of the descendant of a Superintendent of Finance under Philip the Handsome.

Ah, the old families!

The pathological self-centeredness of men in confinement sometimes comes out in an almost unthinking manner. I remember one chance neighbor who called out to me in the exercise yard. That day I had entered my eighth month of confinement. "How long you been here?" his voice asked me.

"Eight months."

The question, as it often happens, was asked only for propriety's sake. You have to pretend to be interested in others before you can talk about yourself. But the essential thing is to talk about yourself. Me, *me, me*, do you understand, *I've* been here for . . .

On the other side of the wall the man gave out a sigh. A short pause; the guard was going by. Then feverish, with an inexpressible accent of suffering, the voice answered me:

"And me for eight days. Eight days already! It's hard! . . . Eight days! Eight days! . . ."

"There are those," I said, "who are doing eight years and who keep their mouths shut."

Prisoners awaiting trial are not allowed to receive newspapers. Their correspondence is censored by the examining magistrate. It is forbidden to discuss anything but family matters. My communications with the outside world were extremely rare. But around me, even in jail, I could sometimes feel the active, although invisible and silent, presence of a sort of freemasonry. When an event which might interest me took place on the outside, I learned of it first, thanks to this clandestine comradeship.

Two men I had known had just been killed: two magnificent rebels gone to waste. As morning soup was being distributed, a somber stare fell on me. Twenty minutes later, as I was passing my mess tin back through the Judas, a newspaper rolled up into a ball fell at my feet.

I felt I was reading news from another planet. There was fighting in Albania. The Montenegrins at Scutari. Monsieur Poincaré. Lord Grey. Wars, epidemics, catastrophes, governmental crises went on without causing the slightest perturbation in the smooth running of that perfect machine: prison.

There are silent encounters. One morning I found myself in an exercise yard whose wire-meshed side was turned toward the high window of a cell. I could see a man's silhouette rather clearly in it; he was tall, bearded, well on in years, and he walked around his cage with rapid steps. Every half-minute he passed in front of the window again, without seeing me. His head was then visible in direct sunlight, in profile: a high forehead, somewhat receding; an arched nose; thick lips; a powerful face, but with something incomplete in the expression, like an involuntary confession of some weakness. He walked, but looked at nothing. Head lowered, he went on.

"Don't you recognize him?" asked the guard who came to get me to take me back to my cell. "That's T***, you know, the murderer . . ."

The murderer? (Since then, I have met many men with bloodied hands, and have learned they are no different from the others.) An ordinary murderer. The kind who slowly tightens his sinewy hands around the neck of an old woman so he can snatch the wad of bills from under a pile of worn, rough linen. I scrutinized that face, by chance a little more ravaged than the ordinary face, with a somewhat higher forehead, its tense muscles and deep lines betraying more concentrated power. The bearded face of an old tycoon with irons in every fire, the kind you meet in banks and in factories, surrounded by the din of work. To complete the resemblance, T*** stopped in front of his window, put on his pince-nez, and read over a letter. Our glances crossed, doubtless without his seeing me. His brown eyes were bewildered and absent, rather gentle: the sickly air of a man suffering migraine headaches.

TEN

Alms and the Almoner

ONLY ONE VISITOR CROSSES THE THRESHOLD OF THE CELL: THE ALMONER, priest, minister, or rabbi. He brings the alms of his presence, the alms of his words and gestures. His faith matters no more than the belief or disbelief of the man in the cell. Guards and officials blend into the walls themselves, the Judases, bars and bolts. You feel in the marrow of your bones that they are no more than cogs in the prison machine. And this is reciprocal: Human beings no longer exist for them. Only such and such a number occupying such and such a cell. The cell counts, not the crowd of inmates, not man. This chaplain is a man. And not an enemy. He is interested only in man. His profession is oddly anachronistic. He is concerned with that undefinable *je ne sais quoi,* the soul.

"The soul?"—laughed an eighteen-year-old inmate, "Catholic" and totally agnostic—"I think it's a dumping ground for the old blues."

Those who declare themselves Catholics, Protestants, or Jews on arrival are visited by the chaplain of their faith. The cell door closes even more tomblike over the "freethinkers": They see no one.

My agnosticism neither shocked nor surprised the Protestant chaplain, an old man of solid bearing and the appearance of a wealthy Huguenot. This pastor, a man of great kindness, open and broadminded, had been carrying on his disconcerting mission as prisoners' chaplain and a prison official for perhaps a quarter of a century.

I remember his low voice, the heavy shaking of his head, his deep sigh when he said to me one gray afternoon:

"Many are those I have accompanied to the scaffold to hide it from them a few more seconds before the end, so that the last voice they would hear would be mine, crying: 'May God help you!' Many . . ."

The whole ambiguous duplicity of the chaplain's calling was apparent to me here, as was the whole revolting sham of his function. Even more revolting because the man was sincere and kind, resigned to his sacerdotal calling with that inner toughness that a social conscience gives to the intelligent bourgeois. The guillotine, doubtless, is not Christian. But the guillotine is necessary to the Christians. The death of Pierre Durand, at a predetermined hour, "by verdict of law," on that seesaw plank, is a horrible thing. But the justice that commands that death is sacred. The pastor's duty is to sympathize with Pierre Durand's final anguish. His "social" duty is to make sure the guillotine functions properly. Christian compassion plays its part, as does the oiling of the blade.

Once a week, the chaplain comes over to the prison. His stomach lined with a good lunch, his hands in the pockets of a well-tailored overcoat, appropriate to the season, his mind occupied by the ordinary things of life, our chaplain crosses the city. On the way over, he is perhaps distracted by the display in a bookstore window, an elegant silhouette, the morning's headlines, the stock-market quotations. In his mind he maps out his day:

Three to five o'clock, prison. Be at the editorial office of *Church Life* at 5:30 . . . 6:30 promised to call on such and such a lady . . .

He thinks, as he approaches the prison, that eighty men are waiting for him in their cells. Including: one condemned man who will not be pardoned; two or three who will probably be condemned; a dozen "lifers"; that little D*** who is so ill; B*** who is always lying and begging for favors; H*** who prays and scoffs; Z*** who is becoming more and more unhinged. The thought of all these sufferings which he sees and cannot relieve saddens the chaplain. Eighty! And the prison is so big. Five minutes to get from the Fifth Division to the Fourteenth. The chaplain is out of breath.

At the gatehouse, the chaplain shakes some jailers' hands . . .

Whenever he hears the sudden clang of the doors being unlocked, the stoop-shouldered boy with the jaundiced face of a sick fox who occupies Cell Number 8–6 feels his heart beating anxiously. The chaplain has just read his card in the file: "nineteen years old, theft. Breaking and entering." The name is unfamiliar. Sad. Let's go in. The hunted man, in his cage, gives an embarrassed greeting. Then he asserts that he is innocent. Innocent. That he is hungry: dying of hunger, the soup is nothing but water. That his father and mother no longer recognize him as their son. That he is without news of his wife, who has had a miscarriage. He is gentle. "I can't go on," he says, smiling, "it's too much all at once." It's true, all too true. Between the two men hangs an invisible balance, and with each little phrase the weights of suffering fall on the guilty man's side, keep on falling. The chaplain can do nothing. Theft with breaking and entering, he thinks: five years' confinement; with extenuating circumstances, two years of prison. And the disciplinary battalions in Africa, in all probability.

"Would you like a Bible, my son?"

Oh! Yes! the nineteen-year-old-theft-with-breaking-and-entering wants a Bible, a book, a fat book.

"Read the *Book of Job.* He, too, thought he was abandoned even by God . . ."

The nineteen-year-old-theft-with-breaking-and-entering will read the *Book of Job.* But the chaplain, knows very well, deep down, that if the Almighty led Job out of captivity and blessed him until "he had fourteen thousand sheep, and six thousand camels, and a thousand yoke of oxen, and a thousand she asses," and "he had also seven sons and three daughters,"

". . . and after this lived Job a hundred and forty years,"

". . . and died, being old and full of days," as is written in Chapter XLII, Verses 12, 13, 16, and 17 of the Holy Writ—this poor bastard here is poorer than Job, and no one will shorten his suffering by a day . . .

The next cell smells bad. The man who coughs in it never opens the window. Very clean, nonetheless, ageless, impassive, as if withdrawn from his own life. An undeniable murderer on his way to the scaffold. The matter is closed. His deepest concern is for his soul. Before this door had closed on him, he never even suspected he had a soul. He hardly ever thought. Gambling, the races, women, Mitzi (whose throat he neatly cut one night with a razor). Now he prays a great deal. His eyes have grown larger, round, shadowy, glassy.

"I go up in two weeks," he says this time.

The chaplain understands the allusion to the next session of the criminal court. With his long experience, he is able to calculate fairly accurately the number of days this man has left to live: there are the three days allowed for filing an appeal, the examination of the appeal, the appeal for clemency to the President of the Republic, the time necessary to prepare the execution. It's now April; all of that will bring us up to July . . . This calculation is rapidly traced in the chaplain's brain. He rests his firm, ruddy hand on the shoulder of the man-who-will-be-guillotined:

"Would you like it if we prayed together for you, my friend?"

Eighty! The chaplain won't be able to see more than thirty today. In two hours, subtracting the time needed to get around the prison, that leaves three minutes and thirty seconds for each visit. At five o'clock the chaplain goes away. At five o'clock, Pirard, Marcel, who is "going crazy" from being alone, suddenly feels crushed, overwhelmed by the idea that the chaplain will not come to see him today, that no one will come for another week. Why—yes, why—did they refuse this evening to give Pirard, Marcel, this last sacrament: three minutes and thirty seconds of human presence?

Twice a month, on Sunday morning, the minister conducts a service. The prison has a rudimentary church, Protestant chapel, and synagogue: everything that is necessary to render unto God what is God's. The Protestant chapel is cellular in construction, and this invention simultaneously brings the science of prisons and the practice of religion to a remarkable degree of perfection.

There is a semicircle composed of several successive rows of cells. A man is placed in each of these compartments, divided from one another by oak partitions. They make you think of vertical coffins. All you can see in front of you are the pastor's pulpit and the two back windows. In one of these windows you can make out the corner of a window ledge. Birds come and perch there. Life! At the foot of the pulpit, looking bored, stands the guard on duty.

The pastor speaks of the Holy Writ and of terrestrial matters to his strange flock of pale men, each motionless in his cell. He sometimes quotes Saint Paul's words, quite appropriate in front of these starving sometime criminals ("Sloth is the mother of all the vices"): *He who does not work shall not eat!* His bass voice is deep; and what he says about the divine legend strikes deeply into these minds unhinged by a hellish existence; what he says about bourgeois morality touches the minds of these unlucky, defeated men to the very quick. Others go to chapel in order to pass a "telegram" from hand to hand: "to Number Seven in the row, look out—, and don't get nabbed!" The latter keep their faces silent in respectful hypocrisy. Their hands joined, they bow their heads during the prayer.

"Our Father who art in heaven! Hallowed be thy name. Thy kingdom come. Thy will be done, on earth as it is in heaven . . ."

On the way out, someone murmurs:

"Go on, you windbag! You get plenty to eat!"

Back from the chapel.

My neighbor, the sad-faced clown, finds a blackish bucket in front of his door. A filthy rag, provided for washing the floor, is floating in it. This hygienic ritual is a dominical affair in our corner of the prison. The bucket gets slimier and slimier as it passes from cell to cell. You drag the nauseating rag across the floor with both hands, while it shreds apart and blackens any water. For long hours afterwards, the dampness seeps through your clothes, making shivers run up your spine.

Obedient ciphers, we wait in front of our doors for the "screw" to come along and lock us up. My, neighbor bends over the bucket, looks up at me and says, mocking:

"'Our Father who art in heaven . . .' He's a nice guy, the Father! Bastard!"

ELEVEN

Capital Punishment

DEATH'S MULTIPLE PRESENCE. TOTAL HELPLESSNESS BEFORE A FATE AS IMPLAC-
able as the end. Sharpened perception of time's flight; consciousness
of death. The will to live weakens. Depression tortures the tired brain.
The huge weight of a life sentence; the near-certain premonition of
dying here. Finally, the ultimate torture of those condemned to die.

Whenever a man is guillotined the knife descends slowly, grazing
thousands of bent, expectant necks. The prostrate multitude feel a shiver
of terror tinged with defiance and perverse attraction.

I have seen a Paris crowd gather around an intoxicating and revolting execution. The hum of the night streets had grown more and more
quiet, more and more uneasy in the dismal boulevards surrounding the
prison, till, in the darkness, it collided, like a front consisting of thousands of livid faces, with the lines of troops. Bizarre revelers arrived
by automobile. Under the street lamps, urchins with queer, mocking
grins traced the gesture of decapitation in the air. Bewildered crowds of
workers and young intellectuals were jostled, divided, dispersed, forced
back in disorder by the black wedges of cavalry or police charges as they
nursed their impotent anger in bitter idleness. Many couples exchanged
vague caresses. You could see them getting out of limousines parked
at the edge of deserted streets, where the expectation of the execution
was no more than a rhythmic humming, rising and falling like the tide
at the foot of a cliff. What cliff of implacable cold stone did the tide of
this crowd beat against: death or prison? You could see them arriving in
groups and bunches from the poor working-class suburbs and from the
depths of the slums—la Bastille, la Chapelle, Charonne, Montmartre
and Montparnasse—pimps and hookers, a world of victims liberated
only by the knowledge that sometimes victims take revenge.

Dawn broke amid violent disorders, amid the cadenced cries of
Murderers! Murderers! doubtless echoed—but with a profound feeling

of being the righteous ones at last—by murderers standing in the darkness of their cells behind the bars of the Santé Prison. Pointless scuffles sent the police charging furiously into the crowd. At long intervals pistol shots rang out, spreading general panic and private joy. People ran off, shouting: "A cop got hit . . ." Slender young women—perhaps nothing more than overgrown girls, with scarves around their necks—eyed the soldiers, their hands resting heavy on their rifles near the arms depots: "Would you shoot at us?" Some of them answered calmly: "Of course!"; others murmured: "Never"; still others turned their dark faces away and grumbled: "What the Hell!" Dawn came up. We saw nothing, except for a whitish tinge which appeared indistinctly at the end of the boulevard above the waves of heads in the jagged foliage of the treetops. We did not hear the rumble of the car from which the condemned man emerged, half-naked, shivering, furious, desperate, alive, horribly alive in every ganglia of his brain, in every fiber of his nervous system. He shouted out his innocence, a macabre joke which no one understood among the guilty men lined up around the scaffold who represented the social mechanism behind Dr. Guillotin's philanthropic machine. He appeared like a phantom among the concerns of pathetic, respectable people—appeared and disappeared, in a rapid movement of the seesaw plank, ending in the double fall: the still-thinking head with wide-open eyes falling into the basket, and the thick stream of warm blood falling onto the pavement of the boulevard, where someone had sprinkled a little sand as a precaution. None of us—the crowd—saw it with our own eyes; but at the exact moment we all had, more or less clearly, the same inner vision. I remember the pallor which suddenly spread over everybody's face, the lips turning blue, the clamor which suddenly spread its huge dark wings over us and over the city, the fury in our chests—the collective feeling of the blade's fall.

In Paris, every traveler approaching that end spends the last stage of his journey in the light-colored cells (the one I was in was painted iron-gray) of the Maximum Security section.

A sign over the door:

"Twenty-four-hour surveillance."

Every five minutes the round "eye" cut into the Judas blinks its metal eyelid; a human eye glows within it, rests impassively for a moment on the condemned man. In the cell, nothing. The rough pottery bowl in which, in other cells, you can wash your face with cool water, is forbidden. The blunt iron penknife you used to be able to buy for three *sous* at the prison store is forbidden. Forbidden is the milk bottle which might be used to knock out a guard or, broken, provide a liberating piece of sharp glass to open your veins. The condemned man changes his clothes when he arrives there: the first stage in dressing the victim for the slaughter. I once caught a glimpse of a young comrade returning from court after being convicted. His hair had just been shaved off; his "civilian" clothes formed a dark pile on the tile floor. Fitted out in old denim worn through at the elbows and knees, his arms dangling, slow tears making perpendicular stripes down his lifeless face, he was staring stupidly at that patch of dark cloth at his feet . . .

Isolation is even more complete in Maximum Security. No more chance meetings during exercise period. The cell door is hardly ever open at the same moment as another. A guard unlocks it; the condemned man, wearing carpet slippers, finds a pair of wooden shoes (rarely his size) at his doorstep. Three paces away, the guard who is to accompany him is waiting. At the end of the corridor, the guard who watches the door leading to the exercise yards. Three pairs of eyes.

The electricity is always left on and burns dully in the middle of the ceiling and in the middle of the sleepless prisoner's insomniac brain. His vague thoughts and nightmares flutter around the incandescent platinum wire until fatigue carries him off.

Almost no graffiti. A scratching, almost level with the floor, hidden, mysterious: *Antoine, guillotined on . . .* No date!

Death is perhaps the most *natural* of punishments; it is everywhere in nature. For the swimmer's recklessness, the mountaineer's false step, man's duel against the tiger in the jungle, his longer duel against cold, hunger, the universe, she permits no other sanction than this—at once the first, and the ultimate one. The death penalty is perhaps the most *human* of punishments in two profound senses of the word. First, because men, for millennia—thus distinguishing themselves from the animals—have made daily use of it, clan against clan, tribe against tribe, city against city, state against state, society against society. The *Thou shalt not kill* of the Decalogue—in the laconic simplicity of its truncated text—is a vulgar lie. No one ever really thinks it. The moral law has always been: *Thou shalt not kill thy brother* in the tribe, the city, the nation or class, and it has always been completed by another imperative, no less categorical: *Thou shalt kill* the man of the other tribe, the other city, the other nation, the other class! It is also the most *human* because it cuts short all suffering. On this last point, modern civilization has arrived at a rather paradoxical refinement in cruelty. Just as it counts on fully exploiting the capacity of poor devils, goaded by hunger, to work, so it counts on the will of prisoners to live. Often, then, society, with calculating, hypocritical sentimentality, prefers life sentences—which death alone ends, as a rule, after long years of torture—to the death penalty. Belgium, Italy, and Switzerland lock up their "worst" criminals for life. France and Germany grant a pardon to certain condemned men by commuting their sentence to life imprisonment—worse, in reality, than death. A great French lawyer who had earned a reputation for chivalry during the Dreyfus Affair, once proposed abolishing the death sentence and replacing it with "six years of absolute solitary confinement," six years' dreadful seclusion, six years of marching through the darkness toward inevitable madness and death! The mailed fist smashing into a skull is no more cruel, in itself, than any act of war—and many acts of peace. It is less so, to judge by the *quantity* of suffering and death inflicted, than that of the shrewd businessman who, through a lucky speculation in coal, brings about a rise in price of three *sous* a hundredweight that will cause the deaths of a few hundred paupers' children in the metropolis before the end of winter.

An act is only as good as the end pursued and the result obtained. Masked or thinly veiled, from time immemorial, they have needed to use the death penalty against us—the working people. We, too, need it, to put an end to all this! Murder will close the circle of murder; for a war can only be ended by a victory; for only the victors can be liberators—having liberated themselves. In the class war, which is like the other kind but stripped of hypocrisy, the greatest humanity must be combined with the most decisive use of force. The class that wants to build a new world, forever cleansed of killing machines, must learn how to kill in battle so as not to be killed. But it must learn as well—along with all those who turn resolutely toward the future—to abolish a past which has put such arms into its hands, to abolish the refined, useless, senseless, gratuitous cruelty of death inflicted by an "act of justice" on guilty men who are sometimes brutes, usually unlucky wretches, sometimes rebels (that is to say, the most ardent of men), and always the inevitable products of the normal workings of society, always victims paying a ransom for others . . .

Nothing, in an opulent and solid society, justifies that abominable thing: the solemn execution, on a set day, at a fixed hour, after complicated formalities, of a miserable wretch who has been kept for sixty or a hundred days in an iron-gray cell in the Maximum Security section, alone with the guillotine blade, that cold line on the back of the neck. You can understand Danton calling for the September massacres.

You can understand the Russian Revolution, encircled like the French Revolution in the past, slaughtering several hundred or several thousand bourgeois on the day when Lenin fell bloody at its feet. You can understand the Third French Republic coldly shooting down thirty thousand defeated Communards; their magnificent blood has not been lost—all debts will be paid. That is the price at which we learn the laws of class war. They hold the secret of a different victory: But your death, Antoine-with-no-name of the Fifth Division, guillotined on an unknown date, seems to me to be something monstrously and ferociously useless.

Totally useless, surrounded by complicated ceremonies, the application of "capital" punishment to the worst victims on the losing side of the social struggle raises the whole system of penitentiary repression to the height of ancestral savagery. The guillotine (elsewhere, the ax, the noose, the garrote, the electric chair—different equipment) adds a symbol of steely clarity to prison. Jail is a machine for grinding up lives slowly. The blade's lightning efficiency grinds better. Modern jails are perfect. Any scaffold, even the most primitive, is perfect. The very permanence of jails and scaffolds testifies to their necessity, and at the same time, to their eternal impotence. They will last as long as the class war in which only one victory can be definitive: that of the destroyers of jails and scaffolds. Your death at an unknown date, Antoine-with-no-name, only shows that you have been treated with all the rigor of the class war—you, who probably never devoted a moment's thought to it.

Once, while returning from a visit with my lawyer, I happened to meet a comrade who was being kept in that deathly part of the prison. M*** was a tall, thin fellow with a long, drab face, a narrow, receding forehead, and flat temples. There was barely a spark of life left in his dull eyes, which were as lusterless as slack water; his face prefigured the guillotine grimace. He was too simpleminded to fool himself. His face barely responded to my greeting: His pupils widened, his eyelids arched; but he raised his long, pale, sharp right hand to the level of his neck and imitated the fall of the knife.

He lived with that anticipation. He greeted its image in a comrade's face. When he walked, the shadow of two uprights crossed by a slanting blade fell before him. His anticipation was not deceived.

When I think of the men I have known well who were devoured by that expectation, the memory of meeting this one, the weakest among them and the most ravaged, rises up to greet me silently with that grave, almost ritual gesture. That gesture: the same one which, years before, during a dawn of execution which became a dawn of rioting, I saw traced by that skinny kid, surrounded by a circle of women in the misty halo of a street lamp . . .

They were five or six in the Maximum Security cells—men of savage strength whose hard, mocking expressions were familiar to me—alone with certain or probable death. They were living as one lives—but better, with more intelligence and will. One of them, with the face of a serious schoolboy and the nature of an impulsive child, divided his hours between calming studies, the orderly daydreams he mistook for thoughts, gymnastic exercises, ablutions—and the long, long walks of the caged man turning, taciturn, around his cage in the dizzying apprehension of losing his head at the end of the road. Nevertheless, the stubborn, unreasonable hope of living still grew within him with such youthful ardor that it was physically impossible for him to think of dying. At the moment when death appeared certain to him, he turned crimson and all the blood rushed to his brain, bathing it in the horrible intoxication of an ultimate act of will. From that first plunge of the guillotine blade right up to the real one, he maintained his self-control, repressing his terror. A fine-looking man, whom I had known less than a year earlier at the height of mature self-awareness, appeared before me on the way out of his death cell. He looked twenty years older, his face deeply lined, feverish, his velvet-brown eyes concealing wild panic under a façade of strained self-control. Innocent, his neck was to feel no other knife blow than that of a death sentence dragging on and on until the day of his "pardon." Defendants in the same trial, we were given the surprise of a chance meeting during a transfer. And I saw how those who felt they were on the road to the guillotine already bore its distinctive mark in their eyes, on their brow, in the fold of their lips, in the jerky movements of their bony, whitened, nervous hands . . .

The iron-gray walls of the Maximum Security section are the most silent of all; but since the prison was built, so many tortured souls have bruised their pitiful wings against the sterility and indifference, brightness and hardness of these walls that the mere thought of it makes you feel their torture going on and on, while one by one their names are lost, without meaning, in the crowd. The same suffering writhes endlessly within these same walls, perpetual from year to year, whatever the names and numbers of its momentary bearers. They relay each other, passing on from hand to hand—not the torch of antiquity—but their severed heads with blinking eyes.

"Tomorrow."

All I saw through the Judas were two rounded eyes under arched eyebrows. The sharp voice whispered but one word:

"Tomorrow."

Tomorrow, what? The four iron-gray walls answer me with their heavy silence. The pages of the old Bible lying open on my table seem to fade, fade . . . What is it that suddenly changes the hue of the walls? As if the sun—but there is no sun—were setting . . . Where does this sudden cold come from—and this feeling of tension in the neck? I am not condemned to die . . . "Tomorrow."

The three sharp whispered syllables will pass from cell to cell. Or the arc of raised eyebrows will pass on their meaning. Or a strange tapping will be heard in the wall. Or the guards will hurry as they make their rounds. Noises, signs, glances, a feeling. All these warnings will cease at the doorstep of one locked cell, but the man within will understand; and if he nonetheless falls asleep tonight, it's because he has known too far in advance, for too many long hours. His troubled sleep, broken by starts, will become calm sixty minutes before dawn, only to be interrupted forty minutes later. The administration estimates twenty minutes as the time necessary to carry out the death ceremony.

Condemned men receive a kind of special treatment. To prevent them from sinking into madness or committing suicide in spite of every precaution, guards or Sûreté agents keep them company. They play cards together. They never speak of *that*. But it is all they think about. And the condemned man learns from his partner's distraction, from a slight unusual pallor, from the tremor of a hand which accidentally touches his, that it's *tomorrow*.

A sharp whistle, coming from the outside, sometimes warns him.

One of them asked his guard one evening:

"It's *tomorrow*, right?"

The guard, flabbergasted, tried to deny it.

"Don't be afraid," calmly replied the head destined to fall less than ten hours later. "I know. And they can all go to hell! Understand?"

Tomorrow.

Tonight the whole prison is listening anxiously. Hundreds of chests are holding in their breath. Brains grow feverish in a communion—perhaps only the contagion of a disease—of the fever of one crazed brain—soon to be a bit of gray stuff, bloodless, rotting slowly—living only in anticipation of death.

Long before the time comes, bare feet make their way toward the locked cell doors in the darkness or pale nocturnal light. Through the cracks in closed Judases the eyes of many brothers in suffering will try to glimpse the man leaving on his ultimate voyage.

Some will perceive—for the space of an instant—a confused image which will remain stamped on their memories forever:

Indistinct silhouettes: shadows, *képis*. Him: a gray profile, deep sockets. In shirtsleeves. Held by the elbow, dragged along, almost carried, fainting perhaps, bewildered. Him.

Then the bars of the window will turn dark against the pale sky and the numbness of chilling dejection.

TWELVE

The *Souricière* and the *Conciergerie*

I WAS INTERROGATED DURING FOUR OR FIVE HALF-HOUR SESSIONS, OVER A period of twelve months, before being sent into criminal court under various indictments, adding up more or less to a ticket on a convict ship headed for Guiana. Prisoners with plenty of money go to their pretrial examinations in a taxi, accompanied by plainclothes policemen. Photographers from the big papers try to catch them on the courthouse steps. They wear ties and detachable collars. They are called "gentlemen." Penniless prisoners are dragged suddenly out of their cells in ragged clothing and bustled into the filthy compartments of the Black Maria. These are known as "guys" or "mugs."

After being locked up for months, the trip in the Black Maria and the duel of interrogation—where a man at bay confronts a crafty hunter lying in wait on the opposite side of a desk, ready to catch his victim off guard, aiming a sudden, unexpected question like a rifle shot—constitute real events . . .

The noise of the car rolling over cobblestones or asphalt. Street noises—the quiet streets around the Santé Prison, whose calm is disturbed only occasionally by an odd passing car, then the bustle of the main boulevard with its countless human and mechanical voices. The feeling of passing, stiff in a vertical coffin, through a street where you often walked with a free and lively step. Peering avidly through the air filter, yearning desperately at the fleeting sight of a female passerby—heart clenched, fists clenched. The moving screen of a trolley car.

On the way out of the Maria, a city trooper, or *'Cipal*, snaps the cuffs on the new arrival and leads him to the *Souricière*.

The name *Souricière*, or "mousetrap," is a fitting one. Two stories of stench-infested wire cages, just big enough to hold a man and a latrine. Two paces wide, five paces long at the most. At one end, the wire-mesh door; at the other, the filthy toilet seat of rusty iron, stopped up to prevent anyone from destroying anything in it. The stench of urine and defecation wafts up over the drawings on the walls. The accused is left to stew there for long hours, frequently five or six at a stretch. How to keep busy? Your defense is ready: Constantly thinking it over only weakens your mind and wears on your nerves. You observe the comings and goings. They bore you in the end: Their variety is a form of monotony. So then you look for the pencil stub which the previous occupants of the filthy stall have concealed in a crevice of the wall under the latrine; or you remove your own from the inside lining of your jacket and add your own page to the prodigious book of the wall.

This wall was once whitewashed. At first glance it appears a solid gray, made up of a tangled, confused, crosshatched network of inscriptions and drawings. Names, stories, rhymed couplets, appointments, confessions: an incredible swarm of writings and hieroglyphics weaves a mad arabesque around the four great human themes: struggle, sorrow, love, carnal lust. The primitive literature of the inhabitants of the social jungle, identical on the walls of every jail. One word of advice is found here again and again, sharp and clear, signed by countless hands:

Never confess!

Someone who didn't sign has etched his experience in little block letters over the name *Adèle* written out in a fine round hand:

I was dumb, I confessed, I'm screwed, it's all over for me.

There is also:

I confessed: 5 years.

Obscenity radiates from the ceiling down to the tiled floor, from the door over to the latrine, in drawings which sometimes attain the lewd perfection of Persian miniatures. In one of "my" cells in the *Souricière*, a life-size drawing of a naked woman took up the whole back wall: lower belly slit open, pointed breasts, mouth twisted, prostituted: The hallucinated artist had not been able to get the proportions right and had been careful and workmanlike only in finishing the sexual parts. The eyes, shoulders, arms might have been drawn by a clumsy ten-year-old child.

(It was only much later and in a very different place that I ever saw pornography comparable to this in imaginative frenzy and in the total absence of aesthetic pretensions. It was in the Winter Palace of Petrograd in the modest soldier's apartment of Czar Nicholas I, one of the masters of post-Napoleonic Europe, one of the heads of the Holy Alliance. In an anteroom off his bedroom there was a cabinet concealing a shower bath and a clothes closet on one side, at the back of which an insignificant painting was hanging. A hidden mechanism, well known to the august hands, allowed the first canvas to be pushed, aside revealing a second one, which was peopled with a swarming mass of purplish, rosy, turgid flesh intertwined in the most complicated positions . . .)

On that same wall someone's fingers had left fecal traces. Someone else had written in blood. The blood letters, having turned brown, looked like streams of excrement . . .

Someone had translated everyone's advice into a single, lapidary phrase:

Shut up or croak.

A municipal guard (two of them for prisoners who are considered dangerous) comes to fetch the prisoner and leads him, handcuffed, to the prosecutor's office. At a turn of the stairs, just beyond a little oak door, you come into a huge hall filled with black-robed lawyers, groups of defendants hedged in by uniforms, law clerks, bailiffs—a whole busy, bustling world where handshakes and dossiers, sudden confidences and premeditated betrayals, are exchanged. Prisoners carrying on surreptitious deliberations at the door of "their" examining magistrate's office. A door too slowly shut reveals an anxious confrontation. A man is in that room, alone, his head in his hands (". . . that's her hair . . .") and, knowingly, like a drowning man who does not want to go down alone, he betrays . . .

Number 12–20 has been dragged from his compartment in the mousetrap, his heart beating wildly (for his fate will be decided today within that curly head glimpsed through a half-open door). So complete is the indifference enclosing him that he might, by shutting his eyes, imagine he was alone. No one, among the people coming and going— too busy and too hardened—notices the anguish of this poor wretch who has been tossed aside on a bench with two other wretches just like him—three grand larcenies. Sometimes a lawyer, suddenly remembering, will touch a hand or shoulder. A hurried conference takes place between Number 12–20's anxiety and the reassuring, distracted defense counsellor's feigned attention.

"Legris!" calls out the examining magistrate's clerk, opening the door a crack.

Legris, Number 12–20 rises, still handcuffed, crosses the office threshold like an automaton, and is dazzled by the light coming from the large window, the corpulent bulk of the gentlemen writing a letter, and the thought that this is the examining magistrate . . .

Another compartment in the mousetrap. Legris feels shattered, caught in the clutches of a cat.

Condemned prisoners returning from their sentencing pass in front of the *Souricière*. I remember the women best: one being led back in tears—hair undone, chest heaving with convulsive gasps—by a fatherly *'Cipal*:

"You'll pull through your six months, my dear. Why, you'll already be out in December . . . Maybe they'll shorten your sentence on appeal . . ."

(It has been known to happen. But more often the sentence is increased.)

"Six months, six months . . ." The bedraggled woman moved out of sight, led off toward the paddy wagon, but her hysterical voice still echoed through the nauseating cages, where the men greeted it with a scornful smile.

"Six months! What a joke! If it were only that . . ."

Another, plump and blond, went by choking with laughter, walking so rapidly that she appeared to be leading her *'Cipal*—one hand on her hip, invective on her lips: savage, furious, unprintable invective pouring over her eighteen-year-old cherry lips like a broken sewer main pouring the pestilence of the city out into the sunlight . . .

A fine figure of a girl: The firm fruit of her breasts standing out under her white satin blouse, the gilded ivory of her teeth between her raging lips, the light golden shiver of her neck, the hot vengeance in her voice, were a fleeting feast for all the males whose locked cages she passed. They learned that someone had "finked" on her, and that she got a year on a "frame-up" for fleecing her clients . . .

I also remember an undergrown adolescent, a precocious lad of fourteen or a backward eighteen-year-old—frail, red-eyed from crying and conjunctivitis, with a weasel's snout and the ragged, rain-washed, tattered, ill-smelling clothes of a shepherd boy . . . His dull eyes were glued to the white gloves of the *'Cipal*, a florid man bedecked with medals, glittering with shining buttons and polished leather . . .

The image of the "outlaw" and the trooper made me think of a title for a sad fable:

The squashed weasel and the cavalry horse.

The *Conciergerie* is the last in the series of traps which lead the prisoner from the threshold of preventive prison to the final oblivion of a dungeon. A few stays in the *Souricière* prepare a man for the plunge into this last trap—the most cramped, the most stifling—encased in thick, centuries-old walls, and buried in the oldest soil of Paris under heavy Gothic arches cemented with medieval blood, the blood of kings. After the massacres of September 1792, Marie-Antoinette stayed in this building while waiting to place her royal head—uncrowned—in the *lunette de Sanson* . . .

Literature! You fall into this pit only to be knocked senseless by a verdict that descends on your head like a bludgeon.

There are so many different levels in the huge old *Palais de Justice,* built over ground honeycombed with underground passages, that I am not really certain whether the ground-floor cells of the *Conciergerie* are actually on street level. You can never shake off the feeling of being held underground when you're in there. The stone arches of its broad, somber, silent corridors are supported by massive columns. In the tiny cells, hardly any larger than those of the *Souricière,* the meager light filters through narrow, barred window slits cut into the thick walls from courtyards lined with tall, gray buildings outside. It is impossible to read except standing directly under the window, and then only at the brightest time of day. The table—at least in the cell I occupied— never gets enough light, except from the electric bulb which burns all night in the middle of the whitewashed ceiling. By day, semidarkness; by night, the irritating glare of the electric bulb. Once, I tried sleeping with a handkerchief as a blindfold to get away from it. The guards, intrigued, dragged me from my sleep. Why this suspicious appearance of a man before the firing squad? They hunt anxiously for suicidal tendencies in all of us.

The cramped monastic cells are separated by walls half a yard thick, which smother noises and hamper communication; they are nonetheless not heavy enough to encase everyone buried here in total silence. For several days on end I listened (listening in spite of myself, distractedly, unable to read, write, or walk in the damp semidarkness of my cell) to the rhythmic sobbing of a stranger, my neighbor, crushed under an unknown sorrow. He cried for three or four days on end, without any shame or pride. I learned the rhythm of his breathing and his despair. He had outbursts of sobbing in which you could sense the outrage of a hurt child, the desolate incomprehension ("No, it's impossible, it's impossible!") of grieved voices at a deathbed. Then there was only a forlorn murmur, dying away, the trailing off of a worn-out sorrow, purged of its substance, extinguished by the exhaustion of both flesh and spirit.

For a few hours you are "removed" from this parallelogram of semi-darkness and stone; you wind your way through the underground passageways, climb the steps of a narrow spiral staircase cut into a tower, and emerge into "the bright light of the courtroom" in front of the twelve jurymen and the judges—old sourpuss bureaucrats whose robes serve to amplify their oratorical gestures. Sham and ceremony. Defend yourself, Legris, show you're a man like the others, neither better nor worse in spite of your crime—your crime of a starveling who turns one day and bites . . . or smashes and pillages a shop window! Deny, confess, repent, beg for mercy from these gentlemen; the rules of the game still allow it, one last time. Nothing you may say or do will have much place in the ritual. You are about to disappear entirely, worn down by the screws, the bolts, the peepholes, the successive traps of the great mousetrap, buried under the three hundred pages of the accusation, the seventeen questions (four aggravating circumstances), the twenty-four grounds and points of the indictment. During one hundred and twenty minutes of argumentation, the eloquence of two thin, contradictory voices waved two false specters before your dismal face: those of a scoundrel and those of an unlucky honest man which, counterfeiter, you never were. Yes, the game is over: You will understand later. On the way. By and by you will scratch these words, simply, into the chalk of a wall:

Eight years for forty-five francs in hundred-sous pieces.

Within these walls I bid farewell (with a nod of the head; both of us were handcuffed to troopers) to a strong, calm bandit who had never killed. He walked away with his springy athlete's gait, a distracted smile on his lips. The redness of his muscular face and the wrinkling of the puffy eyelids over his gray (perhaps metallic, perhaps colorless) eyes were the only things that betrayed the shock he had undergone. "He's taking it well," someone had just told me. He was on his way back to his cell, a convict for the next twenty years. I myself was up for five years' confinement. Seven in the morning.

In the evening an old drunken guard, who had predicted and hoped for my acquittal, came to chat at the Judas of my cell. His lower lip was twitching. He said very rapidly, in a whisper that smelled of absinthe:

"C*** just *passed*. He died like a man. The poison was hidden in the heel of his shoe. He kept his teeth clenched, writhing in death, to keep them from giving him anything or treating him."

The moist, uneasy eye of the old turnkey—twenty-two years of service—betrayed incomprehension and pity . . .

"Why kill yourself? Twenty years? He could have escaped. Been granted a pardon. Anyway, think! With his character, his health, he would have come out of prison at the end of his time healthier than I am, after twenty-two years of service . . . No, it's no good, it's not sensible . . ."

And he went away with a little shuffling step, his shoulders rounded under his greasy tunic with its faded trimmings, continuing his rounds and his quarter century of service, a well-domesticated prison rat with a gray soul like the shadows under these arches, gray and soft like the rag mops which had just wiped up the suicide's vomit.

THIRTEEN

Drunken Boat

IT IS LIKE STEPPING OUT INTO THE NIGHT ON A VOYAGE TOWARD THE UNKNOWN. The march will be long, so long that there is nothing by which to measure its duration, through a relentless night strewn with pitfalls. Falling along the way would be like sinking into a dark lake on a moonless night under a leaden sky in total solitude: No cry would ever be heard. So be silent, then, whatever happens. The fleeting circles would barely break the surface of the still water, which would soon close without a ripple over the drowned man.

A voyage not into space, but into time: forty-six months of darkness to traverse. Fourteen months' claustration have already been covered. That was only a prelude. What will the sentence be like?

The future? Time? Is there a future? The weak and the feckless will fall by the wayside, closing their tired eyes in a prison infirmary. I know that time has two subjective dimensions: The bitter minute drags on eternally; the empty months fly, leaving no more than a bit of dust in the soul. Not even an ash!

En route! The main thing is to have courage at the start and keep it along the way. From now on, the universe has but two spheres: mine and the enemy's. The gears of the machine will grind me from every side, at every instant, for years. In vain will I raise my chained arms in revolt against it. Then let them bear their chains—inescapable burdens—with neither weakness nor vain resistance. I still have the other sphere: The machine cannot rob me of that. We face each other as equals, the huge Prison-Machine and I; our strengths and weaknesses limit each other, locked forever in a stalemate. Until the day of my release, I will be Number 6731, a prisoner, a robot programmed to obey the prison rules. I can do nothing about it. Until the day of my release, I will be myself—a free man, strong, inflexible, without fear—under the chains, the numbered jacket, the harsh, absurd regulations. The machine can do nothing about it. *En route!*

I will walk down that dark road as long as I have to. Until madness or death? No. I have faith in myself: If one or the other brings me down, it will be by violence, in spite of myself, without stooping to fear them. I will conquer prison.

En route.

These resolutions are not particularly praiseworthy in my case. I'm a short-termer. The long terms, the hard ones, begin at eight years. (When I first got in, an old prisoner told me: "Five years? Lucky bastard! That's soon over. I'm doing twenty: fourteen done already. It's a bitch.")

There are only three ways of facing prison. Accepting it as a duel, which many convicts—especially among the true outlaws—do more or less consciously. I have encountered splendid moral strength among them. Giving in to it, head bowed, no inner resistance; letting the prison enter your soul and mold it; sinking into its dank folds, vegetating there—complaining, or passive, or happy to find a good spot. This is how the majority of prisoners act; they are drawn from a variety of social groups where crime is the exception rather than the rule: peasants, middle-class people, lecherous priests, shady lawyers, crooked accountants, corrupt administrators, and those who commit "crimes of passion." Or not resisting at all, and not giving in either; with the will to live broken by the bludgeon of the verdict, you drift along peacefully from one day to the next—for three months or three years—toward the haven of the infirmary where, one morning, you die quietly, having lived, in silence, only the time necessary to die. Real criminals are never found in this category of prisoners. The prison-weathered can always spot these "sad cases" when they arrive; doubly condemned, they carry their fates within themselves . . .

Departure for an unknown destination. I put on my "civilian" clothes, which I had shed the day after my conviction. So many memories of the street are hidden in their folds! Wrists in irons. A boxcar of the train fitted out with cells. In the cramped steel compartment there is no room to stand or to stretch out; my knees are jammed between the wall and the seat, the irons on my ankles further restricting my movement. This transfer coach is dark, dirty, stifling, full of shouting voices. Our deathly silence has a counterpart in the noise made by two guards, ex-noncoms with wine-flushed faces, who are stuffing themselves, drinking, playing cards, talking about promotions, shady deals, good wine, and lifted skirts in a language profuse with scatological exclamations. The foulness of these warm male voices fills our cloistral cells. The coach rolls on, a drunken coach, sinister, as the *bateau ivre* was at times,

Planche folle, escorté de hippocampes noirs[6]

carrying along these two men in uniform, full of animal joy at wallowing in a comfortable dungheap; carrying along too, in the shadow of these living men, four prisoners, excluded from life, chained, motionless, isolated, tortured by thirst, stiff and bruised all over from lack of movement. Coupled to freight trains carrying foodstuffs, uncoupled at a fork, forgotten for hours on a siding in an out-of-the-way station, hooked up again, shunted and jolted amid shouted curses, then returning to the deep silence of a deserted station, our wandering prison rolls and pitches us along its incomprehensible itinerary through time and space. We left in the morning; we hear—where?—the bells chiming at six in the evening. What do we care? But how we would love to stretch our cramped, tingling legs, to straighten our backs, to drink a tall glass of water. That would be good.

The four of us:

Morge—known as *Cookie* or *The Cook*—has the clap. An "anarchist." Twenty-two years old, I think. And twenty years at hard labor. He was the lookout outside the country house where a "buddy" of his, discovered in the middle of a burglary, strangled an old housemaid with his prudently gloved hands, using wet dish towels; then, in epileptic rage, slowly stabbed a seventy-year-old man. The gloved murderer came very close to the guillotine; his precaution saved him. He is free. This pale kid is paying in his place. He will keep silent. He has hopes. His wife (a young, washed-out blonde with TB who, believing in "free love," used to give herself docilely, with soft, immodest caresses, to every chum who came along) promised to meet him in Guiana. It is said the convicts there get plots of land to till if they behave themselves. Illusory hopes of life in a penal colony ferment in this young brain, devoured by rebellions gone astray. Love, too, is perhaps being born there. At a fork in the rails, M. will leave us for another drunken boxcar. (His wife never went to meet him: She died during the year.)

---

6   "A crazy plank, escorted by black sea-horses . . ." The line is from Rimbaud's "Bateau ivre" (Drunken Boat) from which Serge also took his chapter heading. (Tr.)

Horel is sixty years old and looks seventy. His "case" aged him suddenly. He has white hair, a red nose which is always dripping, and wet, bloodshot, spaniel eyes. Horel babbles on and on; from time to time he squeezes a pink tumor on the back of his neck with his old, workworn hand.

"Squeeze it," he says. "Can you feel? The bullet is still in there."

Good luck or bad? He hardly knows himself. Things have gone beyond him. He didn't intend to live; now he no longer wants to die. But six years in jail at his age—and even that through the court's indulgence!—is too much. Horel committed a crime of passion: Jealous of his own son, a handsome lad of twenty, he killed his mistress, a forty-year-old, and attempted suicide. He was brought back to life, after great difficulty, in order to be sent to prison. The drunken boxcar is carrying him toward his fate. Later on, I was to meet him often, his knees and back more and more bent, wearing wooden shoes too big for him, limping, among the old men working in the rope-weaving shop. One hand stuffed into his belt, the other slipped between two jacket buttons to avoid the chill, nose dripping, dull-eyed, slack-jawed, shaking all over with each stiff step like a broken puppet, he tottered on, walled within himself in enforced silence, toward the little prison cemetery. It took several years.

The third one also committed a "crime of passion," although the word seems ridiculous when applied to this fat, pink-skinned boy whose bright cheeks are like ripe apples. He murdered a lad from his village, in a brawl, for playing up to "his wife"—he says "his wife," although she was only his fiancée (but with what triumphant laughter he must have thrown her on her back under the shadow of a haystack on hot afternoons when the pungent sweat of young flesh goes to the brain, headier than wine!). The vigor of his nineteen years will now be employed carrying the soup bucket to the mess hall twice a day. I think he died, too, of pneumonia; my memory may have confused him with another peasant (a hardy lad like him who committed murder under similar circumstances), and I can't remember which of the two died in the infirmary.

We sit in silence, side by side, in the drunken boxcar, unable to communicate. We met only on arrival.

Other temporary fellow travelers got into our coach at a station. I don't remember them at all, as they were headed toward a house of correction while we were being transferred to a penitentiary.

An express train coming onto the track covered our dark silence with the groaning of its couplings. There were jerks, the impact of a stop, the impact of voices, an uncoupling, a voice:

"The cars are there."

Stiff from eight hours immobilized in irons, we stood unsurely, our limbs free, lined up alongside a track while the guards from the transfer service moved from wrist to wrist, putting new chains on us, so that we became a chain of eight men linked together; a caterpillar with eight heads and sixteen slow feet, jangling, balking, staggering, crossing the tracks of the freight depot with our eyes blinded by the signals and our numb feet stumbling against the rails.

A caterpillar crushed under an iron heel; we moved slowly through the thick darkness of the March night. And suddenly my eyes were dazzled, my brain flooded with joy:

The sky!

Above our heads a glittering winter sky, full of constellations, spread out its deep blacks and blues, its profusion of stars, the ripples of light in its shadowy gulfs. Had I ever understood the marvel of a simple starry sky before? For four hundred days I had been deprived of it: and it was a revelation.

I would have fallen, my eyes lost up there, while I stumbled among the rails, the ties, and the cables stretched across the ground, if the other links in the penitentiary caterpillar hadn't pushed me, dragged me, half-carried me toward the lights of the station . . .

The bizarre caterpillar wavered for a moment on its sixteen shaking feet as the station came suddenly to life before it. All the lights seemed to be shining on it: a brutal reminder of a life that had been lost. A stand with newspapers, magazines, books! Tobacco! The people crowding out of a stopped train appeared so close, so *real:* a soldier, a lady leading two kids by the hand, a man opening his newspaper at his compartment window, a man kissing a young woman. How we stared at that ordinary traveler, a sixteen-eyed monster brooding over the joy of his farewell!

Then the caterpillar was sliced in two. A car jolted the four convicts through the lighted streets of the town. They stared out avidly, stupefied that life was still going on, "quiet and easy," just as it was when they lost it.

FOURTEEN

Arrival

WE PASSED THROUGH A SERIES OF THRESHOLDS IN THE NIGHT. THE BUILD-
ings were huge squares against the glittering, deep-blue sky above. A
wardroom; some sleepy-eyed s.o.b.'s who looked at us with insolent
nonchalance; a man in a silver-braided *képi*—bovine, crimson-faced,
massive; *képi* over one ear, breath winy, a ring of keys jangling against
his pants leg.

"This way!"

Unchained at last, amazed at the freedom of our limbs, the sudden
lightness of our bodies (droplets of joy mounting in our veins; how good
to be able to move your wrists freely!), we are led through a poorly lit
alleyway under the dazzling sky. We penetrate another ring of walls,
then a gloomy hall where the air is bad. There we lose each other, surrounded by a single man armed with keys who comes and goes, stands
us in front of numbered doors like wax figures, terrified, under the
glimmer of his dark lantern shining on our faces . . .

"Enter!"

I enter. Where? I don't know. Into absolute darkness. It might be
into the void.

The door closes behind me; the guard's steps fade away below, outside on the pavement. Total darkness. Standing still, I try to make out
my hands, held up a few inches from my eyes. Impossible. I stretch
them out, my fingers moving cautiously like tentacles. I move forward
slowly, feeling my way through the shadows (and still that feeling of joy
flowing through my veins in tiny droplets, vivid and warm; the joy of
moving without hindrance). The absurd memory of that dazzlement
sticks in my mind: It was beautiful, after all, that starry sky! Ah! here's
the wall; follow it. It is clean, without any inscriptions. Four walls, by
Jove, those well-known four walls . . . They are practically old friends,
those four murderous walls. *Nothing else.* I was hoping for a bench.

Let's get comfortable. I make a pillow out of my rolled-up vest and my crushed hat artfully draped over my shoes (what use to me now are these castoffs from the civilized world?). Stretched out full-length on the waxed floor, I dream.

I have no idea of what will come. The lawyers whom I questioned about my sentence exasperated me to death with their evasive answers. They don't give a damn, by God! Once a client ends up here, he is no longer a client.

I saw the dawn rise: A dull gray filled the cell imperceptibly, banishing the darkness; then a pale glow. Slowly, this became light. No idea of the time. Having dressed, I waited for a long while, pacing along the walls as if from habit. Sixteen paces. Seventeen if you turn around without hurrying. Why hurry?

The day began well. The three of us—the passengers of the drunken boxcar—found ourselves together again in a magnificent triangular courtyard . . .

"Terrific," said Horel.

And the little homicidal peasant smiled a broad, broad smile.

There were at least six yards of grass in those ten square yards; and even a little stunted tree, no bigger than a bush, whose buds were beginning to open. We were "free" there, close to the earth and plants, free to chat, three buddies, no?

"We're not part of the system yet," said the little peasant. "It's not possible."

We heard bells ringing, lines of men marching: the cadenced beat of long lines of wooden shoes against the pavement. The cadences of the penitentiary. It was clear to us that we had not yet begun our period of punishment. Besides, our "civilian" clothes were more than enough to remind us of that . . .

We lost them an hour later in the little "first-aid room" of the infirmary, where two prisoner aides in white smocks, a guard, and Sergeant Zizi got us into our permanent outfits. Our old clothes, thrown down one by one onto the floor, searched, pockets turned out, immediately took on the aspect of rags. Zizi, an old bemedaled veteran of the colonial service, seedy and servile, a huge hooked nose hanging over a white mustache piss-colored around the lips from tobacco—Zizi, silver braid running up to his shoulder, dictates his estimate of the value of our effects to an inmate-bookkeeper. Bellowing as if on a parade ground, he calls out:

"One black felt hat: twenty-five centimes . . . Suspenders: ten centimes. One gray tweed suit: one hundred *sous*! . . . One striped shirt: fifty centimes . . ."

Zizi is having a ball.

His appraisal is recorded in an account book, which we sign. The administration takes charge of our effects: They will be returned to us—whatever is left of them after the moths get through with them—when we are released. In case they are accidentally destroyed, the administration, in its honesty, promises to make good their value to the amount recorded here and countersigned by us. We start out by being robbed.

Then, standing naked in front of our little bundles of rags, we wait for our uniforms to be issued: shirts and underdrawers of gray canvas (probably originally white), jacket, trousers, and cap of brown denim. The ones they give us are so worn-out you can see the blue thread of the warp: but they are clean. Wooden shoes.

"Sew this on your right sleeve."

It's a square of white canvas bearing four numbers: 6731. Number 6731, that's me. The wooden shoes make it hard to walk. They go *click clack* with every step, and they always feel as if they're about to slip off.

They shaved my head. My hair has just been swept away along with the last of Horel's white mane. By now I have been sufficiently depersonalized to appear before the administrative authorities. There is nothing left to distinguish me from the others, my peers, our prisoners' rabble. We all have the same stubbly chins, the same shaved skulls—and doubtless the same look of the hunted man.

We appear before a sort of administrative tribunal: the Warden (*képi* covered all over with silver braid), the Controller (*képi* half-covered with silver braid), the Chief Guard (*képi* partly covered with silver braid). *Képi, képi, képi*. Stripes. A fat old man with a mustache who looks like a white wine drinker. A flabby pugnose. A faceless military man who has left no trace in my mind except that of his *képi*. The three of them on a dais behind a long table. Behind them, the Republic: a hunk of yellowed plaster specked with fly shit. Zizi, on their right, is acting as court clerk.

The new man appears flanked by guards, exactly five feet from the dais, in the regulation posture of a soldier at attention. The Warden leafs through a dossier and, depending on the case or his mood:

"Ah, there you are. They say you're a tough nut. Well, you better watch out. We know how to take care of tough nuts here."

A silence. A wave of the hand holding a blotting roller. Bushy eye-brows contracting into a frown under the silvered *képi*. The point has been made, doubtless.

"Dismiss!"

The new man is shoved smartly by the shoulders and thrown out. "Next."

"You're supposed to have character too. Well, in this place, my lad, we know how to round off the corners of character. Understand?"

Shoulders drooping, neck pulled in, a voice which is nothing more than a respectful whisper, the questioned prisoner murmurs:

"Yes, Warden, sir."

The third in today's line-up is a little provincial solicitor who absconded with all the money in his village. The Warden's eye softens as it falls on this sad, pudgy face. This one is neither an underworld character nor an ex-con: a respectable man who went bad, that's all. The Warden suddenly remembers the theory of prisoner rehabilitation.

"Try to behave yourself, Boulin, and we'll see what we can do for you."

To the fourth, an anarchist, the Warden says simply:

"One warning: no propaganda here, or you'll regret it."

Few men in modern society wield such absolute power over their fellow men as a prison warden. The Civilian Controller, who in reality acts as an assistant warden, doesn't control anything. The Warden has, in effect, the power of life and death over the prisoner. All it takes from him is a suggestion to the Chief Guard ("keep an eye on him . . .") and the prisoner, whose number is thus pointed out for the guards' zeal-ous attention, is constantly harassed with petty discipline and loaded down with penalties. The Warden can inflict penalties up to ninety days in the hole: more than enough to send the man thus punished to the infirmary, eyes ruined, lungs ravaged by tuberculosis, throat swol-len, and ears dripping pus. Some die. Each year, the man in the silvered *képi* thus pronounces, in effect, several sentences of slow death, gener-ally for trifling reasons.

FIFTEEN

The Mill

THE PERFECTION OF MODERN PRISON INCORPORATES THE PERFECTION OF THE self-sufficient feudal castle which, despite its economic dependency on the surrounding countryside, was able with its artisans, its men-at-arms, its church, its hospital, its jail, its gallows, its banquet halls, its arsenals, its storehouses, to sustain a long siege. The penitentiary perpetuates the economic and social organization of a medieval *burg* within the modern city. Designed to allow hundreds of men to live and die sequestered within its walls—not by freely accepted discipline as in monasteries, but under brutal constraint—it is a dreary city at once besieged and dominated by the enemy within.

Its outer walls surround vast buildings scattered among gardened, tree-planted courtyards. The single entrance, not far from the guardroom, under the Registrar's offices (for the jail books must be near the rifles), opens onto a courtyard lined by the administration buildings, and closed off at one end by the edifices of the prison proper. The low roofs of the visitors' room and the chapel-*cum*-tribunal stretch out from the administrative offices to the cell blocks. Passing through another gate, the prisoner finds himself in the land of punishment. It resembles an empty back street in a dull little town, lined with white walls and stern buildings with barred windows. The bakery, the kitchens, the laundry, and the various workshops form a quadrangle around a dingy little courtyard. The old prison, a massive parallelogram of white masonry dating back a century, encloses the shoemaking and metalworks shops; on the ground floor, the mess hall. The pointed arches of the gray stone church rise up from a paved courtyard overshadowed on one side by a high wall, and on the other by the four successive rows of the dormitory's barred windows. This dormitory, of relatively recent construction, was designed for the application of the Auburn system—the last word in prison economy: collective work by day, isolation by night. It is built along the classical lines of the star-shaped cell block. Three wings, a central hub; four stories of galleries looking down over a wide hall lighted from the ends by tall ogive windows. The only places where they still use those splendid windows, invented by the cathedral builders, are prisons. The hall is wide; the narrowness of the cells has been carefully calculated: There has to be room for a cot eighteen inches wide and for a man to be able to stand next to it. All the cells are whitewashed, and each has its window, a wide slit which you are forbidden to climb up to . . . A tree-planted court separates the dormitory from an infirmary composed of two rectangular buildings facing each other across a closed courtyard and connected by a glassed-in walkway . . . From the windows of the infirmary (which is painted a suitable white) you can see a grim cube of gray stone dotted with oblong, barred windows—a complete little prison set within the big one, with its own outer wall on which the guards make their rounds, its triangular exercise yards sectioned like a fan—the stockade. Three stories of punishment cells—light, half-dark, dark; in the basement, a double row of "holes." Just as the keep, where the lord of the castle made his last stand, was the soul of the *burgs* of older times, so the soul of the prison—a soul made of implacable rules and of irons—is found within these walls. In the last analysis, discipline is maintained among the prisoners only through fear of the hole . . . Beyond, on either side of a glassed-in corridor, there are workshops: print shop, tailor shop, gold and silver chains, bookbinding, plaited ropes, metalworks. There is also a large yard planted with potatoes. And, somewhere below the prison walls (I don't know where), there is a cemetery . . .

The topography of the penitentiary where I lived for nearly four years remains incomplete and inexact in my mind. The individual prisoner can piece it together only after a long while; through the synthesis of a large number of minute observations. He can see only what falls within a horizon of twenty yards. His movements are regulated by an anonymous power, foreign to his own will. The perfect jail is so compartmentalized that you can live there for years without knowing more than your own narrow sector.

The rhythm of life within this sequestered city follows a clockwork precision. At seven in the morning, three bells, separated by five-minute intervals, announce reveille. At the sound of the first, the six hundred prisoners lying on their cots in the dormitory cells get up. The second gives them a few minutes for folding bedclothes and cleaning up the cell.

At the third, line-up in front of the open cells. Then the silent mass of men is set in motion in a long line through the stairways, across the yards, each man receiving his hunk of bread along the way.

In the workshop, a few minutes are set aside for washing at the faucet. At 7:15 a bell gives the signal for work to begin. At 9 o'clock the bell again: stop work. The bell: line up. The bell: Indian file toward the mess hall. The bell: leave the mess hall; exercise, twenty-five minutes, from 9:30 to 9:55. The bell: back to the workshops. The bell: begin work again. The bell, the bell, the bell: second rest period, exercise, return, work, evening line-up, parade, dormitory, lights out, reveille, begin again: parade, dormitory, lights out, reveille, begin work again, the bell, the bell . . .

The mechanical rhythm of each day, repeated *ad infinitum,* leads to an almost painlessly automatized existence. The bell sets off the same movements, at the same precise instant, in six hundred prisoners. Soon each man has internalized these movements. When a new man makes a slip finding his place in line, the event is absurd enough to attract attention.

The day's rhythm melts into that of the months and the seasons. The monotony of Sunday rest, broken by exercise, trips to church, to the Protestant chapel, to the writing room, does not change it—no more than the wilting heat of August, or the icy cold that makes the robots' teeth chatter when they are lined up for parade.

The rule is work and silence.

Forced labor, usually piecework—that is to say, poured on to the limit of your strength—ten hours a day, from seven in the morning to seven in the evening, with two interruptions of an hour each for meals and exercise and two or three fifteen-minute breaks. Labor, industrial labor, at peon's wages, under concession to different firms by the penitentiary administration.

Absolute, perpetual silence, imposed on men working collectively, torn from life collectively, oppressed collectively. The absurdity of that rule is equaled only by its cruelty. If it were actually enforced and respected, it would be the simplest way to drive the prisoners quietly mad. It is softened by partial abrogation in practice: slackness in supervising and a toleration of words exchanged over the job. As a result, the days of rest are the hardest, and the unenforceable rule is nothing more, in reality, than a pretext for disciplinary harassments . . . The majority of punishments handed out are for infractions of the rule of silence.

The various grades of these punishments, increasing up to those for "incorrigibles," constitute a sliding scale of arbitrary persecutions against those who are put on the black list.

The mill grinds slowly, imperceptibly, after your first resistance has been broken down. And since "you get used to anything," you also get used to this slow-motion existence cadenced by the bell . . . Man thinks he consumes time, which in fact devours him. Reality is too concrete to be terrifying. You need imagination sometimes to realize how oppressing it is . . .

For a long time my neighbor in the line-up was a big flabby fellow with pink skin and drooping cheeks. He used to greet me with a gentle glance and a barely visible smile on his thick lips. The very folds of his clothing seemed to shake effortlessly over his loose-hanging flesh. He radiated a great calmness. He was doing eight years and had a quiet little job in the paper storehouse: a bit of wall behind the latrines for a view.

"Don't let it get to you," he told me between his teeth (and even his voice seemed flat, pale, flabby to me), "that's the main thing. Me, I got used to it in the beginning. It doesn't bother me anymore. You get hold of a quiet spot, and then you take it easy. And it's amazing how time flies: It's slow, slow, and then it's over. I only have three years to go, just think . . ."

He had his little daily pleasures. He ate his stew, bought at the canteen (beans, mutton, thirty centimes), with relish, looking forward to a peaceful afternoon and thinking that tonight there would be a "decent screw" on duty who wasn't too proud to chew the fat for a while . . . Sunday, mail. Next week, a shower. And in a month, only thirty-five more months to serve, sixty-one already done. Time passes! I could read these reassuring little thoughts in his calm, bovine eyes.

"Look at Vallard now," he said to me one day, "how nervous he is! He has only six more months to do."

Vallard was a big, somewhat awkward fellow with a funny, wizened old man's face at thirty-five, a big triangular nose, and steel-rimmed glasses—The peevish look of an old seminarist. He was finishing out a six-year term. We knew he had a wife and two lovely children. He kept silent.

"Look how he carries his six months in his legs!"

True, his step was lively. Once again the man went forward toward his destiny, drawn by a mirage. His spine stiffened; a kind of rejuvenation brightened his careworn face. Only six months more! But destiny found him. Vallard appeared one morning with a bandage on his head. He walked among us for two more days in the lines, with a nervous, tired step. Then we didn't notice his absence. He died in three days, in the infirmary, of an erysipelatous inflammation that ate up his face.

"He let it get to him," said the flabby man. "Can't let it get to you. *Got to be stronger*—Poor bastard!"

SIXTEEN

The Workshop

THE PRINT SHOP IS A VAST BEEHIVE BUZZING WITH THE HUM OF MACHINES. Seventy men in dirty smocks and denim caps work there in unnatural silence . . . The movements of their lips are barely perceptible; their hushed whispering strives at the same time to be audible and inaudible; their glances, sharp under the false humility of their bent heads, follow closely the careless, self-important guard as he moves about among the presses and the rows of type cases. As soon as the yellow-braided *képi* disappears behind a machine, my neighbor bends quickly toward me. His hypocritical mask opens up and returns to life, breaking into a broad, fraternal smile:

"Where you from?"

By sundown tonight we will know all we need to know about each other. Poule is a commonplace little hoodlum totally devoid of intelligence. We have named him after a character in *Les Misérables:* "Ha'penny," *alias* "Two Million." "Squealed on by a fag," he was arrested carrying a bag of burglar tools a block from a building in which there was a strongbox containing, the way he tells it, two million. At this point, a spark begins to glow in the depths of his dull eyes. "Think of it! I could be a millionaire today!"

Does he really believe it? He stands distracted for hours, composing stick in hand, eyes clouded. His stupidity is so staggering that you think he must be putting it on. But fate is playing with him. During his hours of distracted immobility I think he dreams of his lost millions, of fast cars, of Deauville, of half-naked blondes strutting like burlesque queens, breasts firm under artificial flowers. And at night, in his barred cell, the flesh of this depraved, overgrown boy suffers and exhausts itself in dreary ejaculations . . .

After the confinement of a cell, you are dazzled by the size, constant activity, and bustling noises of the workshop. It's a world in itself. So many faces! Then you get used to them; you start noticing things again. Within a span of ten, twenty, or thirty yards, a thousand objects strike the eye. My body revels in its newfound freedom and wealth. Four times a day I am allowed to see the sky, trees, bushes, grass, for the prison yards contain such riches. I don't want to acknowledge these miserable joys, but they are there, in my very limbs. They last for a few days, and then fade without a struggle. Having explored my vista of thirty yards, I know how terribly destitute it is. Nothing ever changes in this beehive, where time weighs down on you like an endless rain of ashes. Soon I strive, in vain, to recapture the first days' wonderment. But every bell reminds me that I am a robot who knows in advance all the movements he will ever make, and all the faces he will ever meet; reminds me that this will go on for 1,300 days (if only I survive).

The presses are right at the entrance, where a guard stands before the locked door. Next come the rows of type cases, extending to the right and along the back; they are handy for hiding from the screw for a moment to exchange a few words or pass a note. There are some glassed-in cubicles along the inner wall: the office of the civilian manager, a gray-haired gentleman who wears an English cap and a printer's smock; those of the proofreaders and accountants, objects of envy because they can talk among themselves. These privileged inmates do little favors. They form a world apart, envied and respected. The back wall opens onto the wire mesh enclosing the storerooms and the glassed-in lithographer's shop. Across from the offices there are windows opening on the latrines, allowing the guards, without moving, to keep an eye on the squatting men. The latrines open onto narrow paved courtyards. The clean-up squad comes in there every day to empty the tanks in the hope of recovering forbidden objects. The perfection of jail! The administration even looks into your excrement!

The work is paid by the day. Some of the typesetters are forced to produce a set number of jobs calculated to squeeze twelve straight hours of hard work out of them. Fortunately, most typesetting jobs can't be parceled out that way. The print shop produces official forms for the Ministries of Colonial Affairs, Interior, Justice, and Health. It also produces scientific and statistical works in which future compilers, coming across the wildest imaginable errors, will stand in amused amazement at what the stupidity of colonial officials, combined with the malice of French convicts, can produce in the way of bizarre statistics. ("Reunion

Island. Marriages: women; 6; men, 6; total marriages, 12." "Imports in Senegal: pianos, by the ton . . . ; ostrich feathers, in cubic yards . . .")

"You see," Gillet, the fat proofreader, explains to a neophyte, "a proofreader is not required to understand what he reads. He follows the copy. The copy is sacred . . ."

His ruddy, sprightly monk's face opens into a smile:

". . . especially when it's pissed out by those idiots." (*He hums to himself.*) "And we don't give a damn, fa-la-la-la . . . Get it?"

We also set up the "wanted" circulars for the police, which keeps us more or less up-to-date on unpunished crimes and their probable penalties. Convicts' hands carefully align the routine abbreviated description and anthropometric photo of next year's convict who is still, at this very hour, hanging around the bars of Ménilmontant, fear in his belly. The women's faces—those strange, sometimes empty, sometimes drawn, sullen or desperate faces of prostitutes and shoplifters, distorted by the police photographer—have secret charms for men in prison. They often steal the proof sheets off the presses to cut out a photo, the portrait of an unknown wanted woman (merely a name linked to the description of a crime: *Marie Chevrillon, 22 years old, thefts*), whose name matters little but who has lovely eyes, widened by fear and confusion, and the lips of a child. Back in his dormitory cell, a man, prey to the most human of all obsessions, will gaze endlessly, night after night, at this mysterious portrait which he carries carefully hidden in his clothes, in spite of the searches. And I doubt that Gainsborough's most charming portraits, or the mystery of Mona Lisa, have ever stirred such inexpressible passions in the depths of the human heart or flesh than these harsh portraits have aroused in the minds of these often perverted convicts.

We also set up the green lists of deserters and draft evaders, the yellow lists of persons expelled from the country, the white lists of three-time losers. The number of crimes, miseries, and sordid struggles which flow inexorably through our captive hands is like the number of the stars . . .

You earn from 50 centimes to 2.75 francs a day working in the print shop.[7] The administration holds back six tenths of this salary (more, in the case of prisoners with a record). Of the remaining four tenths, two are earmarked for canteen expenses, which allow the prisoner to supplement his diet, and two for the savings he will receive when he leaves.

---

7   Wartime figures.

A few francs are set aside in the very beginning: the sum required, in case of death, to pay for a coffin. The first duty of the damned is to pay for his own coffin . . .

It's not always easy. Somewhere there is a rope-weaving shop, where they earn a few centimes a day at the very most. This work is reserved for old men. I sometimes see the rope-weaving crew march by: a dozen old, broken marionettes dragging their wooden shoes, dirty, stiff, bent, gnarled, with mummified faces, hairy nostrils, moist eyes, hands like dried roots. There is one who marches along erect, greasy cap over one ear, his gaunt body bearing a little crimson head with beak-nose on which a drop is hanging: and still, glassy, eyes. ("A hayseed. He set fire to his neighbor's barns. Eight years.") They are sixty to seventy years old and have five, ten, and fifteen years to do. The last in their line is a monster: the Spider. Back twisted, body bowed, legs turned, bent wide apart, his two bizarrely outstretched arms leaning on two canes, this old man, like a lightning-struck tree, made entirely of broken and badly mended bones, crawls along vigorously at the end of the human caterpillar. They say he will never leave this place alive (as if the others were about to leave!). His crime is unknown. Some peasants smashed his limbs with pitchforks and shovels . . .

A dialogue in the first-aid room:

"When you croak, you dirty old beast," says the orderly who dresses the dead, "there'll be some job! We'll have to break up your arms and legs again to get you into the coffin!"

The Spider's blackish mouth, lined with horrible stumps, spits out a whole litany of insults like drool, ending with a snicker:

". . . and don't worry, you'll croak ahead of me." (He didn't know the truth of his words: I saw that orderly die.)

The old men wait for the end as they slowly plait the heavy ropes with their swollen fingers. A stench of filth and organic decomposition surrounds them. Sometimes a young prisoner coming out of the hole is put in with them.

SEVENTEEN

The Will to Live

EVERYONE MAKES HIS OWN NICHE IN THE WORKSHOP, FURNISHES IT AND FIXES it up. The typesetters have the use of a shelf under the type fonts. They add a stool, a cardboard box for type characters, and a little shelf for soap. Dillot, the seminarist, who killed his brother after endless quarreling over a two-thousand-franc inheritance, has made himself a sort of altar out of holy images from breviaries. During the fifteen-minute noon break, he bows his sharp profile over a tiny Sacred Heart of Jesus, turns his eyes away from the world, and prays. My neighbor and good pal, Guillaumet—a jolly hooligan whose Mediterranean good humor almost never leaves him ("When my six years are up"—a broad wink here—"I'll still have fifteen good years left! and I know how to live, you know!")—told me with the air of a connoisseur:

"He gets nuttier and nuttier. Wait and see what happens next."

Another neighbor lives in a strange squalor. He is right in front of me. Whenever I raise my eyes above the type font, I see his naked cranium dotted with dirty-gray hairs around the neck, his greenish skull, livid at the temples. Sometimes I see Dubeux in profile: white-lipped and cadaverous. His movements are slow, mortally slow. He never sits down or rests. He has never tried to communicate with anyone. When you brush by him, he turns on you slowly with a totally inexpressive greenish gaze. At noon, he cuts his black bread into identical little rectangles, lines them up in front of him, and eats them one after the other, motionless, without reading, staring straight ahead or at the ground. His mechanical gestures remind you of a robot. Once a rascal filled his shoes with glue: He's been trailing the same nauseating odor after him for months now. People who pass close by him sometimes give him an elbow in the ribs or whisper obscene insults into his ear, just to see the stupid look in his dirty-green eyes and the slow muttering of his pale lips. They say that he had a small income, that he murdered a woman in a bawdyhouse and that there is a pair of pink silk panties in his bundle at the registry which he would never let out of his sight . . . These are perhaps only legends, but I can very well imagine this blanched little man entering a close-shuttered house with his robot's step, breathing his murderous breath into a terrified woman's face, killing her with those inevitable, automatic gestures that emanate from the depths of his mechanical soul.

"You're too thin," Guillaumet told me. "Get a grip on yourself. Don't mess around! You have three months to react. If you're O.K. at the end of the third, and I see you have guts, you'll pull through. Now, to start off, you better stuff yourself and relax. Here's a bootleg book. Don't get pinched with it; it'll cost you two weeks in the hole and it'll be bad for the club. And here's a cheese someone sent you."

Much, much later, he reminded me of that conversation: "You were so skinny, you see, you looked so beat that some of the boys were saying you wouldn't live the six months for the gravedigger's pint of wine . . ."

Every time someone is buried, the gravedigger, a lucky member of the clean-up squad, marches over to the cemetery and gets a pint of wine for his pains.

"Me, I bet on you. I won. We'll beat 'em!"

I, too, learned how to probe the faces and hearts of newcomers. *I know* if they are going to live. I know when they will supply that extra pint of wine for the lucky gravedigger. I never make a mistake: Their death is revealed to me long before they themselves see it coming. I can't explain this intuition. I pick it up in their glances, from the way their hands rest on the marble where the frames are tightened before being placed on the presses, from the bent of their heads, the curve of their shoulders, their way of walking. I read death in them with an awful clarity I would like to deny, to reject by force of will, but which is there, too strong to be brushed aside. Guérin, for example. He was a rather cultivated, polite man, a small rural landlord convicted of arson. Six years. He claimed to be innocent, but his preoccupied stare and the hard line of his mouth gave him away. His complexion was healthy; he seemed only sad. You had to be sharp to pick up the signs of his weariness, his resignation, his dejection over time passing by. His spring had snapped. He died in six months, simply, as he was destined to die.

I have felt death struggling in others, like a dark bird flapping its wings but unable to take flight. There was one youth whose beautiful wide eyes and deep purple lips must have excited many passions: We sometimes used to meet at the cutting bar, where typesetters shave down leads and space lines. From the beginning, he had the long, slender hands and weak wrists of someone who won't last. And the pale ears too, and the girlish neck where a blue vein stood out . . . Those dark wings! Then one day our glances met; we exchanged a few insignificant words, without moving our lips; I could feel a hardness growing up in him; I noticed his hand, which had become more sinewy, one of those hands which grips and holds on to things.

"What's up?" Guillaumet asked me when I returned to my place. "Does life look so rosy to you today?"

I was smiling at the thought that there would be one less dead man this year.

These were not the tricks of a disordered imagination, but the results of keen observations, too complex to be analyzed, as well as of an inner experience confirmed many times over. I was sometimes afraid of dying within these walls, when I thought of the slow-passing seasons, of the mysterious epidemics that would pass among us, of the inexorable statistics which revealed the same percentage of deaths year after year: It would have been easy to estimate your chances, but at bottom this would be an almost entirely false estimate. I was sometimes afraid, but I knew very well that I would live. And I have seen some astonishing cases of conscious resistance to disease.

The chief proofreader, Lemerre, was a swarthy little man. All of his movements, even all the folds in his clothes, were in sharp right angles. His low forehead was narrow, hard, and jutting. His face was made of three straight lines: the dark line of the eyebrows; the dark, thin line of the mouth; the perpendicular line of the nose. A meticulous, stiff, distant man, I judged him to be firm, very sure of himself, and perfidious. A pharmacist's assistant at the age of twenty, Lemerre had poisoned his boss in the hope of marrying the widow. A mature, calculated crime, aimed at opening his way to a bourgeois existence. A number of stays of execution had kept him from the guillotine and resulted in twenty years at hard labor, which he was serving out in the penitentiary. I met him in his tenth year. He had been turning around this mill for ten years with the same firm, resolute step, never doubting his own strength. The weight of those twenty years didn't break him. Bent over the same galleys in a tiny office choked with lead dust for the past eight years, his lungs were being eaten away by tuberculosis. Every year, in the spring, Lemerre coughed blood. Every year, those who didn't know him well expected him to die. He was made to drink huge quantities of creosote. When the early warmth forced the first buds to open on the shrubs in the yard, and we began to march with a lighter step, raising our heads toward the fresh blue of a sky flecked with soft white tufts, turning in circles to the tramp of wooden shoes in those rounds known as exercise walks, in those days when so much pain was mingled with so much hope in us, Lemerre would have coughing fits and nightly fevers. The infirmary would greet him as an old friend, in a cell on that terrible fourth floor from which few have ever returned. He would spend six weeks there and then reappear, "patched up again," having carried off one more victory against the disease—his narrow, hard, jutting forehead a little heavier, a little harder, his stubborn soul a little surer of itself . . .

One morning we were stupefied to learn that he had died during the night.

"Lemerre? You're sure it's Lemerre? It's not possible," repeated Guillaumet incredulously.

At noon a wad of paper thrown near our feet cleared things up. It was not Lemerre who had died, but Lamarre, the lithographer—an overimaginative businessman who had thought of a way to insure and sell nonexistent shipments—a man generally in good health who had been carried off in a few days by dysentery. Guillaumet said:

"Lamarre, I can understand. But Lemerre couldn't die like that."

Someone else remarked:

"Poor bastard! He was no sicker than anybody else! It's no joke! But as for Lemerre, impossible."

When I left Lemerre, in his fifteenth year of confinement, he said he was feeling "much better."

EIGHTEEN

Some Men

GUILLAUMET LOVES HIS NICHE, OUR ROW OF BENCHES WHICH MUST BE KEPT in perfect order, his good pals he can spot at a distance, this workshop ("the best in the joint"), even this prison ("the best in France"). In a strange way, hatred and habit bind a man to his chain. I myself, months after jail had turned me loose, lying on a dazzling Mediterranean beach, suddenly felt haunted by the memory of my long passage through the "Mill" that grinds up men. I let my head fall into my hands, I closed my eyes. Once again I saw the workshop, the yards where our files of woe-stricken men turned in endless circles, the faces, so many faces; I saw it all again, my heart heavy with a feeling of loss, pity and regret. And isn't it a kind of fascination mixed with pain that makes me write this book? Old chains which have tortured us dig so deeply into our flesh that their marks become a part of our being, and we love them because they are in us.

Guillaumet rationalizes his satisfaction at being here.

"The other pens, you see, are full of short-timers—two or three years. They're stuffed with good-for-nothings, clumsy pickpockets; nervous burglars, run-of-the-mill murderers, petty crooks—you know, the kind of jerks who order a dinner in a restaurant and then try to cut out on the check. Chiselers! But believe it or not, there are hundreds of them who get pinched at it every year!" (The very idea makes him grin with delight.)

You can do anything with that bunch of spiritless, worthless louts: you'd be lucky to find ten real hoods, ten real big-city gangsters in a hundred of them: Moreover, there are twice as many "stool pigeons" there. The administration has set up a system whereby trusties, who are inmates chosen for their good behavior (willing stoolies, in reality), watch over the others. These trusties are thieves, informers, blackmailers, homosexuals; you buy their favor or their silence; you suffer their hatred. They are the ones who work you over when they send you to the hole; there are professional headcrackers among them. Their "exemplary" behavior often gets them released on parole after serving half their sentence . . . Here, in the print shop, we have the fine flower of the criminal courts. "All the crooked solicitors, all the priests who fool around with little girls, all the accountants who are too smart for themselves end up here. They all have connections, people watching out for them, right? So you see, chum, we're guests in a model prison . . ."

His mouth slightly twisted, his eyes wide, Guillaumet continues in a whisper:

"How I'd love to blow it up, your model prison! When I think of all the dynamite that's going to waste, it breaks my heart."

We have a whole miniature society within the walls of the print shop alone. Several accountants, some bankers, brokers, officers, ecclesiastics, teachers, tradesmen, and farmers; thieves, pimps, and gangsters; anarchists. An authentic marquis perpetuates the tradition of colonial administrators. The prison still remembers two famous colonialists "who used to blow up niggers by shoving a stick of dynamite up their ass . . . Do you know what they did to the Negresses? . . ." One winter evening, when the green-shaded electric bulbs made the Workshop seem more intimate, an old-timer passed on to me the horrible legend of the sexual tortures invented by two madmen in the torrid brush of Senegal. Their madness still gnaws at our minds. The sex organs of young black girls, tortured to death fifteen years ago, bleed again today in the souls of prisoners.

Short-legged, pleasant, and stout, ex-Lieutenant-Colonel Desvaux, comptroller-general, former secretary to a prominent Finance Minister, corrects the galleys of colonial statistics along with Lemerre. Ex-Captain Meslier, accountant, takes our orders for the canteen. He has an intelligent, ageless face ravaged by fever, struggle, debauchery, and alcohol. The Indo-Chinese and Sahara campaigns. Alcohol. Left for dead, riddled with javelin wounds, one night of battle in the African jungle. Legion of honor. Alcohol. Wild nights in Paris. Alcohol. But where was the money to light up the town every night? What was left for a worn-out jungle fighter who had battled in the tropics, possessed slaves and houseboys, spilt his blood in the jungle where the panthers stalk; what was left for him after so much plundered flesh, so much squandered wealth, if not alcohol; consumed in bars, at night? Meslier had written to his mistress, a *demi-mondaine* infatuated by this mad hero: "Fifty francs, tonight, or I'll kill you." (Doubtless he used to tell the Bamako chiefs: "Fifty porters and ten maidens tonight or I'll turn the machine guns on you.") Ten years' imprisonment (anyone else would have left his head in the good Doctor Guillotin's machine) soon reduced to five for mercy. Paroled after half his sentence. The African hero paid only thirty months' imprisonment for that slit throat. But he soon returned to the print shop; this time as a forger. Alcohol, alcohol! He had fine, delicate hands, shaky but agile, astonishingly bright gray eyes which seemed a little crazy whenever he stared at something, a friendly voice whose inflections were sometimes tender, the manners of a well-bred scoundrel. In the lines he used to bow to passing buddies, then let fly at them with horrible insults behind a friendly glance. In church on Sunday, he would sometimes sit down at the organ and play amazing pieces by Bach or Handel by heart. Then he would march around with us for twenty minutes, head raised, unseeing.

We have an abbot, a priest, an Ignorantine brother, a sexton: sex criminals, all four. We have respectable middle-class people like Durand, a fat sixty-year-old man who had counted on getting acquitted! In the appeals for pardon which he sends off every three months, he constantly brings up his "long life of hard work and fair dealing"; the fact that his credit had been good, for thirty years, that he was a good father and a good husband. His wife sends him tender letters which he reads over every Sunday morning with moist eyes. In any case, he always has moist eyes, like certain old dogs; and a mouth which hangs open in an expression of vague dismay. He killed his mistress, a twenty-year-old dressmaker, because she was cheating on him.

"I had set her up in a little shop, with furniture I paid for by the month. I thought she was happy, and then suddenly an anonymous letter arrives telling me she has a lover . . . So, while I was working to pay off her furniture, that little bitch could afford to take lovers on my money? I went crazy, Monsieur, believe me, it was too much . . . I loved her so much!"

"My wife has forgiven me, Monsieur; she's an angel . . ."

The other woman, the young blonde with the voluptuous, thrice-perforated belly, must have been a devil.

I look in vain for signs of passion among those who commit "crimes of passion." All I find are impulsive men even less capable of sustained suffering than they are of controlling their anger (which subsides as soon as they act). Anyway, they never act in good faith, since they always hope they will be acquitted. An anemic café waiter killed his mistress out of jealousy. He's the most passive and resigned among us all. There is also T*** the butcher, a shrewd shopkeeper, too practical and too insensitive to really suffer. We used to inveigle him into telling the story of his little donkey, the nice little donkey which he "adored."

"Well, where's the little donkey now?"

"I slaughtered him; he ate too much."

For a short while I had a little old man, crippled by rheumatism, for my neighbor in the leather-stitching shop. At the age of sixty, he began to suspect his wife (who was five years younger than he) of harboring special feelings toward a suspicious-looking neighbor (an old man like himself), and so he chopped him up with a hatchet. "He never had her!" he would blurt out at the end of his story. His simplicity bordered on imbecility. Since he had been a concierge for many years in the provinces, we had him ask the Warden for the job of concierge in the prison . . .

All the middle-class people brought here by crimes of passion consider themselves victims of huge injustices: They have nothing but scorn for the "common criminals." They are pious, submissive, great scribblers, and prone to informing.

The arsonists—or "firebugs"—form another category, even more submissive. For the most part, they are quarrelsome peasants, happy to be able to look down on the "gentlemen" who are forced to wear the same denims and the same numbers as they, but whose office jobs make them envious; they are hostile to the "crooks" out of attachment to private property, hostile to the anarchists out of a love of order. Squealing is the only way they can gain favor with the administration. Their devious mentality helps them ferret out illegal books, love affairs, and "systems" for bringing in illicit tobacco.

NINETEEN

The "Men"

OPPOSITE THIS MOB STAND THE MEN, THE REAL MEN. THE OUTLAW HAS NO illusions about society's values and knows neither faith nor law; but he has self-respect, the knowledge of his own strength, and the respect of other "men"—the strong. "I'm a man!": All his pride is summed up in these words. A man never sells out. A man knows how to take it— and to dish it out—in a knife fight. He knows how to go down into the hole and "keep quiet." The greatest praise you can give him is to say: "He's a man." Safecracker, second-story man, pimp, white-slaver: You can trust him. If he says "count me in," it means for keeps. If he says *no,* it means no; and nobody will ever be the wiser.

Richardeau is a man. You can see it in his face—the face of a stocky strongman—with his black eyebrows, his firm, heavy jaw planted with splendid teeth, his calm smile.

His arms are hairy; he had little, sharply etched tattoo marks on the palms and wrists of his huge hands.

"Do you know what that is?" (an arrow, two dots, a heart).

"No? Well, go ask the boys on the Marseilles docks. They'll still remember!"

All the men, except him, who bear that glorious mark on their wrists are on Devil's Island. There is no more reliable comrade than Richardeau. Tobacco is his only weakness. His neighbor, the arsonist Beaugrand, nurses a patient hatred against him. This tall, flabby, dirty hayseed can detect a pinch of tobacco or a half-smoked butt no matter how well hidden. Richardeau always denies it calmly, even when it's obvious.

"This is your tobacco, right?"

"No."

"It was found in your place."

"Could be."

They gave him two weeks in solitary. Then a month. Then a month in the hole. He's a man; he can take it. But one day somebody threw a hunk of molten lead in Beaugrand's face. Two weeks in solitary, for a "man," is not too high a price for the pleasure of messing up a face like that one.

Laurent is a man. A big blue butterfly spreads its wings across his nose and over his two cheeks. There are blue letters carefully printed across his forehead under his beret, which he wears pulled down like a cap. When someone stares at him, Vincent shoves his cap back over his head with the flat of his hand; and the sergeant can spell out the words: "There's a c—sucker staring at me." All his fingers are decorated with indelible rings. His chest is covered with hearts bearing women's names. He has a President of the Republic on one buttock, and a general in full-dress uniform on the other.

Laurent incarnates strength and despair. Of his barely thirty years, he has spent ten in prison, the African battalions, the road gangs, and jail. When you're at Biribi and you think you'll never get out, you have your face tattooed as an ultimate challenge to society. Laurent only got out by accident, and he ended up here. Ten years and ten years' ban (expulsion from the country, leading to life in prison if they catch you). Laurent has a pale, greenish complexion, a queasy mouth, a fishy eye, a disgusting voice, and a filthy vocabulary. He doesn't bother to hide his half-cured syphilis. One day, during a visit to the penitentiary, an officer with a chestful of decorations stopped in front of this prisoner with his marked forehead.

"So you think you're pretty," said Laurent, "with all that hardware on your right tit?"

Laurent hates the army, officers, brass hats, and good soldiers—"all c—suckers." Laurent hates the rich because they're rich, the poor because they're cowardly, "females" because one of them gave him the clap, because another turned him in to the police, and because he can't get along without them. Laurent hates yokels because "they're scum." Although he is careful, he will stop at nothing. "I'll mess up a few more of 'em before I croak," he says vaguely.

We met once in a room in the infirmary. Something was hurting me inside, and I was going through a very bad time.

"Got the blues?" Laurent asked me.

"Yeah."

He grabbed my hand and squeezed it tightly in a brief show of feeling. His sad eyes communicated a dark warmth to me.

"Stick it out, man! Stick it out. We're men, aren't we?"

The anarchists are men of another stamp. Julien Laherse is leaving in a few days. Despite his bowed shoulders and curved nose, he has the beauty of a young Christ. He stayed in this place for five years, composing stick in hand, patient, unchanging, exemplary, living on a diet of oil, studying German and English, greeting his comrades with a glance of solidarity. When I arrived, he was the first to help me along, out of his own canteen. The sweetness and strength of his character make a faultless, but slightly exasperating, mixture. His language is precise, his ideas have a self-negating clarity. Julien denies all feelings; reason alone should govern man. He practices solidarity through rational egotism. Love? An obsolete expression. A momentary conjunction of personalities and sex needs that's all, nothing more. The rest is nothing but ignorance, outdated beliefs, prejudices, the effects of our reproductive instincts. In two months when he is released, Julien will desert. He will go to Spain, to a sunny land by the seashore, and live a rational life cleansed of the unhealthy needs of industrial civilization: tilling the soil, living on fruit, taking walks through the countryside, swimming with strong strokes against the warm waves, contemplating the world in the light of his lofty, clear intelligence.

Twice a week we get a hundred grams of boiled meat. Julien, who is a vegetarian, used to give his to Miguel.

"Tomorrow," he told him one day, "I'm not going to give it to you."

"But why?"

"Meat is poisonous to the system. If, out of ignorance, you want to poison yourself, I shouldn't help you."

This irrefutable logic was alarming to the comrade, for he was starving to death.

"Julien, that's not the point. You will agree that a thing belongs to the person who needs it and not to the person who owns it without need. You have no right to dispose of food for which you have no use. It belongs to me."

"You're right," said Julien, convinced.

Julien later committed suicide over a woman, in Portugal.

There are a dozen of us comrades in this city of the damned. From a distance I can spot the hard face and square shoulders of the miner, Nicklaus, who wears his prisoner's beret like the leather cap of some hero out of Constantin Meunier. His rude hands, used to handling blocks of coal with their glint of black diamonds, smashed the heads of class traitors during a mining strike. From mine to prison, he merely changed one burden for another, digging even deeper into his hatred. In court, before the judges, Nicklaus had a very clear plan.

"I can do up to six years," he told himself. "I'll be free when I'm thirty-five: I'll still have life in front of me. Eight years, ten years? No. My life isn't worth that. My muscles will be gone and my mind stultified by the time I get out. If they give me ten years, I'll grab the first rotten 'screw' in the gallery and make the jump from the fourth floor with him. One life for another. Mine is worth a thousand times more than his, but the choice isn't mine. Don't tell me that they're not responsible. I'm a determinist. No one is responsible, but they kill us all the same, eh?"

"Once I made that decision," he added, "I wasn't afraid anymore. Only one thing bothered me: Suppose they play a dirty trick on me and sentence me to seven years. I didn't want to have to bargain my life against my will."

Vicenzi is a sort of blond giant, so silent that his mouth has that grave, sealed line you see in certain Italian Renaissance portraits. And pale, water-blue eyes lighting the heavy features of this day laborer who, in olden times, would have made a magnificent *reiter*. On account of his awful calmness in fights, his presence of mind, his surprising agility, he had been put in charge of guarding some precious printing equipment, which he had defended with well-aimed shots from his Browning. We never spoke to each other within these walls, although we had known each other for years. Two or three times a month, we would exchange greetings with our eyes. He would pass by in his impenetrable silence, continuing his march back to life calmly, forcefully, confidently. When he was out on bail, before turning himself over for trial, he told us pessimistically:

"It will be tough. But I'm tough, too." I knew his exemplary integrity and his candor, the candor of a grownup child who believes in truth.

Miguel, Nouzy, and Rollot, all three counterfeiters, are more or less neighbors of mine. Miguel is a libertarian—that is to say, an anarchist-communist; the difficulty of finding a living in the streets of Paris at nineteen with a head so full of ideas and a passion for life so strong that ten hours a day in a factory seemed like ten hours of slavery, had led him down the dark path of "illegalism" (the accepted expression) a demoralizing individualist doctrine to which he was opposed. Nouzy and Rollot—one a forty-year-old stevedore from Rouen; the other, a handsome, fair-haired, twenty-eight-year-old Parisian mechanic—are both individualists, like Laherse, belonging to a so-called "scientific" faction. Because, in modern society, one must be either an exploiter, a wage slave, or an outlaw—three ways of living equally opposed to their ideal—they decided to take up the counterfeiter's trade. They argue with each other about the meaning of life, death, heredity, monogamy, love, war, the transformation of man, the revolution. We manage to get together while working on some job, to discuss great issues . . .

TWENTY

The Mind Resists

SWELTERING AUGUST HEAT. THE PRISON DOZES, BENT OVER ITS TASK. A FEW yards away, the guard yawns on his bench. It's either Réséda, the kindly drunkard, or La Tulle, the nasty drunkard, whose voice and blood-shot eyes have gone soft along with his flabby body. Three men in coveralls are working the hand press in feigned silence. The first—beads of sweat standing out on his forehead—turns the heavy press, straining his arms and body; the second spreads the proof sheets over the text and then strips them off; the third moistens the paper, carries the type frames to the press and removes them. With each turn of the press, the three silent heads come together; in that instant, an astute observer might be able to detect a fugitive movement of the lips, a fleeting expression. The pressman straightens up, the three faces reappear wearing their impassive masks. At that instant, these three men feel like brothers. They will savor the plenitude of their comradeship for long days afterward. Their whispered dialogue grazes the silence of this hell without breaking it—a low-flying bird seems thus to graze the water—searching into *the meaning of life* . . . And perhaps in that instant they are the only men in this jail, in this city, in this part of the universe, in whom the inexplicable flame of pure thought flickers.

The rhythmic clatter of the machines becomes a sort of constant buzzing in our abused ears. The air is heavy.

"The cicadas are singing," whispers Guillaumet as if in a dream.

The cicadas? I blink my eyes like a man suddenly dragged out of darkness, dazzled by the light. There are cicadas in the fields, there are fields, there is a deep azure over the green and russet fields, there is . . .

The thinly painted glass in the windows of the shop has become transparent again in spots. I know where these spots are; I search for a shred of azure in them. A skylight is open. Azure.

Why have you dragged me out of my lethargy, that merciful lethargy of the prisoner that makes us forget the fields, the cicadas, the summer, the world, everything there is, since there is nothing real but our sordid world and time, the time we think we are wasting but which is slowly, inexorably, wasting us? An absurd anger unwinds its dark, serpentine coils in my brain.

"Guillaumet! Hey! Guillaumet!"

"What?"

"She died," I say.

I'm ashamed of having said these two words, but I've said them. Cynically, I return the hurt. These two words come from a stupid popular song—"She died on the bo-o-at . . ."—but they hurt my neighbor, who turns pale, his eyes narrowing. Somewhere—in that unreal world where the cicadas are singing—there is a woman, a woman to whom he clings with his flesh and soul. I long ago discovered the secret superstition which sometimes reduces this self-possessed man to a childish sense of his own weakness. I suffer from the same affliction, and these two ridiculous words unhinge me, too; that's how I guessed his secret. And I hurt myself even more than him, for I'm ashamed. The heat has unhinged me.

I look around me, to escape from myself. Dubeux, with his cadaverous complexion, is swaying slowly to and fro on his feet, composing stick in hand, prey to his usual obsession. Dillot, the seminarist, has his back to me, motionless; he's crazy, too. I can see an image of the Sacred Heart of Jesus under his shelf; and this flame-ringed heart cries out like a piece of living flesh, flesh torn away from the body by sharp teeth (I unconsciously clamp my jaws) and spit out . . .

The guard is half-asleep, the lout. I see two bowed heads through the glass partition of the lithography shop. A crazy old man with a drooping lower lip: I know that during these breaks he draws, painstakingly, for himself alone, on little squares of stolen cardboard, with the scrupulousness of a Persian miniaturist, incredible scenes of intertwined couples caught in insatiable lust. That carnal hallucination is his life. A yard from him, a pleasant German named Füller, his bandaged head tortured by cold sores, hastily copies the tiny portrait of a woman from a photograph; inmates who are sent photographs can keep them for only twenty-four hours.

Returning from the hand press, Rollot the counterfeiter (whose wife is living with another man) bends over the galleys, his brow wrinkled, reading a tray of six-point type. He pretends to be proofreading. His lips move slowly as if murmuring a prayer. I know that beautiful prose, beautiful like a metaphysical incantation, which he wants to keep constantly before his eyes:

The Idea of Nature
At the crowning apex of all things, at the highest point in the luminous, inaccessible ether, the eternal axiom is pronounced, and the immensity of the universe, is but the long echo, the inexhaustible undulation, of that creative principle . . .
. . . All life is simply one of its moments, every living being one of its forms; and the successive orders of things, proceeding from it with inalterable necessity, are bound by the divine links of its golden chain.[8]

At noon the bell gives us a quarter hour for rest. We grab a snack on tables made from old overturned crates. Everyone has his book open in front of him. Dinot, Volume XV of the *General History of the Church*; Laherse, his *German Grammar*; Guillaumet a precious Volume of *"came,"* (the abbreviation for *"camelote,"* contraband books whose appearance has been carefully disguised in the binding shop so as not to differ in the least detail from the works in the prison library), Volume III of Casanova's *Mémoires*. Rollot is reading Balzac. I, too, open a *"came"* book: H. Taine, *On Intelligence,* Book III, *The Knowledge of Mind* . . . Gilles has already covered the pages with marginal notes in a tiny, round hand. The unknown laws of nature (I was about to say "chance," but here in the Mill we like to join our sordidly human chains to the "divine golden links of inalterable necessity") provided rich spiritual nourishment for us when, twenty years ago, they crushed two fine young lives in the flower of their strength.

In those days a little-known tragedy ravaged an old upper-class family, long corroded from within by the seven deadly sins. The children took the part of their injured mother against the father, an old two-faced judge who hid his selfishness and depravity under a hypocritical façade of respectability. One of the sons, an artist just coming into his own, pronounced a death sentence within himself after a pitiless inner debate. Without trembling, with the tempered soul of an avenger, he pressed the trigger of a hunting rifle. He was about to reach the crowning point of his life. The purity and passion of love, art,

---

8   H. Taine: *Les philosophes classiques du XIXe siècle en France,* Paris, 1857.

Paris, the future were just opening before him when, to break a vicious circle of crimes that the written law does not punish, he became a parricide. At the trial, they wanted, above all else, to save the honor of the family; as a result, the parricide shouldered all the blame. The whole family kept silent over the dead man's infamy. The parricide kept silent as well. Influence in high places saved him from the guillotine and the penal colony of Saint-Laurent-du-Maroni in Guiana. He was granted the signal honor of undergoing his twenty years at hard labor in this penitentiary. He only asked for one thing: that his mind be allowed to live. That he be allowed to think. Since he had connections in very high places, he was granted a privilege infinitely more rare than the commutation of a death sentence: that of receiving twenty works by scientists and philosophers in the prison. For the Mill hates nothing so much as thought.

These books, passing clandestinely between safe hands, sent a ray of light through the darkness of the jail. And that light traveled on for twenty years, transfiguring the faces on which it shined. My comrade Gilles owed a new life to it. Before entering prison, this square-jawed, square-headed boxer had known only the life of his muscles and his instincts—which had turned him from a prizefighter into a criminal. At first, imprisonment was worse than death for him. Then the ray of light fell on him. The parricide told him: *Read*. The athlete, his muscles useless, learned that the widest vistas—infinity itself—are embodied in printed symbols. He once wrote me a confession containing these words: "I have no regrets. I'm no longer just a brute."

We defended this treasure with the cunning of savages guarding their totem. Prison tries to stultify: to mechanize all movements, efface all character, desiccate the brain. That is its method of cutting down the defeated rabble of the social struggle which, in the last analysis, is what we are. Those who think, in the Mill, always feel that their mind is constantly threatened. The example of idiots and madmen shows them what can happen. Obsessions, *idées fixes,* dreams, sexual hallucinations, swarm within their brows. "The only mental hygiene," said Laherse with reason, "is to study something, anything: the Bible, German, Siamese." The administration tolerates the study of foreign language on the condition that it remains purely mental: Owning a pencil is forbidden. In my fifth year of imprisonment, I applied for permission to acquire Pascal's *Pensées* and Marcus Aurelius' *Meditations*. Refused . . .

Pascal and Marcus Aurelius nonetheless entered our jail: Jean Fleuriot from Rue Aubry-le-Boucher (known as "One Eye," having left the other on the point of a knife in a Constantine gin mill—burglary, six years) was released, and made a trip to Paris, risking the loss of his parole, just to get them for us. And the lamplighter, accompanied by an affable guard who had been paid fifty francs, picked up a package wrapped in rags behind the prison wall—the *"came"*—containing (a treasure for which any man would have done thirty days in the hole without hesitation) three packets of tobacco, two copies of *Le Matin,* three chocolate bars, a postcard representing a nude from the *Salon d'Automne* (at the express demand of Guillaumet), Pascal, and Marcus Aurelius.

From noon to four o'clock (the bell for mess) the day drags on slowly. The hours are leaden.

TWENTY-ONE

The Round

WHEN THE NINE O'CLOCK BELL RINGS ANNOUNCING THE FIRST MEAL OF THE day, we line up against the shop walls according to the numbers sewn on our jackets. My neighbors in the mess hall are those whom chance has brought to the prison slightly before me, and slightly after. The different kinds of work create, in the long run, divisions based on educational levels, and sometimes even affinities. But on the narrow benches of the mess hall, where we are jammed together behind filthy planks a foot wide, the simple order of our registration numbers provides me with more heterogeneous neighbors. On my right I have Ruelle the accountant, a stiff manikin, disease-ridden, with a bilious complexion, a perpetually open mouth, horrible hands crisscrossed with pink scars, and grimy fingernails. On my left I have a fat, red-faced fellow, an Italian ditchdigger named Zetti, with a fine Roman nose in a shapeless face. He buys a half pint of wine every day at the canteen, pours it into his soup, adds bread and sugar, and then noisily laps up the red, greasy mixture. "Whatever you eat gets mixed up in your belly anyhow," he explained to me politely. The only neighbor I like is a little bright-eyed, twenty-year-old teamster from Luxembourg, who is never separated from his dictionary, a *Petit Larousse illustré*. He reads it, systematically, word by word, page by page. "I'm getting educated," he says with a smile, at once embarrassed and self-satisfied. "Some words amuse me: like *buirette, feminine noun, A haystack*. Sounds like a woman's name. It makes me think of a woman resting in the hay." Martin, you are at the source of all poetry. And the *Petit Larousse* holds more dreams for you than all the tales of Scheherazade.

Men from the kitchen squad go up and down along the benches with heavy wine pitchers, cool and dark inside. You are allowed to treat yourself—if you can pay—to a half pint of wine a day. Those who can't are jealous of the others.

The mess halls used to be part of an old convent: white rooms, with barred windows and tight rows of school desks and benches on either side. We eat in rows, one behind the other: a mournful battalion lined up with our bodies caught at the waist in a kind of rough wooden trap. Each man has a sort of grimy drawer in front of him, under the plank he uses as a table, where he leaves his bread and his fork and spoon, which are never washed. You wipe them as well as you can on a hunk of bread. The utensils stink. Some have been filthy for years. Why be civilized? The need for nourishment is the most basic of our needs. We can eat the most disgusting slops under the filthiest conditions and live. To live is to think. Look at Ruelle's hideous hands with their ornamentation of bluish scars. Guzzle your slops of bread and greasy water and dream of "the eternal axiom which is pronounced at the supreme summit of things." Would you dream about it with the same fervor if there were pure hands here reminding you of the luminous splendor of existence? Eat like a pig, but think.

Whatever scraps are left in the kitchen cauldrons are given out on the spot. "Seconds, seconds?" call the men on the kitchen squad: bare arms, dirty hands, strong sweat. The whole table's mess tins are thrown one into another and sometimes tossed all together into the liquid mash for faster service.

We take our exercise, after leaving the mess hall, in the courtyard, by workshops. Our broad, paved courtyard, divided by grassy plots and enriched by a few bushes, is one of the best. One end is blocked off by the dormitory cell block, with its four stories of narrow barred windows cut into gray stone. But at the other end, above the low buildings of the registry, we can see a row of old poplars. The wind bends their dark branches back and fills them with a sound like waves beating against a beach: Then they spring back swiftly. This simple landscape, set off from an ordinary pale-blue sky, across which scuttle heavy white clouds or milky mists, has for years symbolized all landscapes to me. I greet it every day. I have dreamed poems to these trees, wild and sullen in the cold November rains like helmeted heroes fighting against destiny: svelte and golden in the April sun like proud youths on the brink of some heroic enterprise. I love the variety embedded in their unity, which singles them out to the eye even as they blend together. I imagine them in summer, filled with the peeping of birds and the labor of insects; but distance confers on them that majestic, swaying immobility, that harmony of color and form which must mirror that of the universe.

There is a sea-breeze coolness in their murmuring when the heat beats down on us, turning round and round under the implacable sun ("a sun like a blackjack on your head") to the sharp-hammered rhythm of wooden clogs against the pavement. In the evening they seem to sigh like waves, bringing a fresh wind of life from the open spaces toward which I yearn from my dark cell. I know they line the bank of a lazy river which I have never seen, yet could trace in my mind . . .

The line of men turns around the courtyard like a string of sausages to a military beat. We walk in silence, Indian file, a yard apart, describing symmetrical arabesques around the dreary grass plots. The resulting pattern approximates the shape of a cross. At each branch of the cross a guard is stationed to keep the men in line, silent, and in step. Seen from the infirmary windows, there is no stranger spectacle than that of men strung out like beads on a rosary, in never ending circles, without ever advancing, in a senseless ritual. The guards call out the cadences in turn, aloud: "One, two—one, two . . ." When "Duck Feet," a nice plump old fellow with a waddling gait and an old woman's voice, drops the count, then "Spike Chin," his *képi* crushed down over one ear, his jaws huge and snarling, explodes into hoarse shouts at the other end of the court: "A-one, a-twooo, a-one, a-twooo." He harasses our wretched line, snapping at our heels. "In step, Dubeux!" Dubeux, aghast, is decidedly out of step. "In step, I tell you, goddamn it!" The strings holding up this green-faced puppet seem to snap all at once; if he doesn't fall down right there, like a limp rag, it is because he is carried on by the line, one hundred men in front, one hundred men (the same) behind, inseparable. "Two—hep!—hep!" The cadence is picked up, farther on, by the guttural voice of "The Jap," not a bad fellow, who always seems to be making fun of our grotesque round.

Everybody has his own way of marching: brisk, straggling, listless, or heavy. There is an infinite variety of shapes under the uniform dress. Heads erect, caps smart, or shoulders rounded, elbows flapping; the awkward gait of city urchins, the rhythmic tread of old tramps, the haughty stiffness of Meslier, who seems to wear invisible epaulettes on his threadbare denim. March, men! March. One, two. One, two. There is no end to the round. There is no end to time. There is no end to crime. There is no end to misery. There is no end to the reign of the swine.

I have made my way at least two thousand four hundred times through that eternal round which has continued, starting and stopping, for something like a half century. Slowly, one by one, the beads of that endless human chain are replaced, through the process of life and death. Yet the infernal round is one of the things of this earth upon which time has the least effect. Perhaps Western man must give birth to an entirely new destiny before this absurd circle can be broken.

Gilles, who took liberties in jail, would sometimes wait for me as the line went around in order to whisper me the news. He appeared suddenly before me one morning at the corner of one of the branches of the moving cross formed by our steps: extremely tall, his face a gray mask, hard bitterness in his clenched teeth. He raised his arm, slowly, to his neck, and pressed the edge of his hand against it for a moment. The hammering of wooden clogs exploded suddenly in my ears. On the next turn around, Gilles had his one hand half-hidden in his tunic: Three fingers, sharply outlined, were sticking out. Three. Three fallen heads. I answered "yes" with a blink of the eyes—something heads have been observed to do in sinister experiments. On the third turn around, Gilles was able to say a word:

"Bravely."

One year later; the same time of day; the round continued. Gilles reappeared at the same spot with the same ashy mask:

"Jaurès . . ."

The round carried me on. Those barred windows. A flash of sunlight crowned the poplars with faint gold. The Spider dragged himself, leaning on his two canes, toward the urinary. One hundred and twenty seconds. The path of the human rosary brought me back toward the man whose lips were still sealed over their terrible secret,

". . . assassinated," continued Gilles.

TWENTY-TWO

Night

EVENING COMES, FOR EVEN THE LONGEST AND HEAVIEST HOURS EVENTUALLY plunge into eternity. The sensation of falling softly, slowly, into the amorphous gray depths of the void. Even suffering loses its sharpness, becoming as insensible as decay eating through bone. The occasional cry of despair or madness fades away into the gloom. Our round turns within a void. We have been falling through the void for years, turning in circles. Vertigo. Here is the evening at last: nausea.

The strands of human beads twine rhythmically through the courtyards. If it is summer, the sky is still bright over our heads, vast and calm; if winter, the stars—or the shadows—ignore us. Two long parallel strands meet at the doors of the dormitory cell block, wind up the iron stairs, and line up, bead by bead, before the cell doors. A guard hurries through the galleries counting the motionless puppets standing at attention.

The bolts of the cell door have groaned. Here I am, alone, suddenly still. Or is it only an illusion? The round goes on. The hours fall; our lives fall in a spiraling gyre through the gray abyss: nausea. I am alone in a numbered sepulcher. Third floor, Number 171. Three yards deep by two yards wide. A tiny barred window, hardly more than a slit: but I can see the sky. Chalky whiteness. The cot is monastic. A thin mattress over iron, coarse sheets, gray wool blanket, bedding folded every morning in regulation manner. Being up after the bell is prohibited. About seven minutes for walking in this narrow sepulcher. The sky is fading slowly this evening. My poplars are humming. And now the pale, emerald-tinted azure turns beautifully limpid. If, after so many horrible days, there was only this instant of contemplation, standing before this rectangle of infinitude, hung on the border of day and night, wouldn't life be worth living? I would like to answer: No. Be tough! You're kidding yourself. This moment of vain exaltation redeems nothing. But my whole being cries out the contrary. I can understand that the leper wants to live, his face eaten away, his hands rotting. I can understand that Lamblin, bald at thirty, with his poor, red, albino rabbit's eyes, Lamblin, condemned for life, marching through the round for the past fifteen years without the slightest hope, wants to live, *even like this.* I can understand that Fla-Fla, the idiot, who shakes with hysterical laughter every thirty seconds ("She is there, there, there," he says, with an obscene gesture, when you ask him about his laughter), that even Fla-Fla, if he suddenly understood what death is, that everything will be over, would cry out in terror, because he wants to live, to live, even he. I can understand that they are right: From the depths of their misery, they justify me, as much as the incredible delicacy of the June sky. I am not a coward. One must live. Be tough! Brace up under your burden . . .

Every day at the same moment, waiting in front of my cell door for the end of evening roll call, the same thought draws me slightly forward toward the railing of the third-floor gallery. One leap, a few rapid movements—one second—a fall of perhaps a tenth of a second: about forty feet, a thud, a sharp red pain—skull smashing on the tile floor—perhaps a dull black pain—bones cracking—and the round would cease, time would be vanquished. Giddy temptation.

You can read for a few moments in your cell. You can stare at your secret portrait, copied in pencil by Fuller, hidden under your shirt for fear of the evening search. You can, between two rounds of the guards, ears straining, smoke a cigarette, slowly, the better to savor it and to make sure the odor is dispersed. You can, stretched out on your cot, unfold the shred of the *Petit Parisien* picked up by a man on the maintenance squad in the guard's lavatory: "PEACE CONCLUDED BETWEEN TURKEY AND SERBIA." So there was another war in the Balkans? You can open and read over a *brifeton,* a message scribbled by a comrade or friend, confidences, secrets . . .

Night falls. A lantern at the foot of the courtyard wall throws a pale patch of light, striated by the shadows of the bars, on the ceiling of my cell. Closer, an electric bulb hanging somewhere in the galleries makes a stranger, sharper pattern, superimposed on the first. The cool freshness of solitude; a fresh bath of calm; slowly, I am cleansed of the day's dust, ashes, and mud. How vast the night is! The purity of space comes through the window in great waves and bathes my brow. Faraway train whistles. Gleaming fails, signal lights, stations, a peaceful provincial square in the evening, the lights of a café, a couple embracing on the doorstep of an old house. Man and woman . . . A cry ascending into the night, nearby: "Sentinel, how, goes the watch?" The sudden denseness of a heavy drop of silence. The echo, farther off: "Sentinel, how goes the watch?" A drop of silence, an echo.

I think of power. I extend my free hands into the aerial night. Am I not unbelievably free? Everything has been taken from me. I am chained to the Mill. All that remains to me is to end my life, if I want, by a leap over the railing. I can do it if I wish. It is within my power. No one could stop me.

The world I carry within me has a crystal sphere as its symbol: fullness, perfection. I am free because nothing more can be done to me. Chained to the wall by a circle of iron, I will know how to close my eyes, without a whimper. Let necessity run its course; I am all assent. I have divided the world into two parts: chains, things—and my very flesh, which is a thing—are in *your* power. The crystal sphere, my will, my lucidity, my freedom are irrevocably mine.

I think of the mystery of time's passage. There are minutes and hours which have no end: the eternity of the instant. There are many empty hours: the vacuity of time. There are endless days; and weeks which pass without leaving the least memory behind them, as if they had never been. I cannot distinguish the years that are behind me. Time passes within us. Our actions fill it. It is a river: steep banks, a straight path, colorless waves. The void is its source, and it flows into the void. We, who build our cities on its banks, are the ones who raise dikes against it, who color its waves with the beacons upraised in our hands, or with our blood. Time could not exist outside of my thought. It is whatever I make it. The instant which I fill with light is priceless, like a ray of light from a star which shines for eternity through the space it illuminates. The empty hours and days which I yield to dead things have no more existence than shadows . . . My very dream is the surest reality.

Stretched out on my cot, like a dead man in his shroud (I even like to cross my hands over my chest, like a dead man), eyes open under the pale flickers of the ceiling, I rediscover, I invent, under the crushing weight of the gray stones of the jail, the beliefs which were the refuge and the greatness of enslaved peoples for thousands of years.

The night grows deeper: My thought begins to falter. Notice how the inner flame flickers. Here, on the edge of sleep, comes the poisoned moment. A familiar obsession begins to filter through your veins. You can feel it in all your limbs. Memory again becomes a torture. Is it the city, with all its intersections brightly lit at this hour? Your home bathed in the golden circle of a lamp? the sharp scent of the earth after rain? an innocent, smiling child threatened by the unknown? a woman you desire uncontrollably? Those who have love driven into their hearts pay dearly for it, writhing on their mattresses as on a bed of thorns, ravaged by obsessive jealousy, devastated by the fear of death (for the lives of loved ones seem more fragile than a miracle in this place). Anguish. Lucidity. Madness. The flesh of six hundred males screams in the silence . . .

A sudden glow of light strikes me in the face. The guard passes, stealthy as a thief, a dark lantern in his hand. Then a wild scream tears through the night. The silence, like thick mire, engulfs it.

"Jesus! Jesus! Jesus!"

A strong voice now shouts this appeal; a feverish head beats rhythmically against the wall. Rapid steps clatter up the iron stairs. A door opens. Murmurs.

"Jesus!" repeats the desperate voice; "Jesus!"

Other voices, low-pitched, try to snuff out that voice.

Three giant shadows, three guards, surround Dillot, the seminarist, in his cell. He is in his nightshirt, his joined hands tremble, his forehead is burning.

"'E's loony," says Cauliflower.

"Throw a blanket over his head," whispers Ironsides. "Come on!"

The shadows grow larger around the man in the nightshirt, who finally notices them in his fever, and collapses, sobered by his fear, rolling in the dark blanket thrown over him like a sack. He struggles against it for a few seconds with the fury of a drowning man. His arm finds an opening and his voice, now strident, comes through, no longer calling the Son of Man, but men:

"Help! Murder! Help!"

"Will you shut up," growls Ironsides.

A huge hand crashes down over the lunatic's mouth, choking off his cries with a gag. The silence, like muddy water, swallows up this madman as they toss him, gagged, into a sack.

. . . I slept like a stone. Another day is dawning. I am ready. I shall wear down the Mill.

TWENTY-THREE

The Guards

THREE KINDS OF MEN INHABIT THE PRISON, MORE DISTANT THAN IF THEY LIVED on opposite sides of the ocean. There are the soldiers, sent over from the army post, who take care of outer security. They stand guard in the towers on the outside wall. The guards live inside with us. Many of them have homes and families. They go out to cafés. They wear a uniform with yellow trim which is only slightly different from that of a customs man or traffic cop. But they spend two thirds of their lives inside these walls. The irrevocable condemnation which weighs down the poor oppresses them more heavily than it does most of us. Inmates serve out their sentences, then they leave these walls. Guards don't leave until they are ready to retire, at sixty, only to finish out their days in dismal, provincial wine stoops. On the back streets of little towns you find those empty cafés, still lighted by oil lamps, whose drab furnishings seem to reek of sordid resentments and stale quarrels. That is where Cauliflower, with his bovine brow, Spike Chin, with his copper complexion, Ironsides, with his strangler's grip, and Latruffe; pale and flabby, jangling his cupboard keys in his pudgy hands as he now jangles those of the cell block, will finish out their days; playing pinochle. Seeing these old men holding their greasy cards, a chance observer would feel strangely chilled, as if a shadow, ready to snatch him, had suddenly come between him and life; for the old hands of the "screws" continue to play out the same absurd round on the patch of green felt, under the sign of the queen of spades.

Guards fresh out of the barracks start in at eight hundred francs a year. For thirty-five years, from the ages of twenty-five to sixty, they spend twelve hours a day in jail, under the strictest discipline, forbidden to smoke, to talk to the inmates, to talk unnecessarily among themselves, to sit down or to read on duty, while they themselves are kept under watch by the sergeants and are ready, in any case, to denounce each other for the slightest infraction of the rules.

The uniformed man guards his flock of inmates. The same silence weighs down on him; but we are a crowd, our glances are full of understanding, and the guard is alone, surrounded by false or elusive glances, watched by the whole workshop. Are his hours any less heavy than ours? We suffer for years; he suffers by the day; and in the evening he goes out under the poplars toward his supper, his wine, his newspaper, his wife. Several have the bloated faces of alcoholics. Others, yellow-skinned, have liver and intestinal diseases brought back from the colonies. Some are potbellied: peasants living in idleness on potatoes and sour wine; doubtless they find their life a soft one because their hands, destined for rough work on the soil, are idle.

The guards are no better and no worse than the men they guard. We know them all. We know that Tartarin's sad gaze is sincere; he's a nice old fellow who doesn't bother anybody. We know that the elegant Marseillais has syphilis and that he nearly turned bad, having been in trouble as a kid; that's why he is still a "regular guy." We know that Reseda, also known as Flowerpot, a big awkward fellow with a red nose, has a good heart and drinks because his wife puts horns on him. But the man who called him "cuckold" was put in his place by Richardeau: "Don't be a jerk! Can't you see that man isn't happy? And I'll bet you're more of a cuckold than he is!" We know that Duck Feet, who wears the medal of the Senegalese campaign, is a bit of a nut, friendly but sometimes nasty, and has trouble making ends meet because of his large family. We like Old Gramps, rickety and all white, whose wizened face reminds us of the dead-end kid he used to be. We like him because he once told us:

"Go on, stop complaining. You'll get out of here. Me, I've spent my whole life in this joint: thirty-four years. Twelve more months to retirement. I wouldn't give two pins for the life I've led, you know. And what am I worth now, tell me?"

Not much, it's true. Gramps doesn't care about his job and lets us talk; we watch out so he doesn't get caught. "No point getting him chewed out just at the end!"

There are probably more bad "screws" ("*gaffs*" in French, from the obsolete slang verb "*gaffer*": to see) than good ones. Always on their toes, they have the hunter's instinct. In the workshop, they unexpectedly turn on their heels, throwing the prisoners off their guard, to pounce on a whispered conversation behind the type cases. They notice the thin, white edge of a scribbled note stuffed into an open book, sniff out the vaguest trace of tobacco in the clothes of a man being searched. Every morning they send a whole stack of reports to the Warden. The other guards, if only to avoid being cited for negligence or incompetence, are thus forced to write up a certain number of infractions. They simply pick out a few unfamiliar faces for punishment.

A few of us were talking about the bad ones one morning in the infirmary courtyard: some consumptives, a blind man, and a fellow recovering from typhus, huddling together in a patch of sunlight. Almost every one spoke up in judgment:

"There's Madagascar, who steals our letters to get the stamps . . ."

"Dupart broke a prisoner's arm after putting him in irons . . ."

"Aborton lied under oath and sent some poor bastard to forced labor . . ."

"Cauliflower, when he was a guard in the kitchen, used to steal so much that we nearly starved to death . . ."

"Begaud, you know, the one they call d'Artagnan, steals wine from the canteen and puts in water . . . I saw him . . ."

"And Half Pint got paid twenty francs for carrying a package over the wall and then turned it over to the Warden himself!"

"All of 'em, go on, all of 'em," said someone in despair, "they're all the same. They're no better than us . . .

"They're worse . . ."

"They have more power."

"The ones with more power are the worst."

They are neither more powerful nor worse. Men are without power in the Mill. And the system is worse than the men.

TWENTY-FOUR

The Years

WE SPEND SUNDAYS IN THE WORKSHOP. THE SILENCE OF THE MACHINES STI-
fles our voices. The lack of activity keeps us from moving. We are riveted in our places; the hours drag on slowly, a sluggish river heavy with
the silt of memories. We don't have enough books, especially good
books, to use as a steady refuge. We pass from the idle immobility of
the workshop to the rhythmic round of the exercise yard. The round
goes on and on, sometimes in the heat (our old tunics, buttoned to the
neck according to regulations, clinging to our damp flesh), sometimes
in the cold (nipping our fingers with invisible pincers). Happy enough
if the three trees in the prison yard, frosted with silver dust, remind us
of the enchantment of a park in winter.

Twice a month, on Sunday, from ten o'clock until noon, the inmates
write their families on stationery with a penitentiary letterhead. It is forbidden to discuss the prison or any subject not directly related to personal
affairs . . . Nouzy, writing to his wife, gave her some advice on the edu-
cation of their little boy: ". . . Make especially sure they don't teach him
to respect fetishes; teach him, as early as possible, to see through hypocrisy . . ." His Honor the Civilian Controller summoned prisoner number
6852 into the little workshop accounting office. His Honor the Civilian
Controller Sibour had a sharp nose, a moldy complexion, narrow, square
shoulders, and a beige overcoat which came straight down over his big
flat feet. He pointed to these lines with a stubby, waxlike finger:

"What's that supposed to mean?"

The stevedore from Rouen, a sly old anarchist, narrowed his lively
little eyes:

"That? . . . fetishes? Why, they're fetishes, Your Honor, Sir."

"I'm not talking to you about fetishes. I'm asking you-what you're
writing here to your spouse."

This official savored the word "spouse." "His 'spouse,' Hell!" said a voice behind him.

"Well, Your Honor, Sir, they're my ideas . . ."

"Understand, Nouzy, that you're not in this place to expound your ideas. If I catch you at it again, I'll prohibit you from writing. Write this letter over for me for next Sunday . . ."

"Without the ideas, Your Honor, Sir?"

"You've understood me. You may go."

Happily, few men allowed themselves the privilege of expounding any ideas. Nonetheless, an order from the Warden was posted in the workshop, for the benefit of the half dozen of us who held out, enjoining the inmates to make sure to "write out your correspondence with brevity, dealing, without digressions of any sort, with your family affairs exclusively." Those who had left loved ones behind in life—a child, a woman waited for, dreamed of for years now in the haunted nights of their cells, in the senseless rounds, in the painful hours of sharp despair—these men turned to the task of writing with an uneasiness mingled with anger and disgust. How could they resist writing what they felt, searching for the words to express the inexpressible? How could they forego the urge to vent that stifled, twisted cry, filling a page mulled over, night after night with words of reproach for the letters that never came, plunging their nights into despair, tormenting their souls with unbearable fear and jealousy? But how could they write on that sheet which bears, next to the letterhead, *the inmate's registration number,* that sheet which will be read by Monsieur Roussot, the mail clerk (known as "Pinch Ass" because of his skinny behind), and perhaps by his Honor the Civilian Controller, Monsieur Sibour (known as "Verdigris")?

"When I write my wife," said Guillaumet, "and when I think that cuckold of a Pinch Ass and that eunuch of a Verdigris are going to pick over my letter with sly little smiles, I'd like to throw this iron crowbar into their faces! What a relief that would be!"

Duclos, my other neighbor, whose registration was Number 4552 (which meant that he had survived four generations of prisoners), said in an almost inaudible voice:

"The worst of it is that you can't even bare your soul. They always manage to find it and grab it in their filthy hands. After eighteen years, that's the one thing I haven't been able to get used to."

Duclos, the parricide; became my neighbor during my fourth year. For the preceding fifteen years, he had held an office job that kept him clear of the guards' harassment, allowed him to read and write, and provided him with an incomparable view: ten yards of green grass, a rough stone fountain, and a little pond where goldfish swam about peacefully. The desk of the "general accountant" faced a single window, which looked out over the Warden's little garden. Alone, his stupid task over for the day, his canteen receipts and supply sheets sent off, Duclos would open Spinoza or *Creative Evolution* and, riveted to his chair by heart disease, with his chilly hands hidden nearly all the year round in a muff of old wool batting, his beret pulled down almost to his ears, looking, with his great nose, his bony cheeks, and his fleshless neck, like Holbein's portrait of old Erasmus, he would begin to dream. The years had deadened his sufferings, dulled his memories, worn out his body, drained the blood from his brain. "My intellect," he used to tell me, "has not faltered; but it has grown dim. I have never resigned myself; but resignation has entered me, has bent me down to the ground and told me: 'Rest.' To tell the truth, I'm not sure it didn't tell me: 'Die, slowly.'" His mind, often slack, no longer followed his book with the patience and ardor of an earlier time: Through the bars of the window his eyes wandered over the little garden with its hardy grass, its rosebush and lilac tree, before settling on that calmest of invitations to daydreaming: traced lightly in the water, like our destiny, in a pond as narrow as human life itself, the evanescent arabesques of the goldfish gliding through the water. "There are so many prisons in the universe," thought the old prisoner; "every prison is a universe, every universe a prison . . . Those fish inside their four-foot basin, these men enclosed in their destiny, ourselves in this jail; and all the people who were born and who will die in the airless, lightless rooms of this little town . . ." He could no longer imagine a sky that was not cut into rectangles by bars. And up there, the celestial spheres turned ceaselessly in their immense crystal prison. He wasn't sure if *he* were acquiring greater wisdom or simply moving toward a kind of contemplative insanity. He was as calm as it is possible to be in the Mill. "I was really well off. Two or three times a month I used to get hold of a newspaper . . ." This sinecure aroused jealousies. While Duclos was meditating, Moure, a former attendant in a Jesuit establishment (sex crimes, eight years) lived in his shadow, collecting accounting errors, little favors done in violation of the regulations, oversights of hands numbed by eighteen years of captivity, dangerous secrets . . . Moure had as much patience in his soul as he had unctuousness in his movements, velvet in his voice, pallor in his face, and complacent servility in his eyes and in his spine. His denunciation, ripened over a period of three years, was a masterpiece of irrefutability. They went easy on Duclos, who spent thirty days in the "hole," from which he emerged stumbling, his limbs grown a little more sluggish, his hands a little more gnarled, to become my neighbor. I discovered that he was a man of absolute integrity and rare firmness of character. We were already in his debt for the gift of his books. His presence brought us yet another priceless acquisition.

Moure got the coveted job. The lazy darting of the goldfish excited different dreams in a different brain. Alone with himself, Moure became transformed, like someone possessed. He had always lived burdened with unavowable mysteries, but never had his life been so filled with them as now. In the calm hours of the afternoon, pretending to make clean copies of the *Statement of Supplies Delivered,* Moure opened his secret envelopes. They contained strange little locks of stiff hair, rolled into tight curls; a strange, musty odor clung to them. They were of different shades; and some were attached by white ribbons to paper tags on which was written, in a careful, round hand: "Georgette, November 26"; or "Lucienne, my cute little c . . . my adored one, f . . . on the second day of Easter." These girls' names were always derived from boys' names. In his handwritten inscriptions, Moure liked to link the most brutally obscene insults with love words and coquettish diminutives. Eyes half closed, nostrils flaring, he inhaled the nauseating odor of dried human sperm; lost in his private reveries, his gaze followed mechanically the goldfish swimming in the pool. The soft, sweet face of a corrupted adolescent, with wide eyes and greedy lips like soft strawberries, would form in the reflection of a cloud on the smooth water. A young man's deliciously immodest hands would offer a hot flower of virility to his kneeling lover. Moure then slowly wrote in a date, followed by tender words of affection: "Antoinette, my sweet, my pretty little darling." Then, his mouth slightly twisted, his lower lip trembling, he added some harsh words, obscene to the point of cruelty.

And so the days, the seasons, the years dissolved like thick fumes of smoke, slow to dissipate, but leaving behind no trace.

Spring was the bittersweet season. In April, with the first buds on our stunted trees, the first clear skies, the first warm days, such a powerful call seemed to come from the very heart of life that we all felt we were emerging, our nerves raw, from some great lethargy. April quickened our old, dormant sufferings; but even more, April quickened our failing energies. Three hundred wooden shoes beat more smartly against the pavement in our round; broken marionettes began to straighten up again; gray faces were uplifted . . . Sometimes I wrote poems while marching; I felt so victorious over the Mill . . .

"Only twenty more months!" whispered Gilles, his face radiant, as he passed by.

TWENTY-FIVE

The War

I REMEMBER THE IMPLACABLY BLUE SKY OF ONE SUNDAY. WE SPENT THE DAY on benches along the whitewashed walls of a wide, tree-planted court-yard. Our furtive glances kept watch over the guards, slumped in their chairs in the heavy heat. The sun scorched the grass; you could see the hot air vibrating. The immobility, the heat, the relentless, oppressive brightness were all focused on a new and astonishing thought: war. We had just found out about it, as we always learned about great historic events, through unknown channels. My mind was blank. I tried to imag-ine the monstrous reality of millions of men marching against each other all over Europe, with their rifles hanging in their fists like the stone axes of their ancestors. A few paces away from me was a German, an ordinary lad, simple, strong and straightforward. From time to time, everyone's eyes would turn toward this man, our brother, like all the others, our pal who had suddenly become, without even knowing it, an enemy who in any other place would have been ripe for killing. (We soon learned to say *"Boche,"* but I don't think that term was ever applied to him; he was too real to us, too much like us; hatred, especially the hatred of crowds, needs a certain distance in order to work its distortions.)

That evening Miguel, who seemed feverish, managed to get close enough to stuff a wad of paper into my hand.

"I want," he wrote, "to be outside so I can be the first killed. I want to be in the first battle to throw myself between the French and the Germans shouting: You're all mad, you're all brothers! Everyone called up with me is going to be killed. I belong to a dead year. I already feel like a condemned man the world has accidentally overlooked . . ."

Events presented themselves to us with incomprehensible simplicity. The war burst suddenly out of the void. We knew nothing of its prelim-inaries. We were thus, through the cruelest of ironies, perhaps the only men in Europe in those mad days, to look at it with the detachment of inhabitants from another planet. We were quite certainly among the few Europeans who were not carried away by the terrible war fever of those first days . . .

At night, in our cells, we could hear strange rumblings coming from the nearby town: the "Marseillaise" clamored by delirious crowds in stations filled with departing soldiers, the sudden train whistles, the muffled playing of bands. We would listen, straining, taking in that vague, contagious enthusiasm, then terribly saddened to fall back into the silence, the emptiness, the useless anguish of our nights.

Rumors of victory were circulating. Rollot got a letter which began, like a poem, with these words: "Tonight is a night of victory; I am a happy woman . . ." He read it, blushing, with a twisted smile. He wrote an answer in the margin, for himself. "You are mad. There are only disasters, disasters." The names of conquered cities were whispered about: Mulhouse, Thann, the Cossacks on the outskirts of Berlin. Later we spoke of cities lost and destroyed: Liege, Mauberge, Charleroi, Lille. Defeat passed over the prison like the shadow of a sulphurous cloud. No one knew any details. The guards, questioned at every opportunity, kept quiet. The proofreaders used to listen at the door of the civilian manager's office. They reported this comment on a victory communiqué in which it became clear that Compiègne had been occupied by the Germans: "One more victory like this one, and they'll be in Paris!" Rumors of treason ran rife. People talked about generals turned traitor being shot down in the middle of General Staff meetings. What intrigued our little group of revolutionaries the most was the fate of our comrades. Had they tried to resist? Had they been shot? We imagined them trampled by angry mobs, the war passing over their dead bodies. One of us received a visitor. We primed him with questions to ask. He returned from the visitors' room dumbfounded, understanding nothing:

"Nothing happened . . . nothing . . . Seems that Hervé has enlisted. Almereyda too . . . Anatole France too.[9] All the comrades have joined up. Some of them have already been decorated . . ."

---

9   Gustave Hervé (1871–1944), a leading French revolutionary antimilitarist and editor
     of *La Guerre Sociale,* suddenly turned patriotic in 1914 and changed the name
     of his journal to *La Victoire.* Miguel Almereyda (Bonaventure Vigo) (1888–1917),
     revolutionary publicist, was founder of *Le Bonnet Rouge,* which led the "defeat-
     ist" campaign in 1916–17 until it was suppressed. A self-styled pacifist, Almereyda
     was arrested and accused of taking German money. He was killed in prison
     before being brought to trial, under mysterious circumstances. His son, Jean
     Vigo, became a well-known film director. (Tr.)

Men whose homes were in the North stopped getting letters.

Then the military prisoners began to arrive. A strange joy glittered in their eyes. "Stop complaining!" they said. "You can't imagine how well off we are here!" "I'd rather do five years than go back to living that life at the front, with death at the end of it, and what a death!" The horrors of war were fresh in their minds, and they brought them home to us graphically. Deguy, a police inspector's son with a tiny albino head at the end of a long neck, made a lunge in pantomime: "My bayonet got stuck in this guy's guts and I had to use my feet to get it out . . ." Minot, a deserter arrested in the Pyrenees, his fake pass covered with numbers ("the more there are the better it looks"), told us what happened when he was sent with some buddies to bring back the chow and walked into the Company kitchen. "The whole room was red, yellow, and black; there were no more men; there was nothing left but flesh and scraps of cloth swimming around in the soup and blood on the floor . . . A piece of 155 fell right into their chow cannon; you can guess what it was like . . ." These refugees from the front found our slow torture a soft life. "No; really, you're a lucky bunch of bastards!" Our whole notion of life was thrown into disorder.

The battle moved closer to us. At night a rumbling as of distant thunder came from the horizon: artillery. At noon, when the machines were silent, we could hear the thud of faraway batteries firing across plains and hills where rows of helmeted ants were moving forward in parade-ground order . . . The town fell silent. Anybody who could run away, ran. Our civilian foreman, Monsieur Fouquier, a nasty, plump little *rentier*, moved among us haunted by a phantom; his only son had just been killed at the age of twenty. "Now he's really going to be a bastard," said Guillaumet. "He'll hate us just for being alive." This prediction did not come true. Heavy wrinkles lined Monsieur Fouquier's flabby triple chin. A new pity appeared in his eyes. In a dark corner of the storeroom he showed one of us a snapshot of a beardless young soldier.

An order from the Ministry, so it seemed, forbade the evacuation of all prisons. The guards' faces were damp with fear. "The Germans will be here by Sunday."

Would there be a battle on the river? It made a natural line of defense for the retreating army. Our church steeple seemed to us a perfect landmark for artillery. Poule, terrified, asked me: "Do you really think they'll shell us?" "Naturally," I replied. I lived *alone*, feeling the fear spread from one man to the next. I felt a sort of exaltation which gave birth to a great serenity. The old world was being smashed by the cannon. The Mill would be crushed by the cannon. The law of kill-and-be-killed was reaffirmed for my generation. I would have preferred to take my part in the action, the common suffering, to fall like the others, friends and enemies (for me they were only men bent under the same law); but any end is a good one for the man who takes it standing up, who accepts; each man must fulfill his destiny. Marcus Aurelius taught me acquiescence: "Several grains of incense are on the same altar: one falls sooner, the other, later: no difference . . . Whatever suits you, O world, suits me!" There was profound joy in thinking about this resurrection of the world through the cannon, which had at last interrupted our round.

The cannon moved closer. We stayed in our cells for three straight days; they were immensely serene days. No more rounds of beating the pavement. The Mill had stopped grinding. The Mill, resigned, was waiting for that shell, that great millstone which would grind it up in turn. The guards, terrified, left us alone. I had received an encouraging letter. I was reading the life of Luther. I was alone with my serenity.

During those days, in the neighboring woods, they arrested some spies who were perhaps nothing more than deserters. One of them, a gnarled old peasant caked with mud from head to toe, was brought into the penitentiary before being sent to the court-martial. The orderly, Ribotte, a stool pigeon, was ordered to clean him up. He drove him to the shower room with jabs in the ribs. For the first time in his life he had in his clutches a human being he could martyrize, to whom he was allowed to do anything he pleased. He doused him with near-boiling water. "I says to him: 'Wait and see, this is nothing yet, you bastard! When they tie you to the stake, then you'll really make faces . . . And don't worry, those twelve bullets are waiting for you; you won't miss out on them.' When I gave his balls a good twist, he gave out such a yell that Ironsides came in to see what was happening. I had a big bristle brush in my hand and I was scraping the bastard's belly.

"'What's going on?' says Ironsides.

"'Mister Spy thinks my brush isn't soft enough,' says I.

"'Give him a shot in the mouth,' says Ironsides.

"You can bet I didn't miss the chance. These spies," concludes Ribotte, "just send 'em to me. I know how to take care of 'em."

The battle moved away, the endless round began to turn again. Our daily hunk of bread was cut in half, reduced to 300 grams of brown dough full of straw, beans, and worms (at least they were cooked). Hunger, already an old friend, moved in with us to stay. We were supposed to know nothing of the war. The system added total isolation to total silence: Nothing from the outside was to reach us. The mutilated country bled through countless wounds: Those of her children who were in prison were to know nothing. There were fathers whose sons were fighting, brothers of soldiers, poor devils whose villages were now only heaps of stone still being pounded by the cannon: No one was to know anything about it. We nonetheless had an idea of how monstrous this war was. It reached us even through the bars, the mists, over great distances. The Battle of the Falklands, the English surrender in Mesopotamia, the Russians in the Carpathians . . . Bits of news drifted in to us; all the maps of the world seemed bloodstained to me. Rollot, who had heard about the shelling of Reims Cathedral, told us. Beaugrand, the firebug, ratted on him. My comrade was summoned before the three silver-braided *képis* of the "disciplinary tribunal." The Warden, angry, was drumming on his desk with nervous fingers:

"You seem well-informed, Rollot. Where do you get your information?"

Silence.

"You'd better learn to answer when you're spoken to. Where do you get your information?"

"From the moon, Warden, Sir."

"Oh, so it's that way, eh! I'll put you back in step, my friend. The black hole until further notice."

We were supposed to be ignorant of everything, even the destruction of the most ancient, holy stones of France. We were the only men on earth forbidden to know about the war; but, though we read nothing and could only glimpse, through the double smokescreen of war and administrative stupidity, the general outline of events, some few of us were blessed with exceptional clear-sightedness. I knew enough about the inner decay of the Russian Empire to foresee, at a time when the Cossacks still incarnated the hope of several old Western countries, its inevitable fall. Long before Europe ever dreamt it, we were discussing, in whispers, the coming Russian Revolution. We knew in what part of the globe the long-awaited flame would be born. And in it we found a new reason for living.

Nothing changed. The cannon reigned over all of Europe. A million corpses piled up in the valley of bones at Verdun. France, bleeding through her gaping wounds, avidly absorbed the new strength of Canadians, New Zealanders, Hindus, Senegalese, Portuguese. In the Mill, six hundred men continued their senseless round, attesting to the permanence of order—stronger even than a social cataclysm. We formed an unbelievable island, cut off from the movement of history.

"Perhaps," mocked Duclos, "we will be the last survivors of old Europe. Machine guns, famine, pestilence, and madness will finish out their dance of death, and we will still be marching around these courtyards with Spike Chin and Cauliflower beating out the eternal rhythm."

The bell gave the signal for lights out. Squadrons of airplanes flew over the prison on their way to Paris. The sky turned gold.

TWENTY-SIX

Discipline

FIRST VIOLATION OF THE RULE OF SILENCE: REPRIMAND. SECOND AND THIRD: loss of canteen privileges. Fourth: bread and water. Fifth: Disciplinary Room or solitary. Prison discipline is based on hunger. The disparity between the severity of the punishment and the triviality of the offense is often extraordinary.

Discipline based on arbitrary caprice. The rule of silence is observed by no one. The guards, in their reports, simply mark down the names of men whose faces they don't like, plus a few more, chosen at random, to appear impartial. In each workshop there are a few men who are constantly noted for "bad behavior" and are punished one day out of every two. They are usually tall, skinny kids, with insolent glances—wise guys. "Young hoodlums," think the guards, secretly envious, deep down in their rancid existence, of the youthful vigor of these tough young hooligans. I have always thought there was an element of instinctive envy behind the daily persecution of certain young prisoners by guards past middle age. These men, slowed down by the weight of forty years, themselves bound to our chain, with no future ahead of them, must feel a kind of physical aversion for lives that are still intact, that the Mill can't crush entirely, that will sooner or later take flight toward new adventures, while they themselves will go on and on, guiltless, nonetheless, like the Pharisees, turning in our round until they are sixty . . .

Seated under the yellowed bust of the Republic, the Warden hands out disciplinary justice every morning at the "tribunal." Violations of silence, correspondence among inmates, slackness at work, illicit trafficking in tobacco, brawling—such is the usual gamut of offenses he punishes before going off to lunch. Attempted suicide is punished by thirty days in solitary, as are homosexuality and petty theft. Stool pigeons are treated with a certain indulgence.

The worst privation, after celibacy, is tobacco.

Hautereau, of the print shop, was summoned before the braided *képis,* for having been caught red-handed using tobacco. During the evening search the guard, La Tuile, sniffed something suspicious on his breath and suddenly prodded his left cheek with a yellow, tobacco-stained, finger:

"What you got there?"

"Nothin'."

"Then open your maw and let me see."

Hautereau didn't dare resist the man in uniform, who grabbed his face in both hands, opened his mouth like a box, stuffed two dirty fingers inside his cheek, and pulled out a foul chaw of tobacco (which he had probably spit out himself the day before) from between his rotten molars.

Hautereau—a wizened little redhead, forty-five years old, sinewy, with the flat head of a dried fish—now stands at attention like a soldier before his superiors:

"This is the second time I've caught you at it, Hautereau. Where did you get your tobacco?"

"I found it, Warden, Sir."

"You'd better find a better answer than that. I'll give you thirty seconds. You know the consequences."

The Warden bends his long white mustaches and his ornately braided *képi* over his handsome silver watch. A feeling of well-being, derived from a hearty appetite thirty minutes before lunchtime, gives him great firmness of character at this instant.

Hautereau, his brows wrinkled, is thinking about his pal, the spittoon man, a lucky old devil who lives dangerously. He has enough to pay for the favors of the "prettiest boys"; he lacks nothing. He earns his prisoner's fortune from globs of spit. Since smoking is forbidden within the walls of the penitentiary, most of the guards chew; a few smoke when they are alone; their butts and used chaws end up in spittoons placed around the corridors and the courtyards. The man who cleans these receptacles and refills them with carbolic acid every two days, removes the remnants of tobacco mingled with tubercular sputum. He washes them, rinses them, dries them, and resells them. The butts are resmoked and the chaws are rechewed. Hautereau suppresses an urge to betray.

"Have you thought it over?"

"Yes, Warden, Sir. I found it—that's all I can tell you."

"Forty days in the Room."

The Disciplinary Room is about as big as an average workshop and dark on account of its narrow, barred windows with painted-over panes, and its walls, which are painted black to the level of three feet, and dirty yellow above. A sort of big square wire cage is stuck into the entrance: That's where the guard stands. It makes you think of the tamer's shelter in a bear pit. As in certain bear pits, there are low cement benches placed around the middle of the room about five feet apart.

"Change your clogs!"

Hautereau obeys. He is not allowed to wear his usual clogs: That would be a mitigation of the punishment.

"Go in!"

The ringing echo of wooden clogs beating the pavement in rhythm, the semidarkness, the cage—all terrify him as he enters. He sees a line of frenzied marionettes dancing along the walls, turning round and round with dogged steps, seeing nothing but those walls, the cage, their own backs, hearing nothing but the guard's nagging voice calling out the cadences: "Left! left! left!," aware of nothing but the pain in their feet bruised by unfamiliar clogs, the cramps climbing up their calves, the hunger gnawing at their bowels, and the days that never seem to end. It's another endless round within the larger round. Hautereau enters. Reduced to dry bread and morning soup, the men undergoing punishment march for twenty minutes with their arms folded across their chests, then twenty minutes with their arms folded behind their backs. Every twenty minutes they get ten minutes' rest on the cement benches, legs together, elbows pressed to their sides. Every day they do thirty miles within these walls. Toward the tenth day a man begins to stumble at every turn, carried along by the rhythm, his feet covered with cuts and bruises. If he refuses to walk, they throw him into the "hole." If he collapses, they isolate him in the infirmary for a week; once his feet have been bandaged and his body revived by a few bowls of broth, he resumes his place in the madmen's dance.

"Forty days," thinks Hautereau. "It'll take me at least two trips to the infirmary to do forty days."

What he doesn't know is that he is going mad. But we know it. We call him "the nut." While he turns, prey to his obsessions like all these unhinged marionettes, the worm that is boring into his enfeebled brain will complete its ruin. Turn, old man, turn!

Hautereau's obsession is the most common one, after sex: He is obsessed by his "case." He has been mulling over his case for six years now, more and more convinced each day that he is innocent (which is false), that he has been victimized (which is true), and that there is no justice (which is also true). He broods for months on end over statements he intends to send to the Minister of Justice, to the Court of Appeals, to the President of the Republic. Whenever he is allowed to write; he blackens page after page with close-written paragraphs full of memorized quotations from the Penal Code, precedents in long-forgotten decisions, specious arguments about the testimony of witnesses now dead or vanished, themselves long forgotten. The significant passages are underlined two or three times. Gamekeeper in a woodland, Hautereau used to exercise his male prerogative on the girls who came to gather dead wood on his land. At first a magistrate's court slapped a six months' sentence on him. Six months for lifting the skirts of a girl in the woods, a little thief who was sleeping with all the carters in the next village and who "ran after me herself so's I'd keep my eyes closed"—six months without roaming the woods he used to haunt all year round, from dawn to dusk—this seemed an incredible injustice and an intolerable torture to him. A provincial lawyer advised him to raise the question of jurisdiction and to demand a new trial in a higher court, where an acquittal seemed possible. The Criminal Court slapped a sentence of seven years at hard labor on the poor devil, soon commuted to seven years in the penitentiary at the request of the jury. So many different penalties for so natural an act unhinged his reason.

The dry clack of the clogs echoes endlessly against the walls of the Room. The immobile silence of the pauses cuts like a golden stripe across the gray warp of time. Seven men turning there in endless circles. Asparagus, an Italian bigamist, guilty of illegal correspondence with his wife: two weeks. Two young punks, Floc and Taupin, both pimps, one from the *Porte de Clichy* district, the other from the *Place Blanche*. Floc has legs of steel and a way of looking at people out of the corner of his eyes which is nastier than any insult. Every twenty-four seconds, Spike Chin, whose wire cage doesn't protect him from the evil eye, is struck by that disturbing glance, but since Floc has been keeping in step without flinching for twenty days, the "screw" has nothing to say. He catches up on Taupin, who is by now nothing more than a limp rag, twitching wildly along, his feet bloody. Taupin is so dizzy at times, he thinks he is falling; and that awful burning in his heels, his ankles, the joints of his toes cramped in wooden clogs for twenty-nine days. "Ah, let me die," he thinks. But the screw's voice whips him on: "Faster, Taupin! Hup!" And Taupin, stirred up by that voice like a rag in a gust of wind, lurches forward. Hautereau sees the three other dancing forms less clearly, for they tend to follow him in the rounds and it's only at the turns that he has a clear view of a broad face frozen into a grimace of anger and disgust, another expressionless face wearing glasses, and the last, so blank that it doesn't count. All the figures are dancing. All the masks are grimacing and sneering. The Room is gray with yellow stripes. Nothing else is real anymore.

TWENTY-SEVEN

Latruffe

THE CELL BLOCK IS ANOTHER PRISON WITHIN THE PRISON, TOTALLY ISOLATED by its surrounding wall. Three floors of cells: dark, half-dark, and light. Two rows of dungeons. Triangular exercise yards forming a cement semicircle in a separate courtyard. In a ground-floor cell there is a small, almost comfortable office—cool in summer, warmed in winter by a radiator—belonging to the master of the place, Latruffe, a mountain of pale, swollen flesh, with bluish cheeks. His *képi* seems too small for his pear-shaped head, which widens at the bottom. His sausage-like fingers play continuously with a ring of keys, as inseparable as a Muslim's beads. He greets his victims with a broad, moon-faced smile which exposes his rotten teeth, while he slyly whacks their ribs with his keys. "Pretend you don't notice," explain those in the know. "That's what he likes." Then he goes away laughing to himself and leaves you in peace. But if you make a fuss, he'll never let you go, he'll make you piss blood. He's full of tricks. For instance, in winter he makes you wash your head at the faucet but won't give you the time to get dry; so your teeth chatter till noon. In summer he gives you water you can't drink; I don't know what it is: funny and stale, as if somebody had been spitting into it. I wouldn't put it past him. And at night when you bend over to pick up your mattress, he always manages to give you a poke in the back with his keys on the sly. Don't bellyache! He'll throw you in irons with a report where he says you tried to kill him . . .

"If you're a man, a real one, there's still one good way of talking to him. All you have to do is say to him nicely, like this:

"Listen, Latruffe, old boy. If you want my ass, you'll have it. But me, I'll try to get yours first. Now you can start. Be my guest.

"Only if you talk to him like that, you'd better be serious. That bastard has a sixth sense about whether you've got guts, and he makes bluffers pay double."

Every two or three hours, when the mood strikes him, Latruffe carefully folds his *Petit Parisien,* puts it down on the table, takes his lantern, and goes down to the dungeons.

A dank, foggy blackness, so thick you can almost touch it, reigns in these half-buried cement cells. Each contains a woven mat and a basin. The darkness is so thick inside that your arms seem to hug it, and your eyes absorb it; in a few hours it gets inside you, penetrating every pore. The sense of time no longer exists; the passing days, marked by a hunk of bread each morning, are lost, blurred in the darkness. Reason falters: That inner light succumbs to the darkness. You leave this place a sick man, eyes blinking, soul blinded, like a night bird turned loose in the bright sunlight. Leaving this place, you leave madness, or you take it with you. Four obsessions haunt these dungeons: the horror of injustice (the obsession of the case: "I'm innocent" or "I've been punished too hard, it's unfair"); carnal desire (sometimes jealousy); the horror of death (the death of loved ones, transformed by the darkness into a certainty); the fear of dying. You don't get to choose your obsession.

The human larvae living in these rectangular grottoes hear the guard's soft step approaching from a distance. The man in irons, whose cramped arms are chained behind his back tingling with pins and needles, straightens up with the hope of a few swallows of water. The half-crazed man, turning around and around in the darkness, then lying prostrate on his mat, his brain oppressed by the image of his daughter's death (he sees her blue lips drawn into a last smile, her closed eyelids strangely transparent, her adorable silk-blond hair; he sees it all, again, and again; and, although he keeps telling himself he's crazy, he believes desperately in what he sees), huddles in the corner of his dungeon to hide his tortured face and still not miss the ray of light that is about to enter. That light, and Latruffe's silhouette, attest to the reality of a universe where, perhaps—certainly!—Jeanne is not dead, not dead. Meanwhile the ray of light is prying into the neighboring dungeons, and the dead girl's face rises up again into his tired brain like a drowned body rising from the bottom of a lake . . .

Latruffe moves noiselessly past the dungeon doors. A lamp hanging at the end of the gallery seems to guide him through the silence, the narrowness of the cement corridor, where in a sort of haze the yellow light fights against the gray. This is his kingdom: an insect of prey inspecting the captive larvae on which it feeds. He moves along, neck stretched out, muscles flexed, ears straining: and it's a struggle between him and the larvae. These have even sharper ears: he rarely catches them off guard. But, a patient hunter, he never ceases prying.

Number 6. Latruffe abruptly opens the wicket gate. The lantern dazzles an ageless, emaciated boy sprawled on his mat with both arms outstretched. Latruffe mutters:

"Get up."

The boy gets up slowly. The wicket gate closes again. Latruffe pretends to leave. Actually he is watching at the door. He knows the boy has lain down again. The wicket clicks open again. Again the dazzling light whips the figure stretched out on the cement floor. This time Latruffe opens the door and walks toward the boy, who is standing motionless on his feet now, glued to the back wall.

"What did I tell you?" asks Latruffe in a whisper.

For a moment he savors the terror in those frightened eyes, tortured by his lantern.

"Eh?"

Latruffe sways slowly on his legs. He raises his lantern to the boy's face. Slowly he passes the ring of keys from his right hand to his left: The boy, lips trembling, sees the keys swinging back and forth under the flame. Latruffe raises his right hand slowly, noiselessly, deliberately, and gives that helpless face glued to the wall a sharp slap. The boy's teeth rattle: ti-ti-ti. Tears well up in his eyes. Latruffe raises his hand again, hesitates for a second, and says:

"Enough for today, eh? Tomorrow, try to obey."

Latruffe is laying for Number 8. He's a stocky Spaniard with a hairy face (unshaved for three weeks now) and a shaggy chest. He turns round and round in the darkness, or squats, or lies down; but the same images are always with him. Sometimes it's a woman, his bronze-skinned narrow-hipped Tonine, his Niña, his *niña*, "*niña querida* . . ." Her earlobe is a rose petal, a petal he is constantly nibbling at. And now, for days and nights now, he senses that his Niña has been penetrated, possessed by another man, senses it so vividly that he actually feels the heat of their bellies and the strain of their backs, feels the woman's flesh open to the male's thrust, their lips coming together, the man on top of her like a leech. "A-haa-a . . ." The choked-back cry in his throat is no more than a rattle. Latruffe shoves open the wicket; the light slaps at this castaway's haggard face:

"Silence!" growls Latruffe. "What makes you 'sing' like that?"

Sometimes the man's hallucinations turn his dungeon into a fantastic seraglio. The brunette with the hard, pointed breasts is called Lolita: She offers herself shamelessly, standing, her back arched like a Sevillian dancer's. The blonde is sometimes called Manse, sometimes Lise—after a girl he once knew—and she strips submissively with shy, tentative gestures: The white underclothes fall onto the white bearskin rug at her feet and she shrinks back, desirous yet fearful, before the arms stretched out toward her. Others follow, in pairs and in groups, enfolding, clenching, embracing each other, and in the darkness the man falls into frenzies like a lubricious monkey. Latruffe catches him at last, panting, his organ bared, his hands wet. Latruffe enters quietly with a soft, menacing laugh in his throat:

"What if I put this in my report, Martínez? Aren't you ashamed?"

Martínez buttons up his clothing like a sleepwalker: In the returning darkness he finds himself trembling under the horrid indignity of that cackling laugh. Then he turns over, black in the blackness, his clenched fists heavy as stones.

"Te mataré, cobarde!"

These words spoken aloud ("I'll kill you, coward!") echo against the cement walls which no strong voice ever strikes.

The words soothe like a knife thrust. Meanwhile Latruffe turns back along the gallery, laughing to himself, satisfied, a warm feeling in the lower part of his belly. He makes himself comfortable in front of his radiator and drowses off, twiddling his thumbs slowly over his belly. Inside the low, narrow vault of his skull—another cell containing other larva—obscene gestures caught in the dungeons linger on, multiplying endlessly.

Latruffe gradually acquired his mountain of pale flab from his years in prison. For the past ten years he has been in charge of the stockade cell block. Eight thousand men have suffered within these walls under his hands. It is he who makes prisoners from the chain shop drink purgatives before they are released, to prevent them from making off with tubes of powdered gold hidden inside their anus. Latruffe spreads their buttocks and peers inside. Latruffe probes their excrement with a special forked stick of his own invention. Latruffe accompanies them, at dawn, as far as the registry office, already dressed in their civilian clothes, overcome by that extraordinary anxiety, mixed with boundless joy, of the final minutes in jail. At these moments a broad smile—the smile of a murderous Punch—spreads over his piglike face.

"Try and behave yourself on the outside," he tells them. "Don't forget all we did to put you back on the right path."

That morning, a departing prisoner suddenly turned around on the threshold. Latruffe felt his stomach sink and a streamlet of cold water run down his back. The man lunged his head at him like a serpent, and hissed:

"Shut your stupid hole, you dirty butcher. Try not to forget what I'm going to tell you. If I ever run into you in a dark alley, you'll get six inches of cold steel in the belly just as sure as I'm calling you a piece of shit right now. Understand?"

The departing prisoner had stopped short, turning his back on freedom. Latruffe could feel his short legs beginning to wobble.

"Move on," he said.

But the serpent's head drew closer to him, terrible, with inflamed pupils, phosphorescent in the shadows, like a cat's eyes.

"Do you understand? Answer me, you dumb prick, or do you want me to beat the crap out of you?"

"I understand," he said, defeated, his head lowered.

The satisfaction for the other man was instantaneous; he laughed out loud.

"Yeah, you bet you understood. You're not such a crap-head after all, eh? You dirty pig!"

TWENTY-EIGHT

The Sick

THE INFIRMARY WINDOWS, ALTHOUGH COVERED WITH WIRE MESH, LOOK LIKE the windows of houses "outside." We raise our heads toward that reminder.

Behind those windows you live in unaccustomed calm and whiteness; you are out of the round for a moment, you have come to catch your breath, in a real bed, or else to escape at last, for good, from hope and torment. At times you forget death's sure presence; your existence shrinks to the dimension of this refuge, provided for the weakness of the sick. You are glad not to be walking, marching in step, glad to get a little coffee, naively grasping at the slightest hope of life . . .

My lamp has more flame than oil. My spirit is willing, but my flesh is weak. (I understood why it is that slaves invented the religion of the divine, of the immortal soul imprisoned in contemptible, perishable flesh; I also know very well that the soul would be nothing if it were not flesh. Yet how can I avoid making the distinction between my strength and my weakness?) Every ten months or so, hunger, fatigue, and our peculiar form of overwork mixed with lethargy, break me down: A great coldness penetrates me, my teeth chatter; my heart beats in my chest like an enormous bell. Dizziness, dizziness. The saying goes that you must be at death's door, or close to it, to get into the infirmary. Evidently I am close, for here I am.

Lie down. There is a voluptuousness in the long shivers that precede the inner heat of fever. Relax your limbs and relax your mind. You no longer need your strength, for a while. Listen to the secret invitation to the voyage of fever. Embark.

When you return from the mysterious voyage, when your eyes open again, it will seem to you that a white, airy, almost warm light has filled the room with gaiety. The white beds are lined up in two rows along the light-colored walls. Old Madré is there, his crooked shoulders shaking with silent laughter.

"Well, there you are! I'm very glad to see you here. This is the place where you get patched up . . ."

"Or where you croak," answered a quiet voice from another bed.

Madré seems to turn yellow all at once, his mouth pinched. He shouts toward the back of the room:

"Bullshit. Croak if you want to; but leave the rest of us in peace."

Full of sympathy, this gray-haired fifty-year-old, with one deformed shoulder, greedy lips, a satyr's long, yellow, hooked nose, greenish eyes sparkling with mischief, and smelly breath, helps a sick young man get undressed with one of his affectionate wisecracks: Then tucking him in:

"I'll look after you, Little George. The orderly is a jug-head . . . (he laughs). And a wine jug to boot, by God . . . Lie down."

Through the chatter of teeth a smile answers him from the pillow.

"Come on, go to sleep now: Don't worry about it."

I see these beds, this crooked satyr, the strange sick boy he has just tucked in; I hear these voices in a half-dream bathed in whiteness. Footsteps hammer the pavement, the bell rings in the distance, in the realm of the unreal. Fever.

Another voice—somewhat heavy, like the voice of a fat, gossipy market woman—worms its way into my brain.

". . . More than that, of course! I've seen at least thirty of 'em pass on in three years . . . In every one of these beds . . . There isn't a single place here where somebody hasn't passed on . . . In Number 12, Pirron, a murderer who was doing twenty years (and he had already done sixteen, the poor bastard!) . . . Over there José, Rivol, Andrieux . . . In Number 17, Garon . . . say! He looked just like Van Hoever . . . Yeah, yeah! and he looked at me just like that two days before popping off . . . He died in his sleep, without suffering . . . In Number 19, young Girod; say, Madré, you remember, the young fellow who got married to What's-his-name upstairs . . . In the new man's bed . . ."

(My bed, evidently.)

". . . Poulain, a strapping fellow, carried off in three days by God-knows-what."

Noises. Someone enters. They're bringing in someone new, a big old man, being carried on the back of an attendant. He is breathing noisily. Sharp-eyed, red-faced. His beret is all askew, pulled down comically over his bushy eyebrows. He is greeted by excited shouts:

"Pop Vincent!"

He answers in a loud, hoarse voice:

"It's me. I've been around long enough. Pop Vincent's here to die . . .
Jesus Christ!"

This grinning crowd of dead or dying men is too much for me. I relapse
into my fever, into my dream. Half-asleep I hear Thiébaut, the orderly,
calmly holding forth. His voice reaches me from across a wide white
space . . .

"Dupuis the Controller? Of course I knew him . . . A short fellow,
broad-shouldered, with a pinched chest and a white, dried-up face. He
always looked as if he had a stomachache. A nasty sonofabitch, he
killed a fellow on me . . . A little Rumanian who used to be a counterfeiter . . . I remember, he was right over there. Dupuis caught him
hiding the checkerboard and sent him to the 'hole' for sixty days, when
he came out of the infirmary, because of some wisecrack . . . He came
back from the 'hole' to that same bed, Number 12, and died there . . .
He died telling me: 'Please, Thiébaut, don't forget to have them bring
me my photographs tomorrow morning.' They had just refused him
permission to see his photographs. And they knew very well that he
wouldn't last much longer. But Dupuis had said: 'Let him wait for his
day!' and his day was Sunday, the next day . . . Every three months,
when his day came up, he would ask to see them again, and he used
to sit for two or three hours, as long as they would let him keep them,
looking at his old Mama, a gray-haired lady, and then his big sister, a
nice little thing, and a whole gang of little brothers and little sisters
back in Braila . . . I still think he was just waiting to see them before he
died. When he came back from the 'hole' he was all white, with gray
lips, and he could hardly see. That same day he coughed blood for an
hour. On Tuesday the doctor examined him and told me: 'It's the end;
two or three days. Give him some shots of morphine. Ask him if he
wants some chocolate.' You know, in this place, when you see the chocolate coming you can be sure it's the end. He was a little delirious, he
kept saying, 'Sunday, Sunday,' I guess on account of the pictures . . .
He died Saturday night . . . His eyes suddenly opened up, real wide, as
if he were looking at something awful, and he tried to tell me something, but nothing came . . ."

I listen without eagerness, bathed in a vague feeling of warmth
and security.

"The Scorpion really killed that fellow," continues Thiébaut, "no
doubt about it . . . Would you believe that one time Dupuis went over

to an old paralytic in Room 2 to refuse him something or other, and the old fellow started shouting at him: 'Scorpion! Scorpion! Scorpion!' You should have seen him running away with his little hat in his hand, his overcoat flapping behind him, livid with rage. Think of it! After all, they couldn't throw the paralytic into the 'hole' . . . And he wouldn't shut up, he kept shrieking in this horrible voice: 'Scorpion, Scorpion!' They left him for three days without food."

"And he died?" asked someone.

"He died . . . But that's another story. We used to have an Italian banker here, a swindler, an amazing guy! He embezzled four or five million on the Tunisian railways . . .

Naturally, they pardoned him; he's looking after his liver at Cannes or Menton right now . . . Well, he was a sly one, a mean sonofabitch, old too, completely bald, with a tottering old monkey's head. He used to have the guard bring him tobacco. The old paralytic ratted on him once, and he never forgave him . . . So he poisoned him, slowly, a little bit each day. He was an educated man . . ."

The room was filled with a soft, half-light. His heavy voice was the only one to be heard, but it was enough to fill the room with dark, unsavory memories, with the poisoned breath of the tomb. The night light cast a pale yellow stain on the ceiling, around which our glances fluttered.

TWENTY-NINE

Dying

A CHART HANGING BEHIND THE BED READS: "#5529, VINCENT, AUGUSTIN, welder, 66 years old," and, lower down, in an ugly scrawl: "bronchial pneumonia. 104° of fever, this morning." Three little black dots connected by a line. That means you're on the way out, old boy. Little George went and got a blanket, for your feet, in spite of the heat in here. You couldn't even say thank you, your mumbled words lost in a choking gasp. The boy was terrified by the greenish tint of your face.

"Jesus Christ! My pipes were always good and solid . . . At sixty-six, I'm still as much of a man as I was at twenty."

Last night he was rambling on like that, sitting up in his bed in spite of his worn-out lungs. His eyes bright with fever, he took advantage of the orderly's absence to give joyful reign to his voice as in the good old days. For nearly three years now he hadn't tasted the rare joy of talking out loud.

He went at it to his heart's content, without suspecting that he would die of it in a few hours. Little George's raucous laughter egged him on. He was saying:

"I fought at Beaugency, on the Loire, with Chanzy . . . in the snow, nothing to eat, with holes in our shoes and frozen breechloaders that burned in our hands . . . I lived through that. We were men, all right!"

He was still full of burning energy. The sweat glittered on his forehead. They got him to tell his story, the story of a tired old worker who could no longer keep up at the factory. "The foreman had it in for me, you see. He didn't want any old men in his shop. I get called into the office, they tell me politely: 'Here's a hundred francs, my friend, try to find a nice light job more in line with your strength.' A clerk was pushing me gently toward the door: 'Think about it, M. Vincent. You'll certainly find something else. Our work isn't made for men of your age, I'm sure you understand. You're such a sensible fellow.' I didn't understand anything. Out in the street—I can still see that street corner, the tobacco shop, the mailbox, as if I were standing there now—I suddenly understood that they were showing me the door, after sweating for twenty-seven years. Right away I thought of killing that bastard of a foreman. I went to buy a revolver."

Life was still in him then. Now Vincent's hairy chest is filled with mucous phlegm he can't even spit up. He struggles, coughs spasmodically, vomits into his spittoon. He's had it; he's turning green. His dark, flaring nostrils can no longer get enough air. Was it really worth it to fight at Beaugency, to accept hunger, cold, love, hard work, valiantly, all these long years, only to come to this sorry hour? Madré, mulling over such thoughts, shakes his head as he stands by the window, cooking for himself an appetizing stew: potatoes in onion gravy. Old Vincent is no longer thinking. His face ashen, his mouth drawn, his swollen brows dripping with cold sweat, his eyes closed, he gasps painfully for his last breaths of air. His chest gives out a continuous rattle, and you can hear the phlegm that's choking him rumbling in his throat. The white room is full of that rasping noise and his spasmodic breathing . . .

The guard on duty has come in, cocky, in a white smock, his *képi* pulled down over one eye.

"Well, well, Pop Vincent's kicking the bucket!" he said aloud (perhaps Vincent even heard him). "Better put a screen in front of his bed."

Thiébaut, the orderly, came in to set up a screen around his bedstead, and from every bed, every head turned that way.

"Rrr . . . rrr . . . Ouf! . . . rrr . . ."

This incessant moaning gets louder and louder, its rhythm monotonous. You get used to it. Little George is playing checkers with Madré. Van Hoever is conversing in a low voice with Gobin, the notary.

Madré came over to me a few minutes ago, his mouth twisted in a sickly smile, and said:

"You see that yellow-skinned old hayseed in Number 15? That's Van Hoever, the male virgin—to hear him tell it—really a filthy bastard! The old bigot used to sweep out his village church every Sunday morning, and killed his neighbor's wife because of a quarrel over a boundary wall . . . I hope to see him leave here one of these fine days, feet first . . . If it were only up to me . . ."

He made an "O" with his lips, went "pfuii" gleefully and significantly, then explained: "A fag like that!"

Within this old body, within this old shyster's prison-hardened soul, the little hatreds built up every day, spewed forth in venomous words and gestures as petty as pinpricks, but unceasing. And yet he had his good side, the kindness and loyalty of an old-timer who has seen plenty of hard times. Was he ashamed before my silent disapproval? His tone of voice changed:

"That other fellow, Number 17, that's poor old Gobin the notary, a nice old fellow . . . Just like all the others, by God!—ran off with the cashbox. But it didn't work out for him; he didn't have the temperament. The gentleman, you see, had the soul of an honest man. It's not his fault. So there he is, three more years to do, rheumatism, arthritis, gout, anemia, the whole works! And three months to live . . . The Chief Guard had it in for him on account of an old complaint he once made, and that cut his time-off-for-good-behavior in half. You'll see what a farce it is. He can't eat anything but eggs and milk, which they steal from him. So he's dying from hunger along with everything else . . . And the best of it is that neither of them thinks about anything but their release . . . They watch the others drop dead one by one, overjoyed each time it isn't them . . . That's humanity for you."

Madré began to laugh a stifled little laugh, which made his whole crippled body shake and sent thousands of little wrinkles running around his eyes. Perhaps his thoughts, running ahead of his words, had already settled on some more genuinely cheerful image, for he added, with a wry, gluttonous expression:

"Listen! That old rascal of a notary has two little nieces . . . Wow! Lemme tell you . . . one blonde, one brunette, eighteen, twenty years old, all white, pink, and perfumed, with ruffles . . . They come to visit him, you'll see . . . What tits, what gams, a little wiggle like that when they walk, and little red cheeks like apples . . . Those cheeks, you know, they always made me think of little buttocks just small enough to hold one in each hand . . ."

Over in the corner Van Hoever, Number 15, was racked by a coughing fit. Then he spat for a long time, looking like a broken china gargoyle, his chest fallen in. Gobin turned over laboriously in his bed and bit his lips, probably to avoid groaning. Then the two old men looked at each other. You could hear them picking up the train of their conversation: "He's a bastard," said Van Hoever, whose voice was no more than a whisper. "Just let him croak, that's what I say . . ."

Madré, sticking to his idea, concluded:

"Because, my friend, I'm nothing but an old swine myself. That's the truth, by God!"

A ray of sunlight falls across the window, lighting up the white morning. Little George's hoarse laughter cuts across the dying man's rattle and mingles with it for a moment.

Now that Old Vincent is dying, he has visitors. It seems that a man becomes more interesting before departing. Until now, they didn't pay any attention to him except to punish him; he was never anything more than Number 5231, condemned for ten years. Now that he's dying he has become a human being again.

The room is immobilized. Not a whisper rises from the beds. Madré moves in the background, silent, his eyes lowered, arranging pillows and quilts. The two old men across the way are like two long-dead, dried-out wax figurines. Then comes the sound of self-assured, authoritarian voices. The stout Chief Guard, yellow-skinned from a fever brought back from the colonies, with a bristling mustache and black-and-silver braid running from his cuff to his shoulder, makes his entrance. Then His Honor the Civilian Controller, in a bottle-green overcoat, his hands behind his back, holding a notebook. Under his *képi* he has a little pimply face with rimless glasses. And his eyes, also bottle-green, seem watery. The guard-cum-orderly, known as "Top Kick," follows respectfully, three paces to the rear. We can hear him explaining that this is Vincent, Augustin, and that Vincent, Augustin, is dying.

These gentlemen look at Vincent, Augustin. Can he feel their cold glances falling on his face (where the blood now comes only in rare little spurts), cold glances which see nothing of his pain and misery? His eyes open again. For an instant his pupils are intensely alive. The screen, the uniforms, the white room with, a ray of sunlight clinging to the ceiling, he takes it all in . . . A murmur stirs his lips. But nothing is heard, nothing but the rattle in his phlegm-choked throat.

"Yes, yes," says His Honor the Civilian Controller.

And they leave. An infinite silence falls over Old Vincent. A few more thoughts still wander through his slowly darkening brain. For three years now these people have been watching him die with the same indifference.

Another visitor. The Chaplain, a canon who has come to the prison to replace a young priest sent to the front, moves rapidly on his short legs toward the dying man's bed. The Canon has a kind, decent face, with distinguished, graying temples. His whole person (full, pink, well-shaven face, sharply chiseled mouth, sensual and aristocratic), from his face to the slightest details of his clothing (starched clerical collar and purple ribbon), exudes cleanliness, contentment, and the easy comfort of a well-fed man on whose shoulders life has placed neither fatigue nor undue burden. ". . . My good fellow, my good fellow," he greets us right and left, with a quiet smile. In front of Old Vincent's bed, the Canon lapses into meditation. The man seems to have lost consciousness.

"Ah, Canon!" Van Hoever calls out timidly.

From the depths of his sleep, the dying man no doubt hears the noise and the voices. Why have they come to bother him now? The Canon never thought about Old Vincent when he was dying of hunger, when they gave him five days on bread and water, when he went for six months without a word from his son, alone in the world like an old tree which has fallen, unheeded, beside the road. A last storm gathers in the soul of the old man who fought at Beaugency, worked hard for fifty-one years, and suffered for three years in prison without ever finding any Christian charity . . . The orderly says:

"Canon, I think he's coming to. Look, his eyes are moving."

Yes, his eyes are moving and he is coming back to life, from far away, from that limbo into which his mind was already sinking: So they can't even let him die in peace? The black Cossack offends him and, from the depths his early youth a rage awakens within him. As a child, in the days of anticlericalism, he used to run after priests and vent his spite at them: "Caw, Caw, the crows!" For they are fat and black and don't do any work; they feed off the misery of the poor, to whom they promise paradise at the final agony . . . Is this one going to take Pop Vincent for an idiot now?

Pop Vincent looks up. Then he raises his great gnarled hand, already feeble with death. You can see he is trying to speak; he makes a great effort. His hand rises, becomes a fist: his face convulses, and with a grimace of hate he raises himself up to cry:

"Goddamn you, goddamn you . . ."

Nothing more. Pop Vincent lapses into his coma. But there was so much fury trembling in his gurgling throat, burning in his flickering eyes, that the Canon gets the message. He turns away with dignity and says:

"He is delirious. There is nothing more I can do, my poor friend."

How pained he looks as he says it! You'd really think it does something to him to see Old Vincent die—Old Vincent whom he doesn't know and who is probably his five-hundredth dead man. His elegant hand traces a vague sign of the cross in the air over the dying man. Thiébaut, the orderly, put on a sorrowful face too, and the two of them stare at each other, as solemn as judges, without smiling.

"And my stew is going to be all burnt now!" thinks Thiébaut, scratching his red nose.

THIRTY

Surviving

OLD VINCENT PASSED ON A FEW HOURS LATER.

Madré was telling dirty stories to Little George. Zetti was eating some soup, making annoying little noises with his tongue and lips. The orderly, at the back of the room, was writing at a little black desk. The sky was growing red. Imperceptibly, without a crisis, the rattle grew quieter and quieter, then ceased. Only Van Hoever, whose shriveled, old man's soul trembled ceaselessly at the intuition of death, understood right away. But at first he didn't dare say anything; his eyes opened wide, full of mortal terror.

At dusk, just before the lights were turned on, Van Hoever suddenly felt all alone in the cheerless room, alone with those who dozed, with the Perpetual Sleeper (Number 4627), and with the dead man. The old peasant's eyes searched into every corner of the room. Slowly, with precaution, holding in his already feeble breath, he began to move. His old, dried-up arms—all yellowed and covered with a layer of dirt—pushed aside the stale-smelling sheets. He got out of bed, barefoot, huddling against the chilly air and cold floor. He took a few steps, terribly embarrassed at first in his nightshirt and drawers, and tottering in the unaccustomed, upright position. Then, moving from bed to bed, supporting himself on their iron frames (but careful not to give himself away), Van Hoever slithered toward the dead man's bed. Surely the dead man had not been able to drink his milk since last night. The jug must still be there. "The milk, the milk" thought Van Hoever—"or else *he*'ll drink it, the filthy hunchback . . ." He grinned from hatred, fear, and greed. Ah, the milk! He had it at last; he had only to empty the jug. His face contorted in silent laughter.

But the sacrilege of his laughter before the dead man made him shudder. All he could see in the shadows was the pallor of that large, motionless face, and the dark mouth from which emanated an odor of damp earth. Van Hoever, old and shriveled himself, ready to start out on the same voyage, stared, fascinated by the attraction of the chilled corpse. Terror crept into his dying flesh, soon to be the same shade of green, as cold as a lifeless object. He stood there, terrified, his chin trembling, the jug of milk in his hand. Someone appeared:

"Thief! Thief! old vulture! Ah, I've caught you now, you old bastard, robbing the dead, stealing a dead man's milk, you old vulture! . . ."

Madré seemed to be shaking all over with rage. The two old men stared at each other, consumed by the same anger. They could not see their resemblance, although they were almost identical in their hideous scrawniness, enveloped by the same shadow. Insults rose to their sputtering lips, repressed by one out of fear, shouted by the other so as to rouse the whole room.

"Ha! I hope you choke on that milk!"

The whole room awoke from its lethargy to watch the old Fleming's terror-stricken retreat. He backed away, eyes dazed, moving from bed to bed without answering. He climbed back into his bed, rolled himself up in his covers, paralyzed with fear, hardly daring to stammer out: "Bastard, bastard," and his favorite peasant's insult: "Bum."

Madré ran up and stood over him, his arm pointing toward the dead man:

"Just wait a little, you old thief! You saw how he went off. He was a better man than you. Well, you're going to go too, you can take my word for it. Right here, in your smelly sheets, behind the screen, yeah, and soon, too! You'll be just like him, only uglier, with your hen's ass of a mouth . . ."

The superstitious Van Hoever trembled under that curse. A strange coldness crept into his bones. The memory of sorcerers who make animals die without anyone knowing how, who set fire to haystacks invisibly, and bring evil down on farms where the master has sinned, increased his terror. Madré went on and on; his seething anger against men and the world, repressed for so long, now overflowed in a torrent of furious language:

"Die! Die, you thief!"

The whole room, peopled by thieves and murderers, seemed to turn on the old rascal. Madré himself, carried away by his split personality, that of a once "honest" landlord, who had doubtless forgotten his own trespasses on other people's property.

"Die! And good riddance! Wait till he's three feet underground; then the old carrion won't plague us anymore . . ." The sinister words circled among the beds, where pale sick men listened with abject smiles. The cold wind of death blew on them all. Van Hoever, in the lengthening shadows, raised his shriveled right hand and crossed himself slowly. Now he was stammering: "Holy Mary, Mother of God . . . ," unable to recall the rest of the prayer in his addled brain. His face was like dirty old ivory.

Madré took away the milk. And it was he who got to drink it.

Old Vincent had regained such a simple serenity that nothing of the weariness of his sixty years remained on his wrinkled face. His slack mouth, half-open over his yellow teeth, seemed to be laughing feebly. His eyes were almost closed (although no one had taken the trouble to lower their lids) as if he disdained to see. Even his paleness had become a neutral color, serenely indifferent.

They came for Old Vincent's remains in the evening, after supper. The body, brusquely uncovered, appeared pale, gray, hairy, pressing strangely into the mattress as if it had become very heavy. The big feet stood out; the toes were spread apart and stiffened, probably by a last convulsion. The penis, a fat worm of limp flesh stretched out in its dark bush, inspired pity . . . The belly stuck out too far; the enlarged chest seemed swollen. The limp neck was creased by thousands of wrinkles; the head, hung heavily to one side, mouth gaping, eyes not quite closed, yellow, cold, heavy as stone.

"Is that it?" asked fat Ribotte.

He was breathing noisily. He bent his fat, pale face—the face of a potato-stuffed peasant—over the dead man's head for a second.

"That's it."

Then they lifted up the body by the feet and shoulders and laid it out in an old, piss-stained bedsheet spread right on the floor. The dead man's head and elbows hit the wood hard.

"Doesn't matter," declared Madré. "He don't feel it anymore. Come on."

They folded the arms of the man who didn't feel it anymore and closed the sheet over his face. There was nothing left but a long, bumpy shape stretched out in the whiteness of the shroud. But at that moment a cry rang out, a kind of wild moan. Zetti, his face covered by his hands, bolted toward the other end of the room. Like an epidemic, his terror passed from one man to the next. The two orderlies and Madré, who were bending over, their hands ready to take up the body and carry it away, stood up trembling. And all they saw in the room were two heads drawn together by the same sense of horror, two bloodless, already cadaverous old men's heads with eyes staring out in terror . . . It was only for a second. The dead man was carried off. Voices were heard. Someone even laughed. The terror stayed only with a few; but these it filled with an enormous shadow of despair.

"You scared?" Little George asked Zetti.

Gently, he pulled Zetti's hands away from his eyes, so he could see that fear whose cold breath reached out to touch him.

"You're crazy! What are you scared of the dead for? It's all over for them; and as for him, he lived out his time, didn't he? It was his turn, not ours, right? Old folks, they just gotta die."

"*Si, si!*" the Italian was at last able to say, calmed by that soft young voice.

But across the way, in beds 15 and 17, the two old men shriveled up when they heard those same words: "Old folks, they just gotta die." Van Hoever's eyes searched desperately for something. Now he remembered the little wooden crucifixes country people hang over their beds and toward which the prayers of the dying ascend. "Lord Jesus!" he said. And Gobin the notary, who hadn't prayed for twenty years, repeated involuntarily, his decrepit limbs growing heavy with cold and stillness: "Lord Jesus! . . ." Then, their voices in unison, one clear, the other low, almost inaudible:

"Have pity on us . . ."

THIRTY-ONE

Letters

NUMBER 4627 WAS A LONG BODY, COVERED UP TO HIS EYES, LYING PROSTRATE in almost perpetual slumber. No one could remember the name of this patient, who never spoke and hardly moved. He appeared once every night, like a phantom in his damp bedclothes, dragging himself very slowly from bed to bed toward the toilet. Then he went back to bed. He was dying, by inches, after six or seven years in prison. They used to imitate his nightly babblings, which ended in a comical murmur: "Ben-ben-ta-ti . . . ff."

The prison postman came through the room one evening, oblivious to the greedy looks which clung in the stack of opened letters in hand: "Alexis . . . Madré . . . Van Hoever . . . Poissonnier . . ."

They had to search for Poissonnier, unknown to his neighbors. They found him in bed 19, under Number 4627, the man who was always sleeping, the man who slept endlessly because that was his way of dying. Madré ran limping over to him.

"Hey! Sleepy! Wake up, I tell you! There's a letter for you!"

At last Number 4627 began to stir, showing a puffy face, spotted with tufts of beard, and bewildered eyes. "Poissonnier, yes, yes, that's me . . . here!"

"O.K., you shoulda said so!" said the guard, without any malice, handing-him a yellow envelope.

The postman wiped his tobacco-flecked mustache with the back of his hand. He stood there for another half-minute, set strangely apart. We saw his ruddy, wrinkled little face, his lopsided shoulders, the metal buttons on his yellow-braided tunic; then he became invisible. Only the letters still existed, as if the ignorant and insignificant hands that had handled them, carried them, delivered them, had completely disappeared.

Number 4627 fell back into his perpetual slumber. Madré had to use force to keep him up.

"Come on, do you want me to read you your letter, yes or no?"

Immensely discouraged, he answered "yes," just to be left in peace again.

"All right. Now listen. Don't fall asleep, eh?"

Number 4627 stared stupidly at the letter. His mouth continued to hang open in a sort of drawn-out, unfinished gasp.

"Listen. It's from your wife. Poissonnier spouse, Therese, *née* Michon."

Something of these words must have reached the patient through the veil of lethargy and sleep. His swollen face twisted in an effort of attention: "My . . . my . . . my . . . wife," he mumbled, and he seemed a little bit more awake. Could he understand that "his little Marcel, who had just turned nine, sent him a big kiss?" That his eldest, Marie, was becoming an apprentice and that they both were thinking about their father, who had been away on a trip for so long (in the colonies) and that they were always asking when he would return?

"Sunday night Marcel asked me: 'Tell me, Mama, what will Father bring me when he comes home?' My poor man, I was completely undone . . ." These words could be heard throughout the room. We thought we had heard the child's own voice. Did he understand, Number 4627, with his vague, sleepy stare, that he would never return from that long voyage?

"Did you understand?" said Madré when he had put the letter back in the envelope.

The man shook his head.

"Yes, yes, leave me in peace, let me sleep. Who are these children calling me, and this woman? We are no longer part of the same universe."

He made a face and slid under his bedclothes.

The letters were tiny wings beating in the hands of the men. Each one had its soul, its character, its voice. This one, on fine paper with a sober Chamber of Deputies letterhead, contained only a trite word of acknowledgment (typewritten) which probably cost its recipient five hundred francs. And Van Hoever reckoned up the enormity of the sum which made this bit of paper, with its flamboyant signature, precious: "If he would only do something for me! If he only would!"—this personage who had to be paid so much. A wild hope swelled within the old peasant's heart.

This other, which Madré was reading, came from an extremely old grandmother, spry at ninety-three, whose trembling hand revealed her fear of no longer being around when her "little one"—already nearly an old man—came home. He could visualize her in her black lace cap, raising her eyes, still lively, to him and saying "M'boy" in her peasant accent. He was touched. His grin faded. And as he lost his sly smile he seemed to grow older, to become apelike, a faun without his crown of laughter.

Thiébaut moved his lips as he pored over his letter. A sharp-featured patient had taken refuge near the window and stood staring out across the lilac-colored paper. At the bottom of the page, which was covered with large, uneven writing, there was:

"My darling, I love you. —Simone."

And at that moment, that prisoner felt invulnerable, like someone wearing a talisman.

That large handwriting, offering him a cup of fortifying wine across the distance of years, laid bare a woman's love on the page, initialed by the prison postmaster with a blue-penciled V.

"You can stand anything when you love somebody the way I love you. I know that nothing, nothing can untie that knot that has been tied between us! Suffering is nothing. Dream of me. I am yours and I love you. I tell you so every night, at the times when I know you are thinking of me. There is nothing but you, there is nothing but me, *us*. Love me, wait for me. Come to me . . . A day will come . . ."

He answered:

"Yes, Simone."

This rapture lifted him above his misery. The window offered him a fairly wide view. He stood there for hours, motionless, contemplating a corner of the world. A *quai*-side corner. The river's lusterless surface, with its faint reflections; the towpath with a few tufts of green, a length of wall, a shuttered window. The house was silent. The deserted *quai* seemed silent: But people passed by from time to time. They were unaware that someone followed their steps, and that long after they had passed he still saw them. A little blond girl in a black coat. A workman carrying a toolbox slung over his shoulder. A man on a bicycle, a team of mules. Barges towed by sluggish, black tugboats, of which only the smokestacks were visible. The landscapes unfolded under the sailors' eyes.

The man who gazed out, having been so close to death, was joyful at his own survival. He felt generous, oblivious, selfish, naïve, heroic, poetic.

"Little girl, little girl," he murmured.

The little girl had gone away. A washer woman came and kneeled at the edge of the water. Her bare arms moved rhythmically, and it was good to imagine her regular breathing. From a distance, that female form, at moments, became very beautiful.

From the nearest windows of the stockade cell block rose a cry of lamentation, muted at first, then suddenly frenzied with despair. The dreamer, his head pressed against the bars, imagined he caught a glimpse of a man inside a dark, cavernlike cell, a man in a ragged tunic, head, shaved, shoulders hunched, hands held in the vice of irons, a man crying out his anguish in pain and humiliation, like a beast at the slaughter. Latruffe, pointed snout and drooling mouth, was doubt-less working him over placidly with his keys, insulting him in his little eunuch's voice, stuttering like a clown. A sharper, louder cry brusquely broke the silence.

Ribotte, the fourth-floor orderly, came running in. The sandals on his bare feet went "flap-flap" across the floor. The whole room heard him calling Thiébaut:

"Come quick. Perchot's dying. And What's-his-name is coughing up blood."

"Who's that?" growled Thiébaut.

From bed to bed, these few words passed through the room:

"Perchot's dying."

But we were all right, nonetheless.

THIRTY-TWO

More Deaths

PERCHOT DID NOT DIE THAT EVENING, BUT ON ANOTHER EVENING A FEW DAYS later.

On the fourth floor of the infirmary there were two rows of light-green cells set aside for patients who had to be isolated, with contagious or chronic diseases, or had been placed under special surveillance.

Cell Number 2, closed off by a glass-paneled door, had an outside view. All of the space was taken up by a large, low bed, piled high with covers and clothing. The patient's body was practically invisible, sunk into the hollow place where he had been lying for months. The bed seemed to swallow up the man. Only the head emerged, propped up by bolsters, facing tenaciously toward the window. The sharp angles of bone under the emaciated skin already suggested a death mask: the smooth, high brow of a twenty-year-old, cheeks sunken under a faint growth of beard, but lips that were strikingly red and revealed white teeth frozen in a wide grin. Whatever strength the sick man had left was concentrated in his glowing, watchful eyes.

That morning, after a terrible night—two hours of unconsciousness followed by dull sleep—Perchot half-opened his eyes without entirely emerging from his dream. His side was hurting him. The tops of the poplars swayed from side to side in the distance. White clouds floated across the sky. Catherine was walking across the barnyard in wooden shoes, her arms bare. Chickens were pecking at the ground near the manure pit. A stale smell of rotting straw floated in the warm air where flies were buzzing. Father was calling: "Zidore, Zidore!" The dying Perchot relived these dead things as he heard voices drifting around him. What were they talking about? Catherine went into the kitchen; Maraud, the old, one-eyed watchdog, stretched himself out in front of his kennel . . .

"The doctor said he wouldn't live through the night. Morphine . . . Yesterday, Top Kick gave him a chocolate bar. Better wake him up; I haven't the time. Get the syringe ready."

"Perchot! Perchot! Boy, can he sleep! Perchot!"

Perchot came out of oblivion. The orderly, Ribotte, was pulling back his covers. A new man was attentively filling a hypodermic syringe. The sick man gazed at the steel needle with indifference. The injections no longer hurt him. But the man holding the syringe turned a thin face lit by gentle gray eyes toward him. He said nothing, he propped up the pillow, he folded the clothes thrown on the foot of the bed while the orderly gave the injection.

Perchot wanted to say something to those strangely solicitous eyes:

"Thanks, thanks," he mumbled. "That feels good. It's good medicine, that . . . I have the feeling it's going to save me. Anyway, I've been better for the last three days. The pain has gone away . . ."

Realizing that he was lying too much, he added:

"Last night was only a weak spell. Isn't that so, Ribotte?"

"Sure!"

Ribotte wrote something down in his notebook.

"Yes, you're much better," said the new man at last. "I'll bring you a little coffee: Would you like that?"

Ribotte went out. They were alone. These two men had never spoken to each other before, yet there was an understanding between them. The visitor bent over close enough so that the sick man could speak into his ear without raising his voice.

"I'm going to tell you the truth . . . I heard you talking; I won't live through the night; I can feel it myself. My feet are dead already . . . I can't move my arms anymore . . . I'm finished; that stuff, it puts me to sleep . . . It's horrible! I can't take it anymore."

Tell a lie? The other man didn't have the strength.

"Be quiet. Don't tire yourself out. Don't be afraid."

But both of them were afraid. They read disturbing thoughts in the other's eyes. You are going to die. You are going to live. It can't be helped. It was a moment of silent clarity, in spite of everything. And Perchot felt better. Those eyes meeting his did him good.

"Come back again, come back again," he said, with supplication in his voice. He gazed longingly at that stranger, whose presence somehow reconciled him to the thought of death.

A soft light hovered in the corridor between the two rows of glassed-in doors. It was like being on an ocean liner.

"In Number 4, Old Horta. In Number 6, Father Nicot, the priest. In Number 8, Ollivier. The cells on the other side are empty . . . But the first one is where Miss Roberta died, you know."

The cool air, full of the sound of chirping birds, swept gaily in through the open window. The *quais* and the prison wall seemed bathed in sunlight. The cell, freshly painted, was almost attractive. Ribotte—full of broad smiles, sly little laughs and winks talked about this strange dead man in his thick voice:

"His body was something to look at! Slender as a sixteen-year-old girl. With hips like a regular little woman. And eyes! You wouldn't believe me, but when he was tucked in bed, just looking at his eyes, it made you think of a woman. He was gentle, a real liar, and bitchy when he had it in for somebody, just like a woman. I sometimes used to watch him through the glass in the door: When he was all alone he would curl his hair, pluck his eyebrows, look at himself in a little mirror . . . What faces he made! He would smile, sulk, put on airs, or pout; he used to blow himself kisses and make goo-goo eyes at himself . . . On his good days, he would stand by the window, all afternoon, humming:

> . . . *Amoureuse,*
> *Langoureuse,*
> *La berceuse des amants* . . .

"In the end, just to please him, I got him a lipstick and some powder. He used to make himself up. His mouth looked like a bright red carnation . . . And not a bit afraid of dying, braver than any man, singing 'Fouti-foutu, fouti-foutu' after his attacks of fever; and, when I tried to cheer him up, he answered me: 'Pull through three more years? Who are you kidding? Save your fairy tales . . . But if you want to be nice, tell Coco to come and see me . . .'"

Coco was a young banker, just arrived, in for five years. His wife bombarded half a dozen senators with requests to have him certified consumptive. They finally put him in Number 7, just to make her stop. A tall flabby fellow, who used to do his nails for an hour every morning with special brushes made for him in the workshop. Miss Roberta couldn't get up anymore; she had abscesses in her knees, her thighs, her back; her bones were all rotten, bleeding, full of holes; some days it hurt her so much she would faint. But her arms, her chest and her head were still alive, and that was enough for their love. I saw her—all made up, lips like cherries, white cheeks, languorous eyes—suddenly turn pale, her face distorted with pain. I gave her injections. Coco would come and sit on the edge of her bed; and they would kiss and caress all the time. She was like a little woman who is always sick in bed, and makes everyone look after her . . . He, I don't know what attracted him."

"He . . . I mean *she*, she died?"

"She died. Before she lost consciousness, she said to him again, half-delirious: 'My darling, my little one, don't forget me . . . don't forget me . . . We really loved each other, eh?' Then it was all over. She began to moan and didn't recognize anybody . . . It was just about this time of day, a day like today. You know me, I'm not one of the Boys. They disgust me. They're not real men, they're perverts, dirty perverts. But at that moment I felt pity, I could have cried . . . And then, I'll never stop feeling that deep down, that kid was a woman."

Perchot died at dusk, after a rainshower. Streaks of silver flowed in the river.

Perchot was too weak to cry out. His head—freezing after the burning fever—rolled from side to side on the pillow. There was no life left except in his eyes, where a spark of consciousness still flickered, another tiny flame about to go out.

Ollivier was waiting in the next cell, which was empty. Quick muffled footsteps pattered down the corridor, hurrying past the dying man's closed cell. Ollivier smiled. The door opened noiselessly. Ollivier turned around, his arms outstretched.

"Good evening, dear."

Little George entered, out of breath, his cheeks flushed, his denim tunic floating around his thin shoulders, as fragile as a sapling that will snap in the first storm.

"I really ran. I was scared coming up the stairs. I thought the 'screw' was coming. What a fright!"

They met here every evening, the stooped man and the adolescent who had neither past nor future. They talked quietly together. They sat together in silence. One talked about life, about which he knew everything, as if he were telling a story. The other listened, not really understanding, to that penetrating voice, unlike any voice he had ever heard. Sometimes they held each other close, in the shadows, gazing at each other, at a loss for words. Ollivier waited for that moment when Little George's eyes—slightly off-center, and dark as a pond full of reflections—lost all trace of their normal expression; when his colorless lips became the only sign in that proffered face. The door swung open.

"Beat it, quick!" whispered Ribotte. "Perchot just kicked off."

The guard came upstairs. He touched Perchot's stone-cold forehead and said:

"O.K. Nothing to do until tomorrow. No need to call the doctor . . . The death certificate has been ready since yesterday."

The profile of the guard (the one they call "Top Kick") is sharply silhouetted for an instant against the gray background of the window: comical jutting jaw, bushy mustache, *képi* visor slanting down. He leaves. The dead man remains, his eyes open, empty, and transparent like funeral lights waiting to be lit . . .

I knew Perchot rather well. It was hard for me to recognize him in that emaciated mask. It had been a long time since anyone could have recognized in him the strapping farmboy who had entered a bordello one drunken Sunday. Afterwards he had never been able to understand what had gone on inside of him while he was lying on that passive, indifferent female, who suddenly awoke in fright to discover fixed upon her his wild, hard, inflamed eyes. Later, when they showed him the mangled breasts and belly and he saw his pocketknife red to the hilt with shreds of flesh clinging to the handle, he could hardly grasp what had happened. "What did you do that for?" they asked him. He answered: "I don't know. I still can't believe I did it." Nothing now remained in that white, bony head of the young man's fleshy lips. For years all trace had disappeared, in that inoffensive young lad, of the passionate brute who had murdered. Perchot was paying for an ancestor's crime.

THIRTY-THREE

The Innocent

CELL NUMBER 4. HORTA.

This octogenarian, whose heavy flaccid jowls hung down over his wrinkled neck, had whiskers all over his face, which gave him a pale, bristly look. He used to cock his head to one side and stare out of the corner of one eye, keeping his weaker left eye closed. This gave him the air of having only one huge, metallic, cold-blue eye, through which he stared out at people in hatred. For eight years now the prison had held him in its grip; fiercely bent on survival, his endurance baffled doctors, guards, and attendants, in whom that obstinate eye had at last inspired a kind of terror. Remarried at the age of seventy after living the life of a corsair, tossed between palaces on the Riviera and cells in the Milan penitentiary; legend had turned him into something of a villainous old Borgia, pouring a phial of poison into his young bride's tea. The crime, committed with the skill of an artist, remained in doubt. In the dock, Horta shook his white mane, hurled invective at his judges, railed bitterly at the prosecutor, raised toward the crowd the vigorous hand of a prophet, and cried out in a tragic voice:

"Woe unto you! May my blood bring retribution on you all! I am innocent! Innocent! Innocent!"

Nothing—neither the years in prison, crushing this old man under the weight of a life sentence, the dungeons, the hunger, nor even the illness that had chained him to this bed for the last forty months—nothing had silenced that voice of vengeance. His metallic eye cast the same dagger-glint; his wrathful voice, now hoarse, flung the same furious protest at all who approached him. (And yet in the depths of that cold eye a certain unease betrayed his guilt.) The whole infirmary called him "The Poisoner."

"I'm out of paper," he said to Ribotte. "Ask the Warden for some more immediately. I still have thirty pages to write."

He pulled out a stack of manuscripts, covered with corrections, from under the sheets.

"O.K., O.K.," said Ribotte. "Right away. Only don't tire yourself out writing too much, eh?"

Horta caught a glimpse of me through the half-opened door. With the dignity of an old caged lion he raised his great, heavy body.

"Eight years! For eight years now I haven't got tired! You, the new man! Ninety-six months, two thousand nine hundred and forty-five days . . ."

The words, the numbers, had lost all meaning.

"How long are you in for? Ten years? For me, it's forever, do you understand, forever! . . . The grave. If I live for a century it will still be the same, do you understand?"

He rarely spoke this much, weary of seeing the same faces every day; of feeling his cries fading into the general indifference and—worse than death—feeling his own inability to move the souls of others. But, as he glared at the, his blue eye hardened, his voice rang out with conviction:

"Listen! I don't know who you are. It doesn't matter. Don't ever forget what you have seen, you who are young . . . I am seventy-eight years old. They have been torturing me for eight years, and I'm alive, alive! And every day I shout at them: You have condemned an innocent man! . . . me, I'm innocent! Perhaps you have murdered or robbed, eh? Me, I'm innocent! Innocent! Innocent!"

"Be quiet," said Ribotte. "They'll hear you."

He seemed to lose track of himself. With enormous effort, he sat straight up in his bed. This movement made him wince, for his disease had immobilized both his knees, swathed in bandages, for the past three years:

"Me? Be quiet? Let 'em hear, let 'em hear! Murderers!"

The silent *quai* under the tall, green poplars, the shimmering water where trees trembled in reflection among patches of sky, the path along the bank where a child was running: This peaceful vision of life, glimpsed suddenly through the window, calmed him.

"I'm finishing my brief," he said. "Thirty pages more. This time I haven't left anything out" (the blue eye glittered with pride once again). "My innocence is proven ten times over."

The manuscripts piled up under his hand, close-written line upon line, quite legible, crisscrossed with references and ironical or emphatic exclamation points. Factual arguments—discussed, analyzed, reduced to irrefutable syllogisms—analogies, artfully exploited inductions, brilliant dialectics, subtle, specious arguments which suddenly ensnared the unwary mind like a net, made this a strange and powerful book; and this man must, really have believed at times that his book—which no one would ever read—could and would destroy what he had doubtless never been able to extinguish entirely in himself: memory.

Perhaps even at the very moment when, terrible as an avenger, he thundered his innocence, an image still haunted his brain: his hands calmly uncorking a little octagonal phial and pouring a few colorless drops into the tea, steaming next to a little Japanese ashtray. The young bride came in, resembling one of the white birds gliding across her kimono, golden hair hanging over her temples. Absent-mindedly, she asked, in English:

"How are you today, my dear?"

He watched her sip the amber tea which would snuff out the light in her eyes. The wide falling sleeve of the kimono revealed one delicate bare arm, up to her shoulder.

A thin partition separated Horta from *Abbé* Nicot, a skinny little man, long emasculated by chastity, worn down by a narrow little existence in a provincial vicarage. White-haired at fifty, mouth drawn tight in senility over rotting teeth, low forehead lined with deep wrinkles. Rain-gray eyes, always a little frightened, behind his rimless glasses. Always very neat, retaining a sort of propriety in his prisoner's uniform, he was pitiful and helpless, overwhelmed, submissive, humble, defeated without knowing why.

Every morning, before the attendant got up, sure of not being observed, *Abbé* Nicot would kneel on the floor, join together his tiny, manicured, old lady's hands, close his eyes, and, in the silence of his cell, alone in the world, pray. Then his chest would heave a deep sigh as he returned to his usual view: the white sky through the bars on the window, the landscape of tall poplars, the books on their shelf.

When he thought of his seventeenth-century Latin Bible, bound in buff leather and bearing the signature "Joseph Tommasi, Dauffmann, Dordrecht, Anno Domini 1685," of his breviaries which he had kept since adolescence and which reminded him of the great seminary courtyard, of his *History of the Holy Church* which he had read for ten years without exhausting it, *Abbé* Nicot felt his eyes growing moist. He owned a Bible yellowed by the touch of countless careless hands, a brand-new *Imitation of Christ* made even more vulgar by its pretentious boxing and the red outline on its tiny pages, and Bossuet's *Funeral Orations,* which had come to the prison from a convent library. And no one could imagine what phantasmagoric visions filled his cell at night! The saints, the elect, the martyrs, the blessed dead, the angels, Jesus haloed in silver, God himself at the dazzling summit, Hell with the endless cries of the damned, the dark and bestial Devil with his horned forehead, surrounded *Abbé* Nicot's puerile soul with endless enchantments. That was what gave him his absent expression, as if things only seemed only partially real to him.

"Good morning, *Abbé*!" said Ribotte, jovial. "The Devil didn't visit you last night, eh? old brother?"

The *Abbé* blushed in answering, flustered and embarrassed. "Good morning, Monsieur Ribotte. Always in high spirits?"

He didn't like the blasphemous joke about the Devil. Every one laughed at his simple faith. He used to tell his neighbor, Ollivier, who sometimes visited him in late afternoon: "They laugh at the Devil, and the Devil is waiting for them. No one escapes him, my friend, not one! I am sorry for them."

"How is Perchot?" he asked. "Did he spend a quiet night?"

"Perchot?" answered Ribotte. "Then you don't know he kicked off?"

The *Abbé* bit his lips. He had prayed for Perchot that night, he was hoping. But he said nothing, so as not to appear foolish.

When the attendant had left, the *Abbé* removed his spectacles, wiped them absent-mindedly on his big blue prisoner's handkerchief, and laid them on his Bible, which was opened to the prophecies of Isaiah. He quietly closed the glass door and cocked his ear for a moment: The footsteps were moving away. Then, his mind at ease, he sat down on his bed where he couldn't be seen through the glass door, and joined his hands. The sky's whiteness seemed to enter his myopic eyes. "Poor, poor Perchot!"

A sardonic apparition interrupted his meditation. Madré burst in on him, waggish, a feather duster in his hand. "Dusting" was a pretext for him to wander around the corridors. His old Pulchinello's greenish face mocked him in silence.

"Pax! Oh holier-than-holy Father of charlatans! And how's your itty-bitty health today? Still dreaming of them, eh? those pretty little girls? Go on! They'll be back! You'll see their pink little feet, their pink titties, their pretty little bottoms . . ."

How comical he was, that crestfallen little priest! Madré was laughing with all his might.

Impotent anger made the *Abbé's* lips tremble. He hissed like a furious cat.

"Don't get mad!" said Madré. "That would be a sin. I only dropped in to say hello."

In the old days the *Abbé* liked to entertain the parish children in his vicarage garden. He was hardly bigger than the tallest of his little girls or certain little boys with long bare legs. Sometimes he would hold a young head, with silky blond or dark curls, between his hands for a moment, the better to gaze at it; and his old hands would run gently down along those slender bodies, perhaps retaining in their caress some of the heat of the flesh which he had overcome so long ago. He had let them convict him almost without an argument, overwhelmed by the scandal and the damning, irrefutable accusation of the children.

"He's a nice old nut," Ribotte used to say. "But after all, what a dirty old pig!"

THIRTY-FOUR

The Voice of the Living

IN THE LITTLE INFIRMARY GARDEN, THE SUN HAS DRAWN TOGETHER EVERY-one who can move or be moved. The word "garden" is used here in its most perfunctory sense. A barren, circular pond, usually dry. Four stunted trees forming a square; four cropped bushes, in a diamond shape; four triangular grass plots separating the gravel paths where we hunt for the little white quartz pebbles, so velvet, so soft to the touch, so white that they bring to mind many forgotten things.

This could be the square of some mining village in the North. The survivors sitting here could be victims of the mine gas. After all, one form of suffocation is much like another. We are allowed to walk up and down these paths at will. Divine freedom of the body! We meet, we talk; divine freedom of the soul! The trees are no longer part of the motionless, abstract world of the round: They are real, accessible trees whose bark we love to touch, and on which we watch the ants climbing.

A skeletal young consumptive, half-hidden under his blankets, had been placed to one side on an old deck chair held together with string. Beneath a thin layer of skin, his skull smiles up at life's last sun. Not far off a broken old man, squatting on the ground, lifts a cracked, tooth-less face with red-rimmed eyes toward the sun. He sits there like a bit of debris. Tonnelier, known as "Chemin-des-Dames," is facing him. Expert surgeons, using a triangular silver plate, have patched up his skull, into which a piece of shrapnel bored a hole at Chemin-des-Dames. But three quarters of his intelligence seems to have run out through that hole. He's an idiot. Whatever you ask him, his thick-tongued answer always begins with "Chemin-des-Dames."

Madré, seated on the stone stoop in front of a door, breathes in the warm air. He looks like a Chinese gargoyle. His cheeks puff out one after the other, for he has taken up the habit of chewing tea leaves . . . Little George, with his pointed chin, looks as slender as an anemic, overworked young factory girl. On his arm is young Antoine des Tailleurs—"Toinette." Antoine's head is swathed in bandages; he has a chubby face with beautiful, full lips and long, velvety eyes like a Berber's. A man slashed open his forehead with a pair of scissors. The man is in the "hole": Toinette-Antoine has the blues "something awful." He and Little George walk arm in arm, talking quietly and confidentially like two young girls.

Abbé Nicot is trying to read. In the narrow garden path, cut sharply into sunshine and shade, the gravel crunches loudly under the feet of two men. Laurent, his face tattooed, his neck bandaged, is supporting Filot, the blind man, who walks along stiffly, tapping the ground with his cane. Filot has a strangely frozen face, which seems to be covered with a thin, dull film. His whole face moves in one piece; it is quite large, reddened in the cheeks and around the mouth. A reddish mustache makes an inverted V under his nose, stuck like a peg between two deep furrows. The eyes are glassy. Filot has been blind for two years; he went blind here. Doomed to total paralysis, his legs sometimes give way. He is eligible for parole in two months.

"I don't know what will become of me," he says. "I'll be dragging a paralytic carcass home to my old lady. Sometimes I'd like to put an end to the whole mess. But sometimes I tell myself that my legs are already getting better and that maybe there's hope . . ."

"We're just like lizards in the sun, eh, Father?" Laurent asks *Abbé* Nicot politely.

"Yes, yes," says the *Abbé* smiling. "We're really just like lizards . . . Sit down, Filot."

Filot sits down. It's not easy. Laurent and I have to give him a hand; his blindness and the stiffness of his legs have made him quite helpless. Once seated, Filot turns his dead eyes toward the sunlight. The Sun burns in a cloudless sky, and these sightless eyes are the only ones that can gaze full upon it.

"Feels good," says Filot.

I admire the industrious activity of the ants in the cracks of the pavement.

Madré calculates aloud:

"Perchot is only the twelfth this year. Last year at this time there were already seventeen."

Everyone understands that he is talking about deaths. Just above our heads, behind the half-open window, Number 4627 has entered his death throes.

Someone says:

"Prison is made to kill."

Filot, who has become a deep thinker since the death of his eyes, lets fall some weighty words:

"We are made to die."

That's his way of talking. He speaks only in general terms now. He says "we" as if he no longer wishes to isolate himself from the crowd, whose common suffering he has discovered through his long meditations in the darkness. His thought, in search of the larger truths, moves ponderously along like the leaden clouds of a November sky. When he gives voice to his thought, it seems to project patches of light and shadow.

"Don't we all die a little bit every day, from the first to the last?"

Madré calculates:

"With six hundred inmates, that makes nearly two years of human life every day; in a fortnight, thirty years, a man's life. Altogether, I figured out that we are doing something like three thousand five hundred years."

He bursts out laughing:

"Who wants to count the days?"

"We have plenty of men and plenty of days, all right!" says Laurent. "Just sitting here, what don't we have?"

His restless eyes, dark as murky water, run around our group, pleased to find here men from every kind of background, every kind of struggle, every kind of suffering. Filot raises his hand. We wait for his words. He declares:

"All men are here. Prison is made for all men."

He adds, as if confessing a secret:

"This I know."

And no one smiles.

"All men are here, and all crimes."

"First the thieves," said Madré. "Those who steal in the street, from shop windows; purse snatchers, pickpockets, hotel rats. Burglars: professionals and amateurs. Con men, swindlers, crooked stockbrokers, bigshots who go bankrupt in style. Forgers and fortune hunters. Dumb, half-starved beggars who smash shop windows. Highway robbers, who shake down countryfolk to find out where the loot is stashed. We have thieves, all right!"

"You can see," said someone, "that prisons are necessary!"

"It's too bad," Said Laurent, "that you forgot all the thieves who will never be here, all the ones who don't look like thieves and are the biggest thieves of all."

"Then the murderers. With all the blood they've spilled, you could paint a road from here to Paris . . ."

"With the blood the others have spilled, you could go around the world more than once, eh?"

"The assassins: the ones who kill old *rentiers* in their beds, or stab a fat passer-by near a vacant lot . . . The ones who wait for the bank boy to take out the day's receipts and knock him over the head . . . The ones who kill out of passion, the jealous ones, the mad lovers, the sadists who strangle whores . . . The abortionists . . . The poachers, the smugglers who "pick off" a cop. The unionized miners who want to flood the mines, like you, Thomas. The strikers who kill a scab . . . We have 'em, we have 'em! . . . The firebugs; your type, Citizen van Hoever; the ones who set fire to the store just before inventory . . . *Ah là, là!*"

"Prisons are necessary," some one else continued. "Prisons are necessary."

"I haven't finished," said Madré. "There are more. The pimps, the white slavers, the dirty old men who do nasty things to little girls, the ecclesiastics—I pronounced it right, didn't I, Father? We even have a lawyer who seduced a twelve-year-old kid. Ah, humanity! Beautiful humanity!"

He turned toward Thomas, the syndicalist miner:

"And, frankly, you're really something, getting yourself thrown into prison for God-knows-what, for God-knows-who, for a gang of brutal bastards they call men."

And, like the blind man a moment before, he added: "Me, I know them. I'm one of 'em!"

Van Hoever, glancing obliquely at Thomas, whispered to *Abbé* Nicot:

"They want you to share everything you have. Gotta be pitiless with them. It's not enough to send them to the islands where they couldn't escape . . . better . . ."

"You're right," the *Abbé* approved quietly. "They attack the social order."

The other old man didn't understand those words, but their gravity pleased him because he detected in them a more well-founded condemnation.

Laurent cried out:

"But how stupid can you get? Haven't you learned anything? You talk like the newspapers, like the cream of honest society that you are. Jerks! A bunch of jerks! Have you ever taken a good look at them, at the guys who judge us, who guard us, who go off and live in style in gay Paree? All of 'em, all, from the first to the last? Have you looked at them? Tell me?"

An answer came:

"Yeah, it's true. Like I once knew a judge who . . ."

"Take a look at the guards first . . ."

The blind man stood up, because the ray of sunlight had moved. He longed for its golden warmth. He could feel that the shadows had just reached him. His frozen face sought the light. You could see too, by something straining within him, that his mind sought the truth.

"You can blame it on bad luck."

The miner answered:

"Bad luck is only another name for poverty. And rich people make poverty."

I could hear Van Hoever grumbling: ". . . Pinko! Vermin! . . ."

"It's hopeless," spit out Laurent, with a thin stream of saliva that engulfed a few ants.

"There's nothing we can do," said Madré. "Prisons are the oldest things in the world."

Thiébaut, the orderly, ran across the foot of the garden. Before disappearing, he shouted to us:

"What's-his-name, upstairs, you know! He kicked off."

"It's hopeless," repeated Laurent sharply.

The miner seemed to be smiling, but he wasn't. There was a sharp edge in his voice:

"Let the dead bury their dead!"

Abbé Nicot turned his head quickly toward the man who had spoken the words of the Gospel.

"Hey, you're really funny," said Madré, mocking.

"Man used to live in caves. It's not so long ago since they burned heretics at the stake. Everything ends sometime. Prison will end someday. But men remain, men move on. The old structure is cracking. Perhaps only one good blow is needed before everything changes: It's worth living for, and maybe even dying for. When there is enough bread for everybody, no one will steal anymore. When women no longer sell themselves, when reason prevails, there will be fewer vices and fewer murders. Prison will be destroyed. People will come and stare at the stones that are left, and they won't be able to imagine what we are living through. They won't be able to conceive of our misery any more than we can conceive of their grandeur. Life will become large and free. It will . . ."

Pensively, his sad face turned toward the setting sun, the blind man answered:

"That is far off. Perhaps it's farther off than we know. But it's good to think about it. It's like being in the sun."

"It could begin tomorrow with a general strike."

Chemin-des-Dames, the idiot soldier with the hole in his head, was dancing around our group, staring at the miner in sullen anger. And he, who never spoke, began to shout:

"That's a lie! That's not true! That's not true! I know your phony speeches! You're a defeatist. There's a war on. Guys like you, we send 'em to the firing squad! To the firing squad, I tell you!"

THIRTY-FIVE

About to Be Discharged

IT'S OVER. THREE OF US ARE LEAVING TOMORROW. MY THREE MONTHS'
growth of hair already gives me more individuality than Number 6731
ought to have. Just now Latruffe opened the doors of the stockade cell
block for my last day and night of isolation. A last chance encounter, in
the corridor in front of the dark cells: Bernard (The Slicer) and Rouillon
(Mud Bath) both eligible for release a day after me.

"Are you glad?" I asked Bernard.

"Yes." (A pause) "I don't know."

We've known each other for years. He is an anarchist. His unimpres-
sive appearance—low forehead, narrow eyes, badly shaped features—
conceals an obsessive kind of will power at the service of a strangely
lucid, but unsteady mind. The sharpness of his logic used to make me
think of fine lacework stamped out by machine on low-grade paper. In
jail, Bernard was surrounded by feelings of respect, astonishment, and
secret scorn. In front of him, no one would have dared to pronounce
certain of the most ordinary words. In confinement, Bernard's flesh
had suffered, not more than anyone else's, but just as much. He, too,
had felt himself sliding into madness. The years were too slow, the flesh
too strong, the spirit too poorly armed. Bernard stole a pair of scissors
from the tailor shop. During the nights in his dormitory cell, he laboriously sharpened the two blades. This difficult work, which had to
be done noiselessly, under the covers, grinding the steel against some
pebbles, diverted him from his carnal hallucinations. When the scissors were ready, Bernard made himself—still in the workshop—some
gauze packing and some bandages sterilized in sublimate.

Then one morning he was seen coming out of the lavatory,
extremely pale, both red hands pressing a bandage against his groin,
from which blood was streaming. "I gave myself an operation," he told
the guard, "take me to the infirmary, quick." He tried to walk, but had

to be supported under the arms. At the door of the infirmary, Bernard had not yet lost consciousness: Noticing a cat, he went *psss, psss,* and tossed two shreds of grainy flesh onto the pavement. Cauliflower, the guard, picked this food up in his handkerchief. Bernard had nothing left under his penis but a horrible double gash, which had to be sewn up. The relics of his virility were placed in alcohol; and Ribotte put his new glass jar in the infirmary museum, next to another glass jar, fifteen years old, where a thick worm of gray flesh was hanging.

"Now we have the whole works!" said the infirmary guard known as "Top Kick." There was a whole male organ, in effect, in the two jars: a member and two glands. An inmate, a barber, had cut off his erect penis fifteen years before, with one fatal razor stroke.

We were waiting to be led to our cells for the final hours. Bernard said: "I think we were wrong."

We understand each other. He is thinking of the years, his six, my five, in the jail, of the mark that remains stamped on us. He concludes:

"Life isn't worth that. The most reasonable thing is to get yourself killed."

Mud Bath is jubilant. Merriment is written all over the hairy puss of this troglodyte-of-the-slums. I can hear him purring like a cat, then wagging his head back and forth and singing:

... *une moukère de Mers-el-Kébir,*
... *à Mas-ca-ra* ...

We had a minute alone together. Mud Bath poured his hot breath into my ear, whispering his boundless joy, ready to burst forth in thundering laughter, in yells, jumps, gesticulations.

"My time is up! I've done my six years. They can all go to hell now! And it's long live life! you hear!"

... *une moukère de Mers-el-Kébir,*
... *à Mas-ca-ra* ...

I was unaware that excessive joy could reduce the human beast to a sort of animal-like idiocy. Mud Bath can't find the words to express the gaiety running through his veins: There is only this refrain he picked up in some Algerian dive to the snapping of castanets, this refrain doubtless associated in his eyes with the vision of a woman's belly rhythmically heaving and twisting with the dance as if possessed by invisible demons.

One second, a flash: Mud Bath spreads his arms, throws out his chest, takes a tremendous breath, tensing all his muscles. I could hear his bones crackling. I could even feel the tension of his leg muscles. He emanates the magnetism of powerful, electrified flesh. When Latruffe turns around at the other end of the gallery, Mud Bath is standing stock-still, laughing silently. Once more he whispers:

"It's long live life, eh?"

Now that the guard standing a few feet away from us has his back turned, Mud Bath starts cracking his gorilla fingers—(take, squeeze, break; take, squeeze, break. It's good to be alive!)

We named him Mud Bath because his soul is sordid. Coming out of a conversation with him is like corning out of a mudhole. He never talked about anything but his "case," harping on the same filthy details for years; and his case was a disgusting one: At the end of a drunken spree, his "moll" invited a girlfriend to sleep in their bed. By dawn their frenzies had ended in vomiting, hair-pulling, jealous rage. "My moll must have stuck her at least twenty times with these scissors. She didn't know what she was doing. Me, I didn't do a thing. I was drunk, you see. All I said was: Leave her alone, you bitch, you can see she's blotto. Then I grabbed the other one by her mop and tossed her down the stairs. I swear I had no idea she was dead. You can see I'm innocent, can't you? And they sent me up for six years, the bastards!" The surviving girl is doing twenty years. But at last it's over. A cry of triumph surges up from the very bowels of this brute:

"Long live life!"

Bernard The Slicer and Mud Bath are returning to life with two hundred francs and five years' restricted residence each: enough to live on for six weeks and get sent back to jail for life.

THIRTY-SIX

The World Between

I AM SPENDING THIS LAST NIGHT IN A CELL, LYING ON A STRAW MATTRESS stretched out on the floor, my eyes open, staring into total darkness. I don't know if I have slept or not. I am stunned not to feel, at this dark threshold to life, the enormous joy one expects to feel. A sort of anxiety oppresses me. I am aware of my joy (like a fleeting light at the bottom of a well), only through negative logic: If it were not true, if I were to learn this instant that I would have to take up my place in the round again tomorrow, I would probably kill myself; in any case, the thing that I can most easily imagine after that "if" is the allurement of the third-floor dormitory railing and the flagstones swirling on the ground below; I am lulled by the dizzying prospect. Nothing is more disappointing than the long-awaited fulfillment of a wish: for the reality itself is too concrete and brings with it a certain calm. The exaltation on which one was living disappears, leaving in its place a great void in which things appear only as they are, nothing more.

I hover between this disappointing reality—which is still nothing more than this familiar darkness—and my strange inability to imagine anything else. I will be free in a few hours. *Free.* The enormous word is written in flaming letters before me. But is that all? I can't see beyond it. I don't know what will happen. I can't believe it's really true. Do I still believe in the world? The outside is unreal. I am about to enter the unreal. Like the sleeper who dreams "I'm going to wake up" and doesn't believe himself: I think about the last hours of men condemned to die: They can't imagine what death is. I can no longer imagine what life is.

I begin to love this darkness where nothing obstructs my eyes, where nothing allows me to measure these hours which are perhaps the most endless of my life. I am in a world between, floating down the river of time. Behind me I leave the Mill, where every stone is familiar to me. I am tearing myself away from a world that has become a deep, unforgettable part of me. The old round passes before me enticingly. My heart aches as a corner of the workshop and certain faces reappear before me. I am leaving, they are staying. The Mill is eternal. Three men, three kernels of half-ground grain, will drop out of it tonight, through a clack valve: Nothing changes, nothing will ever change . . .

That must be it; I feel the mark of jail too deeply within me. They no longer brand your shoulder with a hot iron; it is an inner wound that will start to ache tomorrow. For years I was nothing but a thinking automaton whose thoughts and actions were totally separate and unrelated. Now I will have to make decisions every minute, the thousand little everyday decisions which I have unlearned. I feel the same panic as a swimmer who hasn't swum for ten years and must dive in. He has forgotten the taste of the bitter, salty water that washes away our dirt, heals our wounds, and replenishes our being.

I will overcome this. I do not want to carry away with me any defeat. The Mill has not worn me down. I am leaving it with my mind intact, stronger for having survived, tempered by thought. I have not lost the years it has taken from me. We have committed great errors, comrades. We wanted to be revolutionaries; we were only rebels. We must become termites, boring obstinately, patiently, all our lives: In the end, the dike will crumble.

The guard entered with a candle and a suitcase: my belongings.

"Get dressed."

I didn't ask for a light. Why should I speak to this man who only appears to be a man? He is like a part of the wall: He is nothing but a little cog in the machine. I learned long ago that some men are indistinguishable from things.

The cell is filled with a feeble gray light. Dawn. The hour of executions. My blue tweed suit feels strangely light. With unexpected ease I rediscover pockets and the stance of a free man, hands in pockets. I smile at this gesture and the solemn satisfaction it gives me. Here I am dressed again; here is my old felt hat, bought in Belleville. These brown castoffs at my feet belong to Number 6731. Their rounded folds still hold the warmth and the shape of my movements. I see, in this prisoner's denim, my cast-off self.

Dawn is breaking. I stand in this cell, a man whose chains have fallen away. My helplessness now lies in these brown rags that I kick aside. The bolts are still locked, but already I feel free, sure of myself;

somewhere, within me, there is a calm hatred, like a still ocean. I will turn it into strength.

The simplicity of certain gestures. Signatures in the registry office. And then the clack valve of the Mill: a little gate in the great door. The keys turn (I barely notice the automaton-men who turn these keys), I step over a railing and the coolness of the river blows against my face. It is still almost night under the pale sky. The poplars are murmuring on the other bank; the river is there, black, gliding by with a vague, hissing sound; the grass on the banks seems ash colored. I walk quickly under the wall punctuated at intervals by towers sheltering a man and a rifle. I have never seen, will never again see, this landscape of the world between, this landscape immersed in deep shadows and the pale glimmers of the night.

Daylight appears in white reflections on the black water under the arch of an old bridge. You have to cross this bridge, to the right, to go toward the town. A gray form stands out there against the now bluish darkness ahead of me.

This first human figure suddenly transforms into reality the unreal landscape I have been moving through. He emerges in front of me, very tall and very strange, like a barbarian in his shadow-colored overcoat, leather-belted, crisscrossed by the straps of the heavy musette bags hanging at his hips. The soldier's bony face, his piercing eyes glowing in their dark sockets, surges up before me for an instant under the dented helmet which bears, gray against gray, an incendiary grenade. Our ringing footsteps fall in together. This first man I meet at the threshold of the world is a man of the trenches.

Victor Serge (1929)

Serge in English

FICTION

Men in Prison (*Les hommes dans la prison*, 1930). Translated and introduced by Richard Greeman. Garden City, NY: Doubleday & Co., 1969; London: Victor Gollancz Ltd., 1970; Middlesex: Penguin Books Ltd., 1972; London and New York: Writers and Readers, 1977; Oakland: PM Press, 2014. A searing personal experience transformed into a literary creation of general import.

Birth of Our Power (*Naissance de notre force*, 1931). Translated by Richard Greeman. Garden City, NY: Doubleday & Co., 1967; London: Victor Gollancz Ltd., 1968; Middlesex: Penguin Books Ltd., 1970; London and New York: Writers and Readers, 1977; Oakland: PM Press, 2015. From Barcelona to Petersburg, the conflagration of World War I ignites the spark of revolution, and poses a new problem for the revolutionaries' power.

Conquered City (*Ville conquise*, 1932). Translated and introduced by Richard Greeman. New York: NYRB Classics, 2009. Idealistic revolutionaries cope with the poison of power as the Red Terror and the White struggle for control of Petrograd during the Civil War.

Midnight in the Century (*S'il est minuit dans le siècle*, 1939). Translated and introduced by Richard Greeman. London and New York: Writers and Readers, 1981. On the eve of the great Purges, convicted anti-Stalin oppositionists in deportation attempt to survive, resist the GPU, debate political solutions, ponder their fates, and fall in love.

The Long Dusk (*Les derniers temps,* 1946). Translated by Ralph Manheim. New York: Dial Press, 1946. The fall of Paris (1940), the exodus of the refugees to the Free Zone, the beginnings of the French Resistance.

The Case of Comrade Tulayev (*L'Affaire Toulaèv,* 1951). Translated by Willard Trask. Introduction by Susan Sontag. New York: NYRB Classics, 2007. A panorama of the USSR (and Republican Spain) during the Purges, with a cast of sharply etched characters from provincial policemen to Old Bolsheviks and the Chief himself.

Unforgiving Years (*Les années sans pardon,* Posthumous, 1973). Translated and introduced by Richard Greeman. New York: NYRB Classics, 2010. Tormented Russian revolutionaries in Paris on the eve of World War I, Leningrad under siege, the last days of Berlin, and Mexico.

POETRY
Resistance: Poems by Victor Serge (*Résistance,* 1938). Translated by James Brook. Introduction by Richard Greeman. San Francisco: City Lights, 1972. Most of these poems were composed in deportation in Orenburg (1933–36), confiscated by the GPU, and reconstructed from memory in France.

NONFICTION
Revolution in Danger: Writings from Russia 1919–1921. Translated by Ian Birchall. London: Redwords, 1997; Chicago: Haymarket Books, 2011. Serge's early reports from Russia were designed to win over his French anarchist comrades to the cause of the Soviets.

Witness to the German Revolution (1923). Translated by Ian Birchall. London: Redwords, 1997; Chicago: Haymarket Books, 2011. A collection of the articles Serge wrote in Berlin in 1923 under the pseudonym R. Albert.

What Every Militant Should Know about Repression (*Les Coulisses d'une Sûreté Générale: Ce que tout révolutionnaire doit savoir sur la répression,* 1925). Popular pamphlet reprinted in a dozen languages. Serge unmasks the secrets he discovered working in the archives the Czarist Secret Police, then explains how police provocateurs operate everywhere and gives practical advice on security to activists.

The Chinese Revolution (1927–1928), Online at http://www.marxists.org/archive/serge/1927/china/index.html.

Year One of the Russian Revolution (*L'an 1 de la révolution russe*, 1930) Translated by Peter Sedgwick. London: Pluto Press. Written soon after Stalin's takeover in Russia, this history presents the Left Opposition's take on the October Revolution and early Bolshevism.

From Lenin to Stalin (*De Lénine à Staline*, 1937). Translated by Ralph Manheim. New York: Monad and Pathfinder Press, 1973. A brilliant, short primer, on the Russian Revolution and its degeneration, with close-ups of Lenin and Trotsky.

Russia Twenty Years After (*Destin d'une Revolution*, 1937). Translated by Max Shactman (Includes "Thirty Years After the Russian Revolution," 1947). Atlantic Highlands, NJ: Humanities Press, 1996. Descriptive panorama and analysis of bureaucratic tyranny and chaos in Russia under Stalin's Five-Year Plans, based on statistics and economic, sociological, and political analysis.

The Life and Death of Leon Trotsky (*Vie et Mort de Léon Trotski*, 1951), by Victor Serge and Natalia Sedova Trotsky. Translated by Arnold Pomerans. London: Wildwood, 1975; Chicago: Haymarket Books, 2012. Still the most concise, authentic, and well-written Trotsky biography, based on the two authors' intimate knowledge of the man and his times and on Trotsky's personal archives (before they were sealed up in Harvard).

Memoirs of a Revolutionary (*Mémoires d'un révolutionnaire*, 1901–1941) Paris: Éditions du Seuil, 1951. Translated by Peter Sedwick. New York: NYRB Classics, 2012. Originally titled "Souvenirs of Vanished Worlds," Serge's *Memoirs* are an eyewitness chronicle of the revolutionary movements Belgium, France, Spain, Russia, and Germany studded with brilliant portraits of the people he knew. This is the first complete English translation and comes with a glossary.

The Serge-Trotsky Papers: Correspondence and Other Writings between Victor Serge and Leon Trotsky. D. Cotterill, ed. London, Pluto Press, 1994. Includes their personal letters and polemical articles as well as essays on Serge and Trotsky by various authors.

Collected Writings on Literature and Revolution. Translated and edited by Al Richardson. London: Francis Boutle, 2004. Includes Serge's reports on Soviet Cultural life in the 1920s (published in Paris in *Clarté*), studies of writers like Blok, Mayakovsky, Essenin, and Pilniak as well as his highly original contributions to the debate on "proletarian literature" in the 1930s.

Anarchists Never Surrender: Essays, Polemics, and Correspondence on Anarchism, 1908–1938. Oakland: PM Press, 2015. An original anthology of Serge's writing on anarchism translated, edited, and introduced by Mitchell Abidor. Foreword by Richard Greeman.

BOOKS IN FRENCH:

Carnets, Expanded edition with newly discovered manuscripts presented by Claudio Albertani. Marseille: Agone, 2012. Notebook sketches and meditations dating from 1936 to 1947 on subjects ranging from Gide, Giraudoux, and Trotsky to Mexican earthquakes, popular wrestling matches, and death.

Le tropique et le nord. Montpellier: Maspero 1972; Paris: La Découverte, 2003. Four short stories: *Mer blanche* (1931), *L'Impasse St. Barnabé* (1936), *La folie d'Iouriev* [*L'Hôpital de Léningrad*, 1953] and *Le Séisme* [*San Juan Parangarcutiro*]

Retour à l'Ouest: Chroniques, juin 1936–mai 1940. Preface by Richard Greeman. Marseille: Agone, 2010. From the euphoria of Pop Front France in June 1936 to the defeat of the Spanish Republic, Serge's weekly columns for a trade union–owned independent daily in Belgium provide a lucid panorama of this confused and confusing period.

MANUSCRIPTS:

The Victor Serge Papers (1936–1947), Beinecke Library, Yale University. Twenty-seven boxes of correspondence, documents, and manuscripts (mostly unpublished) on a wide variety of subjects from politics to Mexican anthropology. Catalog online:

http://drs.library.yale.edu:8083/fedoragsearch/rest?filter=&operation=solrQuery&query=Victor+Serge+Papers.

The Life of Victor Serge

1890   Victor Lvovich Kibalchich (Victor Serge) born on December
            30 in Brussels to a family of sympathizers with Narodnik
            terrorism who had fled from Russia after the assassination
            of Alexander II.

1908   Photographer's apprentice and member of the socialist
            Jeunes-Gardes. Spends a short period in an anarchist 'uto-
            pian' community in the Ardennes. Leaves for Paris.

1910–1911   Becomes editor of the French anarchist-individualist mag-
            azine, *Anarchie*. Writes and agitates.

1912   Serge is implicated in the trial of the anarchist outlaws
            known as the Bonnot Gang. Despite arrest, he refuses to
            turn informer and is sentenced to five years in a *maison cen-
            trale*. Three of his co-defendants were guillotined.

1917–1918   Serge is released from prison and banned from France.
            Goes to Barcelona where he participates in the syndical-
            ist uprising. Writes his first article signed Victor Serge.
            Leaves Barcelona to join the Russian army in France. Is
            detained for over a year in a French concentration camp
            as a Bolshevik suspect.

1919   Arrives in Red Petrograd at the height of the Civil War. Gets
            to work organizing the administration of the Communist
            International under Zinoviev.

1920–1922   Participates in Comintern Congresses. Edits various inter-
            national journals. Exposes Tsarist secret-police archives and
            fights in the defense of the city.

1923–1926   Serves Comintern as a secret agent and editor of *Imprekor*
            in Berlin and Vienna. Returns to the Soviet Union to take
            part in the last stand of the left opposition.

1927	Series of articles on the Chinese Revolution in which he criticizes Stalin's complacence towards the Kuomintang and draws attention to the importance of Mao Zedong.
1928	Expelled from Communist Party and relieved of all official functions.
1928–1933	Barred from all other work, Serge takes up writing. He sends his manuscripts to France, since publication in the Soviet Union is impossible. Apart from many articles, he produces *Year One of the Russian Revolution*, 1930; *Men in Prison*, 1930; *Birth of Our Power*, 1931; and *Conquered City*, 1932.
1933	Serge is arrested and deported to Orenburg in Central Asia, where he is joined by his young son, Vlady.
1935	Oppositionists raise the 'Case of Victor Serge' at the Congress for the Defense of Culture in Paris. Paris intellectuals campaign for his freedom.
1936	Serge is released from Orenburg and simultaneously deprived of Soviet citizenship. His manuscripts are confiscated and his is expelled from the USSR. He settles first in Brussels, then in Paris. His return to Europe is accompanied by a slander campaign in the Communist press.
1937	*From Lenin to Stalin* and *Destiny of a Revolution* appear in which Serge analyses the Stalinist counter-revolution. He is elected a councilor to the Spanish POUM (Independent Marxist Party) and campaigns against the Moscow trials.
1940	Serge leaves Paris just as the Nazis advance. In Marseilles, he struggles for months to obtain a visa. Finally finds refuge in Mexico.
1940–1947	Serge lives in isolation and poverty. Writes *The Case of Comrade Tulayev* and *Memoirs of a Revolutionary* for his "desk drawer," since publication was impossible.
1947	November 17: Serge dies and is buried as a "Spanish Republican" in the French section of the Mexico City cemetery.

Victor Serge (1890–1947) was born to Russian anti-Tsarist exiles living in Brussels. As a young anarchist firebrand, he was sentenced to five years in a French penitentiary in 1912. In 1919, Serge joined the Bolsheviks. An outspoken critic of Stalin, he was expelled from the Party and arrested in 1929. Nonetheless, he managed to complete three novels (*Men in Prison, Birth of Our Power,* and *Conquered City*) and a history (*Year One of the Russian Revolution*), published in Paris. Arrested again in Russia and deported to Central Asia in 1933, he was allowed to leave the USSR in 1936 after international protests by militants and prominent writers such as André Gide and Romain Rolland. Hounded by Stalinist agents, Serge lived in precarious exile in Brussels, Paris, Vichy France, and Mexico City, where he died in 1947.

Richard Greeman has translated and written the introductions for five of Victor Serge's novels. Cofounder of the Praxis Center and Victor Serge Library in Moscow, Greeman is the author of *Beware of Vegetarian Sharks: Radical Rants and Internationalist Essays.*

David Gilbert is an anti-imperialist political prisoner at Auburn Correctional Facility and is the author of *Love and Struggle: My Life in SDS, the Weather Underground, and Beyond* (PM Press, 2011) and *No Surrender* (Abraham Guillen Press and Arm the Spirit, 2004).

ABOUT PM PRESS

PM Press was founded at the end of 2007
by a small collection of folks with decades of
publishing, media, and organizing experience.
PM Press co-conspirators have published and
distributed hundreds of books, pamphlets,
CDs, and DVDs. Members of PM have founded enduring book fairs,
spearheaded victorious tenant organizing campaigns, and worked closely
with bookstores, academic conferences, and even rock bands to deliver
political and challenging ideas to all walks of life. We're old enough to
know what we're doing and young enough to know what's at stake.

We seek to create radical and stimulating fiction and non-fiction books,
pamphlets, T-shirts, visual and audio materials to entertain, educate
and inspire you. We aim to distribute these through every available
channel with every available technology — whether that means you are
seeing anarchist classics at our bookfair stalls; reading our latest vegan
cookbook at the café; downloading geeky fiction e-books; or digging new
music and timely videos from our website.

PM Press is always on the lookout for talented and skilled volunteers,
artists, activists and writers to work with. If you have a great idea for a
project or can contribute in some way, please get in touch.

PM Press
PO Box 23912
Oakland, CA 94623
www.pmpress.org

FRIENDS OF PM PRESS

These are indisputably momentous times—the financial system is melting down globally and the Empire is stumbling. Now more than ever there is a vital need for radical ideas.

In the six years since its founding—and on a mere shoestring—PM Press has risen to the formidable challenge of publishing and distributing knowledge and entertainment for the struggles ahead. With over 250 releases to date, we have published an impressive and stimulating array of literature, art, music, politics, and culture. Using every available medium, we've succeeded in connecting those hungry for ideas and information to those putting them into practice.

Friends of PM allows you to directly help impact, amplify, and revitalize the discourse and actions of radical writers, filmmakers, and artists. It provides us with a stable foundation from which we can build upon our early successes and provides a much-needed subsidy for the materials that can't necessarily pay their own way. You can help make that happen—and receive every new title automatically delivered to your door once a month—by joining as a Friend of PM Press. And, we'll throw in a free T-shirt when you sign up.

Here are your options:

- **$30 a month** Get all books and pamphlets plus 50% discount on all webstore purchases

- **$40 a month** Get all PM Press releases (including CDs and DVDs) plus 50% discount on all webstore purchases

- **$100 a month** Superstar—Everything plus PM merchandise, free downloads, and 50% discount on all webstore purchases

For those who can't afford $30 or more a month, we're introducing **Sustainer Rates** at $15, $10 and $5. Sustainers get a free PM Press T-shirt and a 50% discount on all purchases from our website.

Your Visa or Mastercard will be billed once a month, until you tell us to stop. Or until our efforts succeed in bringing the revolution around. Or the financial meltdown of Capital makes plastic redundant. Whichever comes first.

Also from 𝕊ℙ𝔼ℂ𝕋ℝ𝔼 CLASSICS from PM Press

Birth of Our Power

Victor Serge

ISBN: 978-1-62963-030-4
$18.95   320 pages

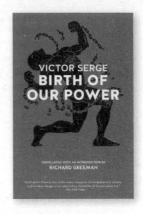

Birth of Our Power is an epic novel set in
Spain, France, and Russia during the heady
revolutionary years 1917–1919. Serge's tale
begins in the spring of 1917, the third year of
mass slaughter in the blood-and-rain-soaked
trenches of World War I, when the flames
of revolution suddenly erupt in Russia and
Spain. Europe is "burning at both ends." Although the Spanish uprising
eventually fizzles, in Russia the workers, peasants, and common
soldiers are able to take power and hold it. Serge's "tale of two cities" is
constructed from the opposition between Barcelona, the city "we" could
not take, and Petrograd, the starving capital of the Russian Revolution,
besieged by counter-revolutionary Whites. Between the romanticism
of radicalized workers awakening to their own power in a sun-drenched
Spanish metropolis to the grim reality of workers clinging to power in
Russia's dark, frozen revolutionary outpost. From "victory-in-defeat" to
"defeat in victory."

"Nothing in it has dated... It is less an autobiography than a sustained, incandescent
lyric (half-pantheist, half-surrealist) of rebellion and battle."
—Times Literary Supplement

"Surely one of the most moving accounts of revolutionary experience ever written."
—Neal Ascherson, New York Review of Books

"Probably the most remarkable of his novels... Of all the European writers who
have taken revolution as their theme, Serge is second only to Conrad... Here is a
writer with a magnificent eye for the panoramic sweep of historical events and an
unsparingly precise moral insight."
—Francis King, Sunday Telegraph

"Intense, vivid, glowing with energy and power... A wonderful picture of revolution
and revolutionaries... The power of the novel is in its portrayal of the men who are
involved."
—Manchester Evening News

"Birth of Our Power is one of the finest romances of revolution ever written, and
confirms Serge as an outstanding chronicler of his turbulent era... As an epic, Birth
of Our Power has lost none of its strength."
—Lawrence M. Bensky, New York Times

Anarchists Never Surrender: Essays, Polemics, and Correspondence on Anarchism, 1908–1938

Victor Serge

ISBN: 978-1-62963-031-1

$20.00   304 pages

Anarchists Never Surrender provides a complete picture of Victor Serge's relationship to anarchist action and doctrine. The volume contains writings going back to his teenage years in Brussels, when he was already developing a doctrine of individualist anarchism. The heart of the anthology is the key articles written during his subsequent period in Paris, when he was a writer and then an editor of the newspaper *l'anarchie*. In these articles we see the continuing development of his thought, including most crucially his point of view concerning the futility of mass action and in support of the doctrine of illegalism. All of this led, of course, to his involvement with the Bonnot Gang.

His thought slowly but most definitely evolved during the period of his imprisonment for his association with Bonnot and his comrades. The anthology includes both his correspondence with his comrade Émile Armand and articles written immediately after his release from prison, among them the key letters that signify the beginning of his break with his individualist past and that point the way to his later engagement alongside the Bolsheviks. It also includes an essential article on Nietzschean thought. This collection also includes articles that Serge wrote after he had left anarchism behind, analyzing both the history and the state of anarchism and the ways in which he hoped anarchism would leaven the harshness and dictatorial tendencies of Bolshevism.

Anarchists Never Surrender anthologizes a variety of Serge texts nowhere previously available, and fleshes out the portrait of this brilliant writer and thinker, who has reached new heights of popularity and interest.

"*Serge is not merely a political writer; he is also a novelist, a wonderfully lyrical writer… He is a writer young rebels desperately need whether they know it or not… He does not tell us what we should feel; instead, he makes us feel it.*"
—Stanley Reynolds, *New Statesman*

"*I can't think of anyone else who has written about the revolutionary movement in this century with Serge's combination of moral insight and intellectual richness.*"
—Dwight Macdonald

Also from SPECTRE CLASSICS from PM Press

William Morris:
Romantic to Revolutionary

E. P. Thompson

ISBN: 978-1-60486-243-0
$32.95   880 pages

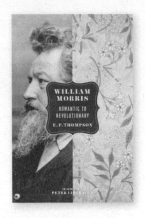

William Morris—the great 19th-century
craftsman, architect, designer, poet and
writer—remains a monumental figure whose
influence resonates powerfully today. As an
intellectual (and author of the seminal utopian
News from Nowhere), his concern with artistic
and human values led him to cross what he called the "river of fire" and
become a committed socialist—committed not to some theoretical
formula but to the day-by-day struggle of working women and men in
Britain and to the evolution of his ideas about art, about work and about
how life should be lived. Many of his ideas accorded none too well with
the reforming tendencies dominant in the Labour movement, nor with
those of "orthodox" Marxism, which has looked elsewhere for inspiration.
Both sides have been inclined to venerate Morris rather than to pay
attention to what he said. Originally written less than a decade before his
groundbreaking *The Making of the English Working Class*, E. P. Thompson
brought to this biography his now trademark historical mastery, passion,
wit, and essential sympathy. It remains unsurpassed as the definitive
work on this remarkable figure, by the major British historian of the 20th
century.

"*Two impressive figures, William Morris as subject and E. P. Thompson as author, are
conjoined in this immense biographical-historical-critical study, and both of them
have gained in stature since the first edition of the book was published... The book
that was ignored in 1955 has meanwhile become something of an underground
classic—almost impossible to locate in second-hand bookstores, pored over in
libraries, required reading for anyone interested in Morris and, increasingly, for
anyone interested in one of the most important of contemporary British historians...
Thompson has the distinguishing characteristic of a great historian: he has
transformed the nature of the past, it will never look the same again; and whoever
works in the area of his concerns in the future must come to terms with what
Thompson has written. So too with his study of William Morris.*"
—Peter Stansky, *The New York Times Book Review*

"*An absorbing biographical study... A glittering quarry of marvelous quotes from
Morris and others, many taken from heretofore inaccessible or unpublished sources.*"
—Walter Arnold, *Saturday Review*

Also from ▌SPECTRE▶ from PM Press

Catastrophism: The Apocalyptic Politics of Collapse and Rebirth

Sasha Lilley, David McNally, Eddie Yuen, and James Davis, with a foreword by Doug Henwood

ISBN: 978-1-60486-589-9
$16.00   192 pages

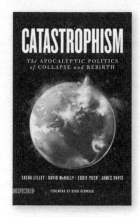

We live in catastrophic times. The world is reeling from the deepest economic crisis since the Great Depression, with the threat of further meltdowns ever-looming. Global warming and myriad dire ecological disasters worsen—with little if any action to halt them—their effects rippling across the planet in the shape of almost biblical floods, fires, droughts, and hurricanes. Governments warn that no alternative exists than to take the bitter medicine they prescribe—or risk devastating financial or social collapse. The right, whether religious or secular, views the present as catastrophic and wants to turn the clock back. The left fears for the worst, but hopes some good will emerge from the rubble. Visions of the apocalypse and predictions of impending doom abound. Across the political spectrum, a culture of fear reigns.

Catastrophism explores the politics of apocalypse—on the left and right, in the environmental movement, and from capital and the state—and examines why the lens of catastrophe can distort our understanding of the dynamics at the heart of these numerous disasters—and fatally impede our ability to transform the world. Lilley, McNally, Yuen, and Davis probe the reasons why catastrophic thinking is so prevalent, and challenge the belief that it is only out of the ashes that a better society may be born. The authors argue that those who care about social justice and the environment should eschew the Pandora's box of fear—even as it relates to indisputably apocalyptic climate change. Far from calling people to arms, they suggest, catastrophic fear often results in passivity and paralysis—and, at worst, reactionary politics.

"This groundbreaking book examines a deep current—on both the left and right—of apocalyptical thought and action. The authors explore the origins, uses, and consequences of the idea that collapse might usher in a better world. Catastrophism is a crucial guide to understanding our tumultuous times, while steering us away from the pitfalls of the past."
—Barbara Epstein, author of *Political Protest and Cultural Revolution: Nonviolent Direct Action in the 1970s and 1980s*

Also from ■SPECTRE▶ from PM Press

Capital and Its Discontents: Conversations with Radical Thinkers in a Time of Tumult

Sasha Lilley

ISBN: 978-1-60486-334-5
$20.00   320 pages

Capitalism is stumbling, empire is faltering, and the planet is thawing. Yet many people are still grasping to understand these multiple crises and to find a way forward to a just future. Into the breach come the essential insights of *Capital and Its Discontents*, which cut through the gristle to get to the heart of the matter about the nature of capitalism and imperialism, capitalism's vulnerabilities at this conjuncture—and what can we do to hasten its demise. Through a series of incisive conversations with some of the most eminent thinkers and political economists on the Left—including David Harvey, Ellen Meiksins Wood, Mike Davis, Leo Panitch, Tariq Ali, and Noam Chomsky—*Capital and Its Discontents* illuminates the dynamic contradictions undergirding capitalism and the potential for its dethroning. At a moment when capitalism as a system is more reviled than ever, here is an indispensable toolbox of ideas for action by some of the most brilliant thinkers of our times.

"These conversations illuminate the current world situation in ways that are very useful for those hoping to orient themselves and find a way forward to effective individual and collective action. Highly recommended."
— Kim Stanley Robinson, *New York Times* bestselling author of the *Mars Trilogy* and *The Years of Rice and Salt*

"In this fine set of interviews, an A-list of radical political economists demonstrate why their skills are indispensable to understanding today's multiple economic and ecological crises."
— Raj Patel, author of *Stuffed and Starved* and *The Value of Nothing*

"This is an extremely important book. It is the most detailed, comprehensive, and best study yet published on the most recent capitalist crisis and its discontents. Sasha Lilley sets each interview in its context, writing with style, scholarship, and wit about ideas and philosophies."
— Andrej Grubačić, radical sociologist and social critic, co-author of *Wobblies and Zapatistas*

Also from 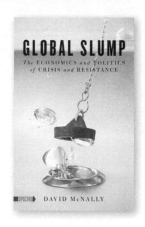SPECTRE▶ from PM Press

Global Slump: The Economics and Politics of Crisis and Resistance

David McNally

ISBN: 978-1-60486-332-1
$15.95   176 pages

Global Slump analyzes the world financial meltdown as the first systemic crisis of the neoliberal stage of capitalism. It argues that— far from having ended—the crisis has ushered in a whole period of worldwide economic and political turbulence. In developing an account of the crisis as rooted in fundamental features of capitalism, *Global Slump* challenges the view that its source lies in financial deregulation. It offers an original account of the "financialization" of the world economy and explores the connections between international financial markets and new forms of debt and dispossession, particularly in the Global South. The book shows that, while averting a complete meltdown, the massive intervention by central banks laid the basis for recurring crises for poor and working class people. It traces new patterns of social resistance for building an anti-capitalist opposition to the damage that neoliberal capitalism is inflicting on the lives of millions.

"In this book, McNally confirms—once again—his standing as one of the world's leading Marxist scholars of capitalism. For a scholarly, in depth analysis of our current crisis that never loses sight of its political implications (for them and for us), expressed in a language that leaves no reader behind, there is simply no better place to go."
—Bertell Ollman, professor, Department of Politics, NYU, and author of *Dance of the Dialectic: Steps in Marx's Method*

"David McNally's tremendously timely book is packed with significant theoretical and practical insights, and offers actually-existing examples of what is to be done. Global Slump *urgently details how changes in the capitalist space-economy over the past 25 years, especially in the forms that money takes, have expanded wide-scale vulnerabilities for all kinds of people, and how people fight back. In a word, the problem isn't neo-liberalism—it's capitalism."*
—Ruth Wilson Gilmore, University of Southern California and author, *Golden Gulag: Prisons, Surplus, Crisis, and Opposition in Globalizing California*

Also from ▇SPECTRE▶ from PM Press

In and Out of Crisis: The Global Financial Meltdown and Left Alternatives

Greg Albo, Sam Gindin, Leo Panitch

ISBN: 978-1-60486-212-6

$13.95   144 pages

While many around the globe are increasingly wondering if another world is indeed possible, few are mapping out potential avenues—and flagging wrong turns—en route to a post-capitalist future. In this groundbreaking analysis of the meltdown, renowned radical political economists Albo, Gindin, and Panitch lay bare the roots of the crisis, which they locate in the dynamic expansion of capital on a global scale over the last quarter century—and in the inner logic of capitalism itself.

With an unparalleled understanding of the inner workings of capitalism, the authors of *In and Out of Crisis* provocatively challenge the call by much of the Left for a return to a largely mythical Golden Age of economic regulation as a check on finance capital unbound. They deftly illuminate how the era of neoliberal free markets has been, in practice, undergirded by state intervention on a massive scale. In conclusion, the authors argue that it's time to start thinking about genuinely transformative alternatives to capitalism—and how to build the collective capacity to get us there. *In and Out of Crisis* stands to be the enduring critique of the crisis and an indispensable springboard for a renewed Left.

"Once again, Panitch, Gindin, and Albo show that they have few rivals and no betters in analyzing the relations between politics and economics, between globalization and American power, between theory and quotidian reality, and between crisis and political possibility. At once sobering and inspiring, this is one of the few pieces of writing that I've seen that's essential to understanding—to paraphrase a term from accounting—the sources and uses of crisis. Splendid and essential."
—Doug Henwood, *Left Business Observer*, author of *After the New Economy* and *Wall Street*

"Mired in political despair? Planning your escape to a more humane continent? Baffled by the economy? Convinced that the Left is out of ideas? Pull yourself together and read this book, in which Albo, Gindin, and Panitch, some of the world's sharpest living political economists, explain the current financial crisis—and how we might begin to make a better world."
—Liza Featherstone, author of *Students Against Sweatshops* and *Selling Women Short: The Landmark Battle for Workers' Rights at Wal-Mart*